# Dog Duty

## Bobby D. Lux

Cover art by Tory Hoke. www.thetoryparty.com

ISBN: 1502330156
ISBN-13: 978-1502330154

## FOR NIPPER, ERNIE, AND MISSY

I hope your real-life adventures when our family was asleep
were as exciting as I imagined them to be.

## ACKNOWLEDGMENTS

With many thanks to:

Family, friends, mentors, and teachers all along the way. This book doesn't get written without you.

Thank you for giving this book a shot. Without you, it doesn't exist.

# CHAPTER ONE - ON THE JOB

I focused on the criminal I was chasing between the buildings on the outskirts of Grand City's industrial section. A part of the city the taxpayers would have left off the map if they could've. That's where I was. I felt right at home.

My first mistake was thinking it was just another night on patrol. After eight years on the job, it was an honest mistake. I was guilty of getting caught up in the routine of day-after-day, every day. Eight years, also nearly three-quarters of my life up until that point. There had been talk around the department that they wanted to retire me two years prior. Once I again passed all the required tests, they couldn't find a legitimate reason to send me packing. Not that I was complaining. What else was I going to do? What else was there to do?

Nothing and nothing, that's what.

The mundane in this case was the one-hundred-and-sixty pound bag of sweat I was gaining on. I'll give it to this guy, The Perp, he was fast. Not fast enough. Nobody was.

His attempts to lose me were comical. Faking right before turning left, as if something so trivial would throw me off. I could still see, even if only in black and white. I could run through the arteries of those back alleys in my sleep. They didn't go on forever. This human clot would soon find a clogged one.

The Perp got tired of trying to lose me and resorted to knocking things over to try and trip me up. A sure sign of desperation. This chase would be over in no time. Then I smelled the distinct reek of rotten tuna.

It was dinner time for a fat cat who was about to feast on a half-opened can of fish. I know humans have a different definition of fat cat. For me, in this setting, it was all too literal.

My fat cat was perched atop one of the stacks of boxes The Perp hoped would slow me down. The Perp made a swipe of his right hand and sent the boxes, the rank tuna, and the cat flying my way.

They say cats can adjust themselves to land on their feet in under a second. The look of panic smeared across this guy's face told me that he was going to need help with his landing. I've never had the same problems with cats that other dogs do. I don't particularly like them. I don't dislike them either. They're just cats. I jumped over the boxes. I figured, since I was up there anyway, I might as well catch the damn thing. It really was the least I could do.

"Nooooooo!" the cat screamed as he fell nice and snug into my jaws. The poor jerk didn't even have his claws. We landed safely, and I dropped the cat. My hunches were right. He plopped flat on his back before getting up to his paws. "Don't eat me."

"I'm not going to eat you," I said.

"Oh, you're a cop," he said as he stared in awe at my collar engraved with *Grand City K9*. "Thanks, officer."

"Fritz is fine."

Introductions aside, I had other pressing matters. The Perp's distraction bought him a smidgen of time. I'd make up those extra yards in a few seconds. I took off again down the alley. Again, this was all too routine for me.

I'd lost sight of him. I followed the sticky scent of sweat and the sound of pounding feet. I rounded another corner and found myself facing a dead end. There was a wall directly ahead of me, too high for The Perp to climb over. The footsteps had stopped, but the scent was right there. The sirens were still in the background. I was on my own while backup played catch up. Not that I needed it. If the sweat didn't tell me where to go, the shivering refrigerator box may as well have had a neon sign above it with an arrow pointing down. *The Perp was right there.*

I should have just kept my position. I should have started barking. I should have waited for backup to arrive and skipped this entire mess that is about to follow. Instead, I was dulled by the routine ease I'd experienced up until that point. I pounced on that box and tore through it. I got a good, deep bite on The Perp. Suspect detained. I could keep him at bay without having to tear his arm off.

"If I were you," a voice rumbled, out from behind me. "I'd let go of him right now."

I swung The Perp around and took my first glimpse of Clay, a Rottweiler custom built with one-syllable efficiency. Bite. Maim. Kill.

"This is none of your concern," I growled, out of the side of my mouth that wasn't holding onto The Perp. "Turn around, and go home."

"If you're smart," a voice said, one that hovered near Clay's shoulder. A voice that sounded like the screech of air from a balloon. "You'll be the one who lets go and goes home."

"Shut up, Scamper," Clay said.

Scamper, a Jack Russell terrier, and Clay's parasitic sidekick, stepped out from behind Clay. The lightweight wasn't my main concern. That was saved for the dog with shark eyes who descended upon me.

"This is official police business," I said. "You'd best be advised to leave."

"Oh no," Clay said. "That's where you're wrong—"

"Stop barking," The Perp said, crying out. He relaxed his arm as best he could, considering the circumstances. Too many people think their arm is stronger than it really is and have tried to shake me off. They'd have better luck trying to swim up a waterfall. Some have tried to use their other hand to pry my mouth off. An excellent way to lose fingers. This Perp was smart. He knew his way with dogs. "Get him. Clay, attack!"

"Dead wrong," Clay said, finishing his threat.

I let go of The Perp in time to maneuver away from Clay's pounce. The Perp got up, took his shirt off, and wrapped it around his arm. Clay and I circled around one another.

"Don't worry, Clay," Scamper said, who appeared behind me, showing his needle teeth. "He can't leave now."

"Maintain silence during the operation," Clay said.

The Perp darted into one of the buildings. I made after him. Clay took me down with a precision bite to my arm. He pulled it out from under me. I was pinned down, and Clay was going for my neck.

"Oh, my Lord," Scamper said, taunting. "I've never seen such a beating delivered in all my years of watching this most brutal of all sports. I thought I'd seen it all until tonight. This is carnage at its finest or worst, depending on your perspective."

I kept my head moving so Clay couldn't get a good crack at my neck. I got my hind legs under Clay's chest and pushed him off me. I shook myself off, and we were face to face. It was time for Clay to be another notch on my dance card. A lightning bolt shrieked up my tail.

I yelped and turned. Scamper was trying to take my tail home for a souvenir. The dirtiest move a dog could pull on a fellow canine. It's the human equivalent of a kick to the jewels.

"I got him," Scamper grunted through his closed jaw. "I got the cop. I did it."

"You got him," Clay said, "but I'm gonna finish him."

I kicked my leg back and caught Scamper clean in the skull. He let go, and I turned back as Clay lunged on me. Clay was on my leg pulling it out of socket. I could feel the muscles peeling away off my bones. My body froze with pain while Clay's jaw grinded into my leg. I jerked at my leg to free it. Instead, Clay bent it in the wrong direction. No half measures with him.

So this was it. I tried to get back on my feet and failed. I wasn't going to lay there and let this happen. I heard the tendons pop and snap near my foot. I couldn't stand. I looked like a fish trying to flop its way off a boat and back into the ocean.

"He's done," Clay said, his teeth coated with my blood that was smeared across his face.

It was The Perp who saved me from a further mauling. He distracted Clay by lurching his head out above the safety of the other side of the wall. My neck was fully exposed, and my head felt like concrete.

"Clay, Scamper," he said. "Let's go. Come. Back to the docks..."

And that was the last I remembered before the pain and the darkness squeezed out the remainder of my sight. There was no time to process the ridiculous possibility that "dock" might have been the last word I ever heard in my life.

I must not have been out long because when I opened my eyes I saw Scamper balanced on a shaky ladder of boxes, trash, and broken appliances. He moved his hips back and forth trying to generate the momentum to jump over the wall.

The voices of the other officers approached, calmly giving The Perp's description into their radios. Male white, early thirties, six feet, hundred-fifty pounds, dark hair, wearing a black, long-sleeved shirt, blue jeans, unknown weapons. I barked so they would know where to find me.

I tried to get up. I couldn't. My head was spinning. I saw the blood around my body. I wanted to let everyone know I was okay. The Perp was getting away, and I saw which direction he went. He went through the building. I could still get him. I just needed someone to get me back up on my paws, dammit. My partner, Officer Hart, was the first to find me.

"K-9 unit down," he said into his radio. I barked and tried to point my head in the direction of the building. "It's okay, Fritz. Just stop right now. Relax."

The barking made me dizzy. It bothered me that Officer Hart didn't seem to care about catching The Perp. I wanted to bite Officer Hart for not going after The Perp. I was fine. Officer Hart kept his hands on my leg to stop the immediate bleeding. My blood was already all over his dark pants. It wasn't until more officers arrived that they continued the search and established a perimeter. The Perp was probably already long gone by that point.

As if things couldn't get worse, Nitro was with the officers arriving at the scene. He was a rookie. Typical. A cowboy who relied solely on a unique belief system that got him through each day. Himself. Nitro's partner let him off the leash, and he ran over to me.

"Which way did they go?" Nitro said.

"He went into the building," I said, shivering. "In that door over there, nearest the wall."

"How long?"

"Maybe four minutes ago. I don't know. I was out."

"You couldn't stay awake?"

"I don't know what happened."

"So much for the investigation then."

"The other two went over the wall," I said.

"What other two?" Nitro said. "There was only the one guy."

"He had two dogs with him here in the alley."

"Fritz, the only one who cares about any dogs around here is you."

"I see they still keep you on a short leash," I said.

"Not for long, Fritz. Tough break."

"It's not broken, Nitro," I said.

"I'm not talking about your leg," Nitro said as an ambulance pulled up to the end of the alley. Two EMTs jumped out and came over to me. Officer Hart stood, wiped my blood off his hands as the medics tended to me, and conferred with Nitro's partner. "This is my case now. It's about time they let the real cops on the scene. Your ride is here. Your chariot awaits."

Officer Hart and the EMTs scooped me up and placed me into the back of the ambulance. My leg seized, and I cried out. The larger of the EMTs put both gloved hands on my leg and tried to hold it steady. I had to control every instinct I had not to bite him. They gave me a shot in my good leg, and any fight I had left in me evaporated.

Before they closed the door to the ambulance, I watched Nitro make a show of going to the building I pointed him toward. Nitro sniffed around the door then he looked up and barked to make sure all eyes were on him. When they were, he scratched at the door with one paw.

"Excellent work, Nitro," Nitro's partner said as they entered the stalagmite of a building.

"Don't worry, Fritz," Officer Hart said. I could barely hear him over the sirens as we rolled out of there. "We'll take good care of you. You had a good run, boy. Real good."

Then my eyesight lost a battle to the suffocating nothingness. For the second time that night, everything went black.

# CHAPTER TWO - JUST ANOTHER HEAD ON THE WALL

The lights were darkened. There I was up on the new big-screen, high-def TV for my peers to see. A TV ostensibly intended for detailed viewings of grainy surveillance footage. Instead, one that found more use on Sunday afternoons in the Sergeant's office during football season. I realized how much fur I'd shed since those early days. I was a halfway-decent-looking dog. I couldn't have been more than a year-and-a-half old when this clip was filmed. Chief Lennox, Officer Hart, and I had gone to visit the kindergarten class at Twain Elementary School for my first recorded public relations spot. Now it was being displayed as the beginning clip of my *greatest hits* collection at my retirement celebration.

According to the vet, I was lucky to still have my leg, and I would never be the same. Someday, I might be able to run again. Maybe. They rushed me into emergency surgery and repaired everything. Some repair job. Repair means back to normal. This was back to we-don't-need-you-anymore. This was sayonara, Fritz. Thanks for the memories.

I should have been more embarrassed that this video was being shown to my sworn comrades. Not that they were all watching. Most of them were typing away on their cell phones. Their sense of nostalgia seemingly matched mine.

Not too bad looking up there, sure, though I was embarrassed to even make eye contact with myself. I had no on-camera experience, and while it may seem easy to sit there and act natural, try doing it while being fully aware that you're trying to seem like you're just being yourself. It's a real mind trap. Go ahead, try it. Act natural. I'll be here waiting for you.

I looked more nervous on screen than I actually was thanks to my eyes anxiously darting across the room. I had to force myself to stay seated. The scent of whatever contraband the teacher had concealed in her middle drawer tugged at my attention.

"Since I've been sworn in as the new chief here in Grand City," Chief Lennox said, the star of the video, "major crime has dropped in every category including auto theft, assaults, and even cheating on homework." Chief Lennox leaned in and winked at the students. They were instructed to laugh, and some of them did. "Crime is down big time. And it's thanks to the hard-working men and women of The Grand City Police Department. But it's also thanks to our citizens, who we rely on to be our eyes and ears out there and to let us know when things are happening in their neighborhoods. So that means when you see something or someone who doesn't look right, you pick up that phone and give us a call. And if it's an emergency, just dial 911, and we'll be there faster than Fritz here can chase down a bad guy. And that's pretty fast. Speaking of Fritz, he's the newest officer on our roster, and this is our way of introducing him to the citizens of our wonderful city. Come on up and say hi, kids. He's friendly as long as you're not a bad guy."

A few pre-selected little kids ran up and rubbed and wiped their dirty, sticky, little hands all over my fur. One in particular kept coming in over my head even after they were all told beforehand to not touch my head or face. They pinched, pulled, and tugged at me while Chief Lennox wrapped up our promotional video.

"The children of Grand City love our police dogs," Chief Lennox said as he walked toward the camera, "and if I know Fritz, he loves them right back. The Grand City Police Department and our K-9 unit, it's what keeps you safe."

The director, who stood behind the cameraman, waved her hands at me. When she had my attention, she softly clapped her hands at me with pleading eyes. That was my cue to end the commercial with a playful bark. It took Chief Lennox six tries to get his speech right. I nailed the bark on the first take.

The lights in the Elk's Lodge came up just long enough for Chief Lennox, the evening's emcee, to switch tapes. The VCR popped and cracked, and the lights lowered once more. I looked away from the screen up to the ceiling. The string holding the middle section of my retirement banner had given way at some point during the previous video. The banner now draped in a depressed U-shape.

A cheer came from the lodge full of officers when the familiar beat and opening "Huh!" from the "Cops" theme song charged through the speakers. It was the *Grand City* episode featuring my segment with Officer Hart.

Fade in on Officer Hart behind the wheel as we patrolled northbound on Honor Drive. The camera whipped around to me in the back. I was all business now. No kids and no scripts for miles.

"A lot of people don't respect these dogs," Officer Hart said, too loud to the camera as he balanced his attention on the road and the camera. As I looked up at that screen and heard what Officer Hart had to say, I really wanted to smile and let my tongue hang out, but I wouldn't. If I smiled it meant that I accepted what they were doing to me. Not a chance. They decided that my days of riding in a squad car were over. Some piece of metallic tape playing in a machine was nothing to feel happy about. "Not just the criminals but even some officers think that dogs like Fritz are a prop or something, but not me. He's my partner. He's got my back, and I have his. People need to understand just how valuable these officers are. They can outrun, outjump, outlast, and sometimes, most of the time, really, they can out think just about any suspect we're after. They get to places we can't and have no fear. And that's just the run of the mill K-9. Now Fritz back there—"

He went on for a bit more about me. I'm uncomfortable relaying word for word how good he thought I used to be.

"Grand City units," a dispatcher said through the radio, "be advised on a confirmed stolen vehicle last seen travelling southbound on Honor past Marbush. Red, ninety-nine Ford pickup, plate similar to four, India, seven, eight, five, one, three. Driver is a male white, thirties, possibly on meth."

"Here we go," Officer Hart said as he grabbed his radio and looked to the camera. "This is K32, we're ninety-seven the area. We'll be checking southbound."

No sooner did he tell me to keep my eyes peeled did the stolen truck zoom by us on the other side of the street. Officer Hart spun the wheel hard, and the cameraman fell back into the door. It made for a hell of a shot. While he cranked the wheel, Officer Hart uttered a few bleep-worthy words that earned laughs from the audience in the lodge. We've all been there.

"K32," Officer Hart said, "I have visual on the vehicle, in pursuit southbound Honor approaching Highwater." The lights, and unfortunately, the sirens went on. Contrary to popular belief, not all stolen-car suspects took you on chases that spanned hours and hours and got news choppers flying above you. More often, they give up and pull over like this guy in the truck did. Officer Hart rolled down my window. "We're stopped with the suspect vehicle on Honor, just north of Hightower. I have one at gunpoint."

"K32, ten four. One at gunpoint."

Two hands came out from the driver's window with the fingers spread out. Officer Hart exited the vehicle with his gun drawn toward the truck.

"Stay behind my car," Officer Hart said to the cameraman. "You, in the truck, keep both your hands out where I can see them. Now reach down and open the door from the outside. Slowly!"

"Don't shoot me," the driver said, slurring from inside the truck.

"Shut up and do what I say. Tell him you're here too, Fritz. Speak."

I barked and snarled. They were always more scared of me than they were of a bullet. Bullets missed sometimes. I never did.

"Is that a dog?" the driver said. "Okay, I'm coming out. I'm coming out. Keep the dog away from me."

He opened the door and slowly got out with his hands up. He froze when he saw me and the gun staring him down.

"Get down on your stomach, face down, legs spread apart, hands behind your head!" The driver obeyed without a fight. "K32, I have the driver proned out."

Maybe it was the cameras, maybe it was fear, the meth, just plain stupidity, or a combination of all four, but suddenly the suspect hopped to his feet and made a run for it into oncoming traffic. Did he think he was going to get away? From us? From me? Officer Hart couldn't safely get after him and was yelling foot pursuit into his radio. He didn't have a clean shot on the suspect. I'd seen enough of this. I leapt out of the car and was across four lanes of highway like it was nothing. The cameraman cared not for his well-being and ran after me, forcing cars to slam on their brakes. By the time he caught up to me, I had the car thief face down on the center divider screaming in tears. Officer Hart pulled me off the guy and cuffed him.

Jump cut to us stuffing the crook in the back of another squad car. What didn't make it to the final cut :

"I didn't get a good shot of the bite," the cameraman said as he panted. "I was running after him, and the camera was too shaky. That dog's fast. Anyway, can we let this guy go and let Fritz get him again?"

"What?!" the cuffed man cried.

"A lot of guys will let us do that if we missed the shot," the cameraman said. "We don't have to, you know. Just if you want to make it more realistic looking, we can get a better shot, that's all I'm saying. Tell him to take another bite at least. Let's see if we can get the guy shaking or screaming real good before we take him in. This is about making people at home scared to mess with you guys. Come on, Fritz. Get some."

"I'm going to pretend like I didn't hear you say that," Officer Hart said.

"I would've ripped him up," Nitro said, sitting next to me back at the lodge. "Look at you. The biggest show in the industry and you're just standing there growling like some Chihuahua chasing a stuffed toy."

"There was no need to rip him up," I said. "He was detained. Look how out of breath he was already. I didn't need to do anything."

"Who said anything about *needing to*, Fritz? All I'm saying is that when I'm on that show, you better believe that the first chance I have to use full force I will be all over that like Nitro on a car thief. Get my drift?"

"Yeah. I get your—"

"That's a nationwide show, pops. You could've been the baddest dog in law enforcement. Instead, you look like a domesticated guard dog. Shame."

"I've used full force when the situation called for it, and you know it."

"Yeah, like the other night? How's that leg? You need a walker? Do we need to do a welfare check on you?"

My blood bubbled. The fur on the back of my neck stood at attention. My tail thumped, and my nails gripped into the tile floor. A rookie fresh out of the academy with the pre-packaged nerve to lecture me about police work. Me? The dog who pulled back-to-back twenty-hour days when this pup was still climbing through a litter to get some attention from mommy.

Being a cop is the highest calling a canine can seek. I know a few mutts who are into the whole Hollywood thing. You'd never catch me under the bright lights complaining about the catering. Not me. I was a cop, and that suited me fine. I was happy with where I was and where I'd been. I had no want nor need to be anything more than what I was; I had everything I wanted and wanted everything I had.

The clip finally ended with us processing the car thief back at the station, which thankfully brought an end to the video portion of the evening. Chief Lennox reassumed his position as the center of attention.

"Well, Fritz, it looks like the years have been kinder to some of us than others," Chief Lennox said. "You've earned your gray, my friend. Me, I sat at a desk and waited for mine. And when the day comes that they invent a proper dye that makes hair look natural without looking, and I quote you out there, Sgt. Lewis, yeah, I see you sitting out there, 'like you spray-painted your head with badger color,' well that'll be the day that I erase my gray hair for good. But Fritz here, he's earned his. It distinguishes him, and he wears it well. We're going to miss you around here, Fritz. So on behalf of the entire Grand City Police Department, I want to wish you a happy, healthy, and very long retirement full of relaxation."

Chief Lennox led a surprisingly decent applause in my tribute. That applause taunted me like steady rain on a day off. Slap, slap, slap on the concrete and across the face. Guess what, pal? You don't have a say in where you're going today.

I looked up at a quartet of faces not shouting out at me. Not calling my name. Not showing any emotion whatsoever beyond a startled clam. Just four sterile faces staring off into the great big whatever. The four elks heads mounted up on the wall directly across from and above me, overlooking the hall. They too had seen much better days.

"Time for some new blood," Nitro said, slicing through the ovation. "It's been that way for a long time around here too."

"You think there's room for one more up there?" I said.

"Stop embarrassing yourself," Nitro said. "You're making me uncomfortable with all this boo-hoo nonsense. How about you do us all a favor and take it like a real dog, will ya?"

There was plenty of room for me up there with the other heads. They wouldn't have to rearrange the other fellas for me to fit. I could fit snugly between any two of them or off to either side. A trip to the vet, a quick shot in the arm, and I wouldn't feel a thing. I'd fall asleep, and they'd pull out the shears, or saw, or sword, and when my eyes awoke, I'd have the best seat in the hall, next to my new friends: Okie, Salmon, Mickey, and Reginald. I'd be all head with no body to worry about anymore.

My leg wouldn't hurt, and I wouldn't feel bad about resting. Aesthetically, the best place for me would be right in the center of the four, placed a foot or two higher than the rest so that we'd come to a slight point; a pyramid of mounted heads.

These were the thoughts of a fool. They only succeeded in drowning out the cheers from my former co-workers. Of course there's no place for a German shepherd on a wall full of elk heads. That's a damn shame.

"And because Article Twelve, Section Forty-Seven of the Grand City Charter says so, we are forbidden from giving away city property," Chief Lennox said, "so we will now perform the informal ceremonial auctioning off of the dog." *Property?* With a showman's twirl of the arm, which revealed conclusive evidence of massive armpit stains, Chief Lennox turned to me and gave a bow. The elk heads looked down on me across their big stupid fat noses. Even their lips snickered in amusement. "On behalf of Grand City, I'm proud to offer a fine specimen up for grabs. A canine crime fighter the likes of which Grand City has never seen before."

"And one soon to be forgotten by canine crime fighter two point zero," Nitro said. "That's a computer reference. You know, for those of us that don't count our kibble on our paws."

"And we're going to start the bidding at one dollar," Chief Lennox said. "Are there any takers in the house?"

One hand went up.

"Going once?"

No other hands.

"Going twice?"

Still just one.

"Three times?"

Now this was insulting.

"Sold. To Officer Peter Hart for one dollar. That's quite a bargain you got for yourself."

"A dollar?" I said.

"Would you give it a break?" Nitro said. "It's the tradition, and you know it. We all get sold off for a buck at the end. I mean, I figure I'll net three or four myself, but that's me. When you factor in inflation, I bet I pull in double digits, but that's not gonna be for many, many years. But you, Fritz, a dollar is about all the market can bear."

Nitro was right. They squeezed every cent out of me they could. We don't earn a salary, but dogs on the force live better than just about every dog imaginable. Don't waste my time with those pampered mutts who go to salons; that's not being a dog. We were fed perfectly portioned meals at ten hundred, eighteen hundred, and ten hundred hours again the following morning on the dot (on holidays they gave us warm turkey and ham); all the fresh water we'd ever need; we were groomed often; our kennel was never anything but flea-less; and we were provided with every tool necessary to do our job to the best of our ability.

I've been shot at. I've sniffed out bombs, drug paraphernalia, and crime scenes. I've chased killers and gang members in the rain. I've been punched and had my fur ripped out. I've rescued people from collapsed buildings. I've been attacked with all sorts of weapons, both blunt and sharp, and I've had to bite an incalculable amount of people who'd been who knows where. At the end of all that, I'm worth a dollar. It takes Officer Hart approximately seventy seconds to make that amount.

Officer Hart stood up from the crowd and approached the stage. Like any police officer worth putting into a story, Officer Hart was taller than most and skinnier than nearly all of our fellow cops. He chose not to wear a mustache, which informally forever disqualified him from being a motorcycle officer. The stress of the job was starting to take its initial hold on Officer Hart. It gets to everyone sooner or later. If you're not careful, it clings to you. At first you think it makes you stronger. You're carrying the load. Someday, it's that load that's going to make you buckle when you're most vulnerable.

Officer Hart's hair was thinning, but not to the point where you'd say he was going bald. He kept up the last time we jogged together. I did have to slow my pace. Nothing noticeable to him. I didn't want him to think I was taking it easy. If anything, he might have thought it was me who had lost a step. Confidence is very important for a police officer. Call me melodramatic all you want, but when it's a matter of going back to your kennel at the end of the night or not, confidence in your abilities is all you have. I won't take that away from anyone. Not anyone I cared about. Officer Hart reached into his back pocket and retrieved his wallet.

"Do you take cash or credit?" Officer Hart said. More humor that fell deaf on my lone ears.

"Cash only, Hart," Chief Lennox said. "We're old fashioned around here."

I nearly expected Officer Hart to appear with one of those giant checks they ambush unsuspecting senior citizens with at their front door. A few years ago we busted a ring of burglars who'd duped seniors with those checks. That was a fun operation. Our detectives found the website the crooks hooked their victims with. A crude design that promised the elderly a chance at millions and a comfy retirement. All that was required was a name, address, phone number, and an optional social security number. We supplied the information for one of our safe houses.

They called a week later and told us that our entry was a finalist and gave us a date and time to be home at the address we provided. We hired an actress from the local playhouse to appear in the front window of the house when the nondescript unmarked van with no plates pulled up out front. The actress got cold feet at the last second, and we made Norton, a baby face right out of the academy, dress up in a wig and a muumuu.

The three crooks got out of the van with their prop check and cameras while Norton waved and welcomed them with a phony high-pitched voice. As soon as Norton opened the door, he pulled his gun and yelled "Freeze!" still using his granny voice. The rest of us swarmed on them from around the side of the house. One tried to make a run to the van, but I had him down before he was two steps off the porch. He split his jaw when his face slapped into the cement. Oh well, next time don't be a scumbag.

"Come here, Fritz," Chief Lennox said as he held Officer Hart's limp dollar bill high like it was an unearthed chunk of gold.

I popped up to my feet. My hip buckled, then my leg flinched, but it was nothing. Cops like it cold, and the air conditioning was cranked up too high. I stood between Chief Lennox and Officer Hart for one final photo op for the department photographer and a guy with a hole in his pants from the local free paper, The Grand City Metro Review.

The uninformed will tell you that dogs don't smile. I didn't when cameras were around because it was usually at a crime scene or a standoff situation. Neither is appropriate for mugging at the lens. But when our mouths are open and our tongues are draped out to the side, what do you think that is other than a smile? Next time you see a picture of a dog, look at the ears. Are they straight up or out to the side? Check the eyes. Wide open or just regular open? Is the head tilted up? These things matter. I tried to work a smile, I really did.

I saw the picture from the department photographer a few days later. The Chief and Officer Hart held the dollar up over my head, oblivious to how disrespectful it was.

"And on a final note," Chief Lennox said, "I also don't want to forget to mention the work of Nitro, our newest K-9, who played an integral role of getting us closer to our suspect, a known dog-fight operator."

"That's my cue, old man," Nitro said.

I could do a lot of things, but I wasn't going to stand around like a sucker while they paraded my replacement in front of my face. I left through the back door and no one noticed, not even Officer Hart, who already had returned to his seat. My tail wasn't tucked completely between my legs, but it was too close for comfort. If anyone had seen me, they wouldn't have noticed a tail drooping a few inches lower; it was just another tail to them. But not me. That was my tail.

## Chapter Three - The Long Leash Goodbye

The *Grand City Police Department Kennel* was my home for eight years. It was modest, and that suited me fine. I've always stood firmly alongside the notion that a coddled officer was an ineffective officer. Some argue that having nice things to come home to is the motivation you need to get you through your shift. They're wrong. That comfort makes you soft. My sole luxury was my bed. I could rest my chin on the side, and my body would float on a cloud of cotton padding until the next thing I knew, Officer Hart was there with a treat, and we were ready to go out on patrol again.

My kennel was where I decompressed after a long night. It was a place to spend a quiet evening with my thoughts. I analyzed what worked out there and what didn't, how the criminals reacted and how I reacted to them. Did something surprise me? Could I have been more effective in the same scenario?

As you pulled into the department parking garage, I was off in the back on the bottom floor through a door marked "The Ears and *Knows* of the Department." I shared a wall with the holding cell and the drunk tank. You might think that would've been a problem, your place of rest and wonder being in such close proximity to the nightly derelicts. One thing about cops is that we look out for one another. If a prisoner was too inebriated, we'd play a little game with them. Red Johnny.

When a drunk was too loud for their own good, and if they looked gullible enough or were under the influence of the right concoction of illicit substances, the jailer would issue them a stern warning.

"You may think this is a load of garbage," a typical Red Johnny warning began, "but if you don't pipe down, you're messing with some powerful stuff."

"Oh yeah," began a typical response. "What are you guys gonna do? Get ten of you in there to come kick my ass? Huh?"

"No. That would be easy. We don't go into Red Johnny's jurisdiction. He's gonna handle you."

"I don't see no Red Johnny. What're you talking about?"

Depending on the jailer or the booking officer, some details changed with the storyteller, but the by-the-book story is as follows : The jail was haunted by the ghost of, guess who, Red Johnny. Johnny was an old Grand City bootlegger who was finally done in by the law back in 1927. They only caught him because he was marching around the town square stark-raving mad as a result of rabies, which had eaten away at his brain. Hours later, while waiting for transport that was delayed in a terrible storm, Red Johnny succumbed in that cell. He was clawing away at the wall and growling and barking at the ceiling. From that moment on, that cell became the unofficial property of Red Johnny. To this day, he haunts the cell where his last breath was taken from him. There was only one thing Red Johnny hated more than spending eternity in that cell. It was when someone else was there who wouldn't let him rest.

"I don't believe in that stuff," was the typical response to a Red Johnny tale, regardless of any appended details.

When I heard "Red Johnny," I waited for a few minutes, and then I barked as loud as I could and scratched at the wall. The jailers would pretend not to hear anything when the drunk complained about the noise. After all, Red Johnny's powers were of another world, and it wasn't the jailers who were bothering him. The longest it took me to shut someone up was just over four minutes. When it was over, the boys would reward me with some extra treats, usually a day-old doughnut.

Most of my peers from other cities lived with their partner, but not me. I was fine with that. Officer Hart visited me every day, even on his days off. Sometimes he brought his family with him so they could get to know me better. His wife would let me smell her palm and scratched my cheek. There was one time in particular when she brought a new visitor with her and Officer Hart. At the time she was pregnant, smelled like a hospital room, and otherwise kept her distance from me. The unexpected guest was another dog with them on a leash.

My initial reaction was *unremarkable*. That's not fair. *Normal* is a better choice of words. Very normal. A regular dog for a regular family. Maybe with a touch of German shepherd in him but the ears sagged too much for me to respect him.

"This is Fritz," Officer Hart said as he walked the leashed dog closer. "You want to say hi?"

Officer Hart led him over to me for a sniff through the chain link. From nowhere, this guy gets the nerve to raise his lip and show me some teeth. In my own kennel. I snarled and showed this guy what real teeth looked like, teeth that were capable of snapping more than milk bones. Out of respect for Officer Hart and his wife, I didn't make a bigger deal out it. I rose up and stared him down until he lowered his underdeveloped head. Officer Hart got between us and passed the leash back to his wife, who said something about rescuing that other dog like she wanted to do in the first place.

You don't do that to a dog in his home, showing your teeth like that, unless you're ready to take that home and make it your own. And nobody was taking my home from me that day.

"Who do you think you are?" Nitro said, having been led into the kennel by his partner.

"Leave it alone," I said.

"You got to upstage me one last time, huh?"

"I wasn't upstaging anyone. I just wanted to leave."

"Oh, I see. Whining and yelping to anyone who'll listen that even with a bum wheel he can still work but now you just want to up and leave. Look, I took your spot whether you like it or not. You want to say I'm playing politics, old man, fine. For them to remember me they have to forget about you. That's how it works. By you making your little escape back there, you know what the first thing everyone said was?"

"Really? They asked for me?"

"You should have heard them," Nitro said. "'Where's Fritz?' 'Is he okay?' 'Hey, do you think this whole thing is a mistake?' 'Let's take a vote. Who here thinks Fritz still has that *it* that he always had, huh, whadda ya say?'"

"Wow," I said. "What was the vote?"

"No. I'm kidding. No one noticed you vanished except me. Fritz, you should be happy—"

"Happy?"

"Let me finish," Nitro said as he circled around me. "Listen, you made it out. You have a hobble, so what? It'll probably heal. If not, it's a reminder of, you know, all your battles."

"I don't need a reminder."

"No more chases. No more late nights. No more stress. No more putting on a happy face for the press. You can finally relax. You know, plenty of dogs in our field don't get to enjoy this. Are you listening to me? I'm giving you some solid advice here."

"Fine. You want to trade places with me then?"

"Seriously? You trying to be a comedian? Trade with you? No way."

"There's cops on this force who can barely zip their pants up, and I'm being forced out. You don't get it, Nitro."

"I don't get what? Let me take a guess what the big mystery is. Someday I'm going to be in your place, and some younger, faster, stronger, quicker, smarter, sharper facial structure, buffer, leaner, and just better overall dog is going to take my spot? Okay, fine. But you know what? That's not happening today, and it's not going to happen tomorrow, so I'm not losing any sleep over it tonight."

With that final salvo, Nitro went over to my bed, the only bed I ever remembered sleeping in. He unceremoniously dragged it to the other end of the kennel, next to the shared wall with the holding cell.

"No, you don't get it," I said. "There's a reason why they don't bring the old-timers around to say hi. A very real reason."

"Blah, blah, blah. I have a big day tomorrow. It's time to start the rest of my life. So yeah, just uh, get all your stuff because if it's here tomorrow, I'm chewing it."

I don't know what hurt more the knowledge that it was all over or knowing that I didn't even fight back. I stayed up as long as I could that night because I knew when I closed my eyes and fell asleep that as soon as I opened them again it would be over. It would be time to go for good. Perhaps, I expected a stay of execution, hoping that Chief Lennox would burst in during the night to tell me that Officer Hart's dollar was no good because he changed his mind. I wanted to take in every last moment I had in there. It wasn't long before I gave up on giving myself moments. They decided I'd had enough.

"Can't even leave on your own four feet," Nitro said a few hours later between bites of his breakfast.

I hobbled out of the kennel for the final time to Officer Hart's waiting Intimidator (last year's model). Mrs. Hart waited for me with the trunk open and the tailgate down. When humans are discharged from a hospital, they roll them out in a wheelchair just to be safe. If they're not healthy enough to walk out, why send them home?

I got a few steps away from the kennel with Officer Hart when he put me on a leash. A new one, from the smell of it. A few of the guys came up to scratch my ears on our way out. The morning shift already had their briefing and was dismissed, so there weren't too many around to say bye. Actually, that was a good thing. I didn't want them to see me being walked out. You don't put a professional on a leash.

Maybe they were worried I'd tried to go back. Maybe they thought that I didn't know where I was going or what was going on. That's probably the biggest mistake people make with us. We know.

I put my paws up on the tailgate and was ready to hop up when Mrs. Hart pulled me back by my collar.

"No, no," she said. "Peter. I need help getting him in. Can you help please?"

"One, two, three," Officer Hart said as he grabbed me around the ribs and hoisted me into the Intimidator. I shrugged him off and shook myself. When people seize you like that it messes up the fur and makes taking a breath tougher than nature wanted it to be. "He couldn't jump in on his own?"

"He looked like he was struggling. I didn't want him to get hurt."

"Awww, well, we don't want our Fritz-o here getting hurt now, do we?" Officer Hart said, in a tone I'd never heard before and never wanted to hear again. It was sloppy, goofy, and high-pitched. *Frtiz-o?* Who was this guy, and what had he done with my partner of eight years? "Now you just go lie down, buddy. We'll get a treat for you once we get going."

Leaving the force was one thing. Actually, it was more than *one* thing, it was *the* thing, but for this very moment, it was just one thing. You can't yank a dog from all he knows, then, as a last kick in the teeth, his partner, his buddy, the guy who watched his back and vice versa, his fellow cop, was now acting like a civilian?

And for the record, I could've gotten myself up there on that tailgate just fine. I think.

Officially, they're called suburbs. We, and I'm talking cops, have a few other names. Night off patrol. Real crime not allowed-ville (a good idea, but far too wordy). The call of the mild. Yawn shift. Feel free to invent your own.

On the contrary, dogs only need one word for them in their vernacular. Jackpot. For every dog with a weekly-gardened lawn to grow old in, there are a thousand other hounds chasing their tails in apartments, condos, or worst of all, mobile homes. Others choose to travel solo down the road looking for scraps and a dry patch of dirt to curl up in for the night.

I'd encountered a handful of suburban dogs in my career, and while they seemed nice enough, I was never impressed. A bit too well-fed. Too relaxed. Too comfortable for my liking. For a dog to be a dog, he's got to still have that itch. No, not fleas.

Through no fault of his own, a dog is naturally drawn toward laziness. Even I am not immune toward a want to indulge in some quality laziness. You must resist that urge and stay lean and hungry. Lean and suburbs only have a passing relationship.

Making it to the suburbs guaranteed a dog a life of laziness. There was nothing left to worry about anymore. Food and water? Taken care of. Shelter? Covered (literally). Affection? As long you didn't bite the little ones, you're golden. Some people even bought gifts for the dogs. Gifts. And you don't have to do anything for them other than sit down when they ask you to. Some will demand that you lay down, but for a dog, that's never going to be a problem. It's what we do. Not *me*, of course. You could even bark and yell at the sirens when they bothered you. Just don't take advantage by keeping at it after they're out of human earshot.

So when I tell you that making it to the suburbs is akin to getting six balls out of six on the lottery, I am in no way exaggerating.

Me? I've never be a gambler.

The Intimidator pulled away from the department with me in the back next to a bag of soccer balls. Officer Hart honked at Cary, the crossing guard, as we rolled through the intersection between the department and Fair Oaks Blvd. We were out of eyeshot before I had a chance to poke my head up to say goodbye.

Officer Hart and Mrs. Hart sat up front. Simon, the Hart's ten-year-old boy with hair and freckles in every direction, rode in the backseat. He sat sideways with his back to the window, the seatbelt somehow wrapped around both of his arms and waist, and his shoes up on the seat. When prisoners pulled that nonsense with the shoes up on the seat, Officer Hart put an end to it quick.

"High side left!" he'd call out and then slam on the brakes, making the prisoner tumble over in the back. This worked especially well on the overly inebriated. On occasion we could high side them until they puked all over the back and would make them clean out the car when we returned to the station.

"Honey," Mrs. Hart said. "Please take your shoes off the seat."

"Fine," Simon said as he used his toes to peel off the heels of his crisscrossed, superhero-movie-tie-in Velcro shoes. He shook his ankles until the shoes, and an inch of sand, flopped onto the floor of the Intimidator. He kept his feet and wet socks up on the seat. I smelled those feet immediately. You want to know what human feet smell like once and for all? Just plain unnatural. A smell that you wouldn't expect to exist on the same planet that's home to barbecue sauce. A smell that hits you with the same force as when someone who (wisely) doesn't live with cats enters the dwelling of someone with several feline roommates. The smell isn't going to kill anyone, and it goes away as you get used to it, but that first whiff is like sprinting into a fence.

"Your mom told you to take your shoes off the seat."

"I did, dad."

"Honey, stop," Mrs. Hart said. "Aren't you excited about Fritz, Simon?"

"I like Nipper."

"Don't you like Fritz?"

"I like Ernie."

"Ernie is fine too, but let's focus on Fritz, okay?"

"I even like Missy."

Nipper? Ernie? *Missy?* Fine names on their own, but I didn't know where this kid got off thinking he was going to start changing my name. You'd run into a guy in cuffs on the curb, and he'd start in with the same one-liners: *here poochie pooch; hey, Fido; c'mere, Lassie.* If no one was looking and I caught some scumbag saying that to me, I'd bite 'em just a little. But you can't even take just a little nibble on a kid, not that I'd want to. I got up and put my head over the seat to see what Simon was talking about.

"Move, Fritz," he said as he pushed my head back. "Jeez."

"Honey, you can't push Fritz like that," Mrs. Hart said. "We talked about how he's different."

"What's going on?" Officer Hart said as he looked back while he kept the Intimidator straight. Mrs. Hart put her arm up as to grab the wheel with a "honey" that rang more critical than the "honey" Simon received. Hasn't she seen him drive before? We've gone triple digits off road through the rain on chases, and she's worried about him turning his head?

"Fritz's shadow is blocking the TV, Dad. I'm trying to watch this, so I made him move."

"You can't do that with Fritz," Officer Hart said.

"I do it to the other dogs."

"Fritz isn't like other dogs—" I didn't even care what he said after that. Those five words were the only bright spot I'd had in days. That's right; I wasn't like other dogs. I'd run twelve miles without as much as a pant, even in the sun. I sniffed out the best hidden contraband; try hiding it in a baggie in your rewrapped plastic-shampoo bottle, I dare you. I ran in after they threw the tear gas and yanked the hijacker out by his arm. I pulled an all-nighter in the cold chasing someone through a forest, and I still looked good on no sleep for the PR gig in the morning. I dodged bullets when I had to. I bet you couldn't name another dog who'd done all that and was still standing. "—so you can't treat him the way you treat other dogs, you understand?"

I understood perfectly.

"Fine," Simon said, reaching over to scratch my head. "Sorry, Fritz. Just don't get in the way of my TV again, okay?"

By this time, we were somewhere between the third and fourth levels of suburbia, beyond the supermarket and hair salons and just getting to the churches and parks. The deeper you got into this place, the bigger everything became. The houses were all painted from the same palette of light hues. The boats were all the same color of blood. The sports cars were painted like the moon. The flowers smelled like poisons. The Intimidators and their kin were dark and shiny. And somehow there I was riding in the back of the Hart family Intimidator on my way to the rest of my life in the suburbs. My leg was still bandaged, but I kept myself occupied trying to pull that thing off before we got home. Home. There's a concept.

Then it hit me. I hadn't had a clean place to mark in years. I couldn't remember the last time when I was the first to claim a spot for my own territory. It might have been that time out behind the Atlantic Octo-Plex movie theater when I wanted to cover some unsightly graffiti. They discouraged us from marking on the job. It didn't look professional and I agreed. Maybe somewhere else that's no biggie, but that's not how we did things in Grand City. I'd been everywhere and now there was nothing left for me. Just high-end tract homes with too many pesticides in the yards. There was nowhere left for me. To mark or otherwise.

The streets were as flat as the lawns. The driveways were inclined. Pigeons didn't sit on the streetlights. The mailboxes were all cemented into the sidewalk. The fences were all the same height, just too high to peek over without a ladder. The trees lining the sidewalks were all decades older than the homes and did an excellent job of keeping the power lines out of sight.

One thing distinguished the Hart residence from the others – a carved, rustic-looking wooden trinket that hung below the address numbers and said, "Home is where the Harts are!" with a silhouette of a mom, dad, son, and a dog carved into it. One of those things you got at the swap meet for the same price as the bag of organic coffee being sold the next booth over. In the academy, they tell you to never give away your position when you're in the field. There was no need for a strategic advantage out in that neighborhood.

"Are you ready for your new home, Fritz?" Mrs. Hart said, turning to me. Officer Hart killed the ignition.

Did I have a choice?

# CHAPTER FOUR – SPEAKING IN THE SECOND DOG (IN THE ROOM)

You know the anticipation you're supposed to feel, but don't, when you're standing outside an open door waiting to go in somewhere you've never been before? You ever been at a place where you recognized every smell, but none are familiar? You ever not know what was on the other side of that door and not care? You ever look around and not be interested in anything in any direction?

You ever felt the slight push of the air as the front door opened, pulling you inside like water down the drain? You ever tried to stay outside as long as you could until she nudged you in, complaining about how cold it is outside? You ever get promised a treat just for entering? You ever smelled another dog off to your left? You ever heard your nails go tap-tap-tap on the floor? You ever stopped walking because you don't know where to go next? You ever realized how dumb you must look standing there like a fool when everyone else just went in and got on about their business like it was nothing? You ever not believe them when they said, "This is your home now," and they dropped a treat in front of you that snapped in three pieces as it hit the linoleum? You ever know that you're being told the truth and you wished it was a lie?

You ever think about how many chemicals went into making something look and smell clean? You ever tried to figure out where you're going to sleep for the night within two hours of waking up? You ever looked around to find where someone else decided was the place to leave your food?

You ever think it was over there?

You ever think it might have been over here?

You ever think it was in another room?

You ever get suspicious when that smell from the other dog hadn't moved or changed its slow breathing? You ever thought that you needed to figure out who else was in that room before you worried about food and shelter? You ever smelled scented dog shampoo? You ever wondered if they got vanilla confused with just plain, old, cheap soap? You ever feel relieved when the kid runs off into the house and you wouldn't be stuck having to play with him? You ever smelled a roast from the kitchen and knew that you weren't going to get a bite of it, and if by some chance you did, it was going to be the lousy overcooked center?

You ever wondered if that other dog knew you were there? You ever finally walked down off the circular step a few feet beyond the door into the living room? You ever wondered why they put a step there in the first place? You ever realized that in a fire, or some other kind of pressure situation, to take a single step up a few feet before the front door is a hazard for most humans?

You ever felt like an idiot when you discovered that what alerted your senses and put you on guard was a sleeping Poodle, curled up in a puffy bed next to the television? You ever choose to have some fun at someone's expense only to instantly realize that you were overcompensating for feeling a moment of weakness? You ever crept up on a sleeping dog to see how far you can get before it woke up? You ever justified your bit of cruelty by saying that you were testing to see if you still had some of the same functioning skillset you had three years ago? You ever heard him in the background tell her to not worry and that you've had the best training in the world while being totally aware of the apprehension that reverberated through his words?

You ever felt like a common criminal because you knew that you were acting like a bully but that it was too late to back out because you were inches away from someone you should've just left alone? You ever pondered what someone was dreaming about while you watched them sleep? You ever saw eyes awaken and leap from zero-to-terror in a heartbeat? You ever watched a white bundle of fur shoot straight up and fly across the room, nearly crashing into the table leg?

You ever heard them scream, "Missy, it's okay" and your heart dropped?

You ever felt like a fool?

You ever been told that, "Well, this experiment failed," and that you were going to be an "outdoor dog" now?

I have. And I bet you have too.

## CHAPTER FIVE – YOU EVER READ *NO EXIT?*

"I know it's no department kennel," Officer Hart said, sounding more like the partner I remembered, "but I'd say it's a nice place to retire, buddy."

He closed the French doors behind us and walked me into his backyard. My final resting place. You know, you toss a roof on a backyard and you essentially have yourself a jail cell. Let that rattle around your dome a bit.

"Dammit," Officer Hart said, tripping over a Wiffle ball bat and spilling most of the water he had for me in the bowl. He placed the bowl off to the right of the doors, a few feet away from the barbeque–a big, long, metal furnace built into the wall. What I assumed was my new water bowl was placed next to an old pot, one big enough to cook a few pounds of pasta in. That too was also filled with water, not that it was fresh water, unless your definition of fresh included floating strands of grass and clotted dirt at the bottom. The bowl Officer Hart set down was constructed with dogs in mind–it was plastic and looked like it would slide across the concrete with a slight gust of wind. It even had a fading police badge painted on the front side of the bowl. "Well, here's some water, Fritz. I'm sure you're thirsty. Don't drink the other water. This bowl here is special and just for you. The food is over there on the other end of the barbecue, and it's for everyone. That's about it for now, Fritz. I'm sure you'll find plenty of toys around here if you look. I'll be back in a bit, so just relax and enjoy your new surroundings. Good luck with your new neighbors."

He knelt down beside me and scratched behind my ears, right on the sweet spot, the place where otherwise you'd spend hours trying to dig your paw in as deep as you can. A really good scratch requires digits with the ability to form into a hook shape. Alas, we dogs can't pull that off. The singular flaw on an otherwise superb creation by nature.

Like any good ear scratch it wasn't long enough. Just as I turned my head into the pressure, Officer Hart stopped. He patted me on the spine (a popular human gesture, but one that falls severely short when compared to the ear rub) and went back into the house.

I was alone. With no one around me. No other dogs. No people. Maybe this wouldn't be such a bad thing after all. I could hear myself think again. Thinking is one of those mundane things you don't know you're missing until you sit down and do it again. So, not wanting to waste any more time, I took a moment on the patio to just think. The trouble was trying to decide what to think about. Now that my life had stopped, more or less, there wasn't anything left to consider. All the interesting stuff had already happened. If I'd stopped to think about it when it was going on, I would have missed it. Thus, giving myself nothing to think about. It wasn't like I could do anything about the past, which brought me right back to trying to come up with something to think about.

A ha! I remembered a smell from my past, from my youth. I couldn't place its origin and had a hard time deciphering what it even was, but there it was lingering right out there in front of my nose. Maybe a dog I once met? I didn't know if I was chasing a memory or if I was experiencing one of those smells that meant there was something wrong with my brain. I was suddenly exhausted. You're not supposed to feel your brain working. It's supposed to be going on automatic, feeding on instincts.

The instincts. That was it. Instincts. They always came back when the mind was clear. I decided that's what I would think about. How they never let me down. Not once. Your guts put you in a scary situation on the job, and the instincts got you out. The trick to being in tune with your instincts was to not think about them, just let them be. That's what I remembered. In fact, thanks to those instincts, I knew that while I sat there on the side of the Hart house, I was being hunted at that moment.

My thoughts would have to be placed on pause for the time. Without turning my head, I twisted my ear enough to the outside to know I was being watched from above and from behind. I heard something crawling, something large. One sniff confirmed a familiar smell. Human child, male, approximately twelve years of age, with processed cheesy puffs smeared around his mouth. I turned, and he froze. He was in the next yard over hanging on top of a wooden play fortress, and his ratty eyes were aimed at me.

"You can't get me, stupid dog," he said, taunting.

Oh yes I could. Before he'd have time to soil himself, I could have vaulted off the patio table, pushed off the cinderblock wall, and took his arm home as a souvenir. But I'd been trained to know better. Instead I stared, sans growl. That rattled the little brat, but his distance from me seemed to only re-inflate his confidence.

I watched him shove his foot into a corner of the wooden fort for support. This play set was huge and a waste of space; far too big for one child to play on alone. I didn't break eye contact with the varmint, but peripherally, I counted three swings, a rope climb, monkey bars, and a two-story slide. He gingerly balanced himself and stood straight up on the cross beam. To put it in perspective, his knees were parallel with the top of the block wall that separated the two properties.

"Freeze," he said, reaching around to the back of his camouflage shirt and retrieving a bright pump-action water gun with a long tube of sloshing liquid connected to the foot-long barrel. Not the first time I'd found myself in the sights of such a weapon. Only three months into my career, I led a charge into a drug lab that was disguised as a foreclosed home in the projects. As I flew down the hallway, a junkie popped out of the closet and fired a similar weapon at me. He didn't get a second shot off, but it wasn't until my adrenaline wore off that I felt my right arm burning and saw that my skin was singed and my fur was gone. I licked the bare skin, and whatever he must've shot me with made me sick. I doubted this ill-footed child was packing the same heat. "I said freeze. Don't move, and I'll make it quick."

One of the things you learn while working as a tool of the public-relations division is that sometimes you have to take one on the chin. But since I technically was not a Grand City employee any longer, I wondered how many of the old standards I needed to heed. While I was busy thinking (that old trap), the kid shot me in the head. I wrongly assumed he would need to pump up the air pressure first, but no, he climbed that fort loaded and ready for battle while I was still getting used to the notion of a backyard for life.

The rope of water slapped me in the side of the head and across my shoulder. A clean hit with some zip to it. The water dripped below my eye and around the side of my jaw.

"Ten points! Ten points! Ten points for me! Yeah! Whooooo!" the water hunter shouted.

He threw his arms up in the air like a victorious prizefighter. In that same motion, he also threw himself off the fort. An excellent lesson about momentum and balance. His gun hung in the air like a cliché before joining with a clang to match the boy's thud and tumble down the slide.

And yes, I found that funny. As should you.

"You should have been there, man," said an unknown, flippant voice. "The rush was something else. Especially when you stop in the middle of the street and just stare at them until they swerve. If you can make eye contact with them, they always get out of the way."

"What happens if you don't make eye contact?" another voice said, this one trying too hard to be condescending.

"You better keep running."

"So let me get this straight. You almost get hit by a semi, and it's the time of your life?"

"Bingo. Hey, why you think they penned us in this morning?"

"I don't know, but don't worry. I'll figure it out."

"Yeah. Sure, Nipper."

Then the two of them came around the corner, and the three of us stopped cold. There was that smell that teased me minutes ago, the same one that lost its ticket and was wandering around my mind looking for an empty seat.

"Who are you?" the first one, Nipper, the one closest to the side of the house who was about my size, said. Shorter, not as thick, but a better-than-average-sized dog. Clearly, he had some Shepherd in him but not enough to correct the ears hanging low on both sides of his head. He had eyes that didn't reveal a whole lot of depth, and his arms were skinny. "What are you doing here?"

"Hold on–" I said.

"I asked what you're doing here."

"Relax, Nipper," the other one said. The other one was short, thicker than me, rust-looking, and built like a replacement engine. I had no idea what breed he was supposed to be representing.

"Whose water is that?" Nipper said.

"Mine," I said.

"Impossible."

"C'mon, pal," the other one said. "What's really going on?"

"If your partner would breathe and relax his tail back there–"

"Don't tell me what to relax, bub. This is my, our, me and Ernie's yard and we don't appreciate loiterers."

"Actually, you mean to say I'd be trespassing," I said. "Loitering has to do with remaining in a public place for an extended period. It's a law that's meant to give police the ability to break up potentially unruly groups of people, the homeless, but no, what you think I'm doing is trespassing, but that's beside the point. And really, I'm not actually trespassing either because I was invited here, and no one has asked me to leave."

"Oh, a wise guy," Ernie said.

"The point is that I'm not trespassing, and no, I'm not loitering."

"Could've fooled me," Nipper said.

"Somehow, that doesn't seem a task too difficult to achieve," I said.

"What'd you say, pal?"

"You heard me," I said. Nipper took a step toward me. I took three steps toward him. He lowered his head. I went lower. He puffed up his back. Un-puffed, I was still bigger. "And we aren't pals by the looks of it."

"Hold on," Ernie said, getting between us and facing me. He backed Nipper off and then came up to sniff me, sticking his snout under my chin and eyeballing me. He smelled sweet, like fresh dirt. Clean fresh dirt. Yes, there's a difference between clean and dirty dirt. "I'm sure there's a perfectly good explanation for what this guy's doing here. Wait a second, were you crying?"

"Was I *what?*" I said.

"You look like you were crying, no offense."

"Looks can be deceiving, Shorty," I said.

"Did you just call me Shorty?"

"That's what I said. Shorty."

"Look, I don't have a problem with you yet. I don't even know your name. I just call it the way I see it, and what I see is that it looks like you've been crying."

"He's crying, Ernie?" Nipper said. "That's hilarious."

"It's water from that jerk next door," I said. "He shot me."

"Sure he did," Nipper said.

"Hey, what in the–" Ernie said as something caught his eye. He walked behind me and stopped at my water bowl. He sniffed it and took a quick sip. I hadn't drank from it as of yet, so I had no official claim to that bowl. I nudged Ernie aside and stuck my nose in for a gulp. Now it was mine.

"Just to clear that up," I said.

"Whatever," Ernie said, under his breath. "I already got one. Besides, that one's not yours anyway."

"What?" I said, licking my chops.

"That's his."

"His who?"

"His," Ernie said, pointing to Nipper. "Hey Nipper, remember your old water bowl? The one we thought they lost?"

"My cop bowl?" Nipper said, still sitting but bouncing on his hind legs like he was working up the nerve to walk over.

"Here it is. I found it."

"This is it," Nipper said, joining us at the water bowl. He batted it around with a paw until the badge showed. Nipper sniffed the badge. "How'd you get this?"

"Officer Hart gave it to me."

"I don't believe you."

"And I don't care what you believe," I said. "He gave it to me. It's my bowl now. As far as you and I are concerned, it's always been my bowl, got it, Jack?"

"Jack?" Nipper said. "What are you talking about? Who's Jack?"

"It's cop talk," Ernie said. "I heard it all the time on the streets. They call you Jack when they're trying to act like they're friendly, but really they're about to bust ya."

"Ah, I see," Nipper said. "So this crybaby here thinks he's gonna get tough in my yard, with my bowl."

That was enough. I'd been insulted by worse and challenged by much better. There comes a time when words have failed and all that's left is for you to drag your paw and draw a line through the sand. I put my paw in the bowl and slid it behind me, under my tail.

"You want this bowl?" I said, whispering through my grin. "All you have to do is make me move, and then you can take it. It's yours."

"Nipper," Ernie said.

"He's bluffing," Nipper said.

"Am I?" I said, licking my front teeth so I knew that he'd get a good look at them. Of course, I'd never do this in real life, but this goofball was hardly real life. It worked. Of course it worked. And, of course, I was bluffing. I wasn't going to do anything to this guy. I'd never disrespect Officer Hart like that. I knew Nipper wouldn't try me; not even in an alternative universe somewhere on the outskirts of the cosmos was Nipper going to do anything other than step back, which is what he did. "Now can we put this issue of the bowl behind us?"

"Good idea," Ernie said.

"Fine," Nipper said. "It's just a faded old bowl that no one here wanted anyway. You know what, after taking a good look at it, it's all dented up anyway. Water probably tastes worse in that bowl, so you might as well have it. Otherwise, they might as well just throw it out with the rest of the garbage."

That one hurt. It hurt worse anything else he could have done to me in that yard. And it wasn't like some stupid joke from Nitro. Nipper was more right than he knew. That bowl belonged to me, after all. At least Nipper had no idea what he'd done. One good thing about the encounter was that it momentarily allowed me a chance to forget how badly my leg was throbbing, but as soon as I realized that the pain was gone, it had a tricky way of jumping right back into place.

# Chapter Six – Be on the Lookout

EXTRA!!!! EXTRA!!!!
WOOF-ington Bank Robbed!
Subjects unleashed and considered dangerous. Rabies not ruled out!

By Col Lee

(AP) A gang of canine bandits have struck again, this time nabbing over 10,000 pounds of chew bones from the Woofington Bank vault late last night...

Or so read the plastic chew toy next to me in the corner of the yard. The fact that they actually paid someone to come up with that nonsense story to put on a squeaky plastic toy still amazes me. Who was it for? Certainly not for us. Other than the dogs working on the force, I can't think of any who could read a word. Never mind that, who would want to? Honestly, I don't even think that what we do is reading to begin with. Over time, you see humans perform similar behaviors around certain letters and symbols, and eventually you can piece together enough of a vocabulary to be able to plough through a sentence or two of human. And then there are all the languages you have to deal with, as if interspecies communication wasn't already a difficult enough road to navigate. I don't know who came up with the idea for humans to have different words for the same thing, but I'd guess they were no fan of law enforcement. The only word that everyone seems to agree on is *no*. Thankfully, it's one we used a lot. I can't count how many times I sat by while humans yelled at each other with no one knowing what the other meant. The more someone didn't understand, the louder the other would get. As if volume somehow translated to comprehension. That only worked for us. It was always the person who relied on increased volume that ended up hogtied in the back of the squad car. Pick one language, the one that most humans understand, make that the rule, and be done with it.

We dogs got it right, same with just about every other animal, with the exception of birds for whatever reason. We can bark anything, and no matter what breed we're rapping with: Boxer, Spaniel, whomever, it all makes sense to us.

My point is that the little story about the bank robbery was meant for humans. I dread meeting the human who finds that amusing. Odds are it's the same type you encountered on a drunk call. Here's the secret to crafting a successful dog toy— you only need two things – the ability to be chewed, and noise-making capabilities that simulate pain when you bite it. That's it.

Not that I ever had time to play with toys in my youth, and I was far too old to start playing with them. I was put off by how many toys Nipper and Ernie had scattered across the yard. In addition to the newspaper, there was a mini-football, a collection of gnarled, drool-stained tennis balls, assorted rubber bones, a thick multi-shaded rope with a frayed end tied to a ball with plastic spikes, some long feather-and-stick combination item that looked better suited for a cat, and an old stuffed monkey, which I assumed belonged to Nipper.

"How long you gonna be here?" Ernie said. Ernie acted like an unofficial mediator between me and Nipper. I kept my distance from Nipper and Ernie. They stayed on one side of the yard, I stayed on the other. I took to the northwest corner of the yard, away from the neighbor's fort. For the first tense hours after my arrival, Ernie brought messages from Nipper to me and asked if I had anything to offer back in return.

"I just want to take a nap," I said. "By the way, do either of you sleep here?"

I wasn't accustomed to sleeping outdoors, but I felt the change of scenery would be good for my fur. Thanks to a poor choice of lawnmower, or a case of canine laziness rubbing off on Officer Hart, the grass in the extreme corner was a few inches higher and provided a nice bit of cushioning for me. As an added bonus, my location guaranteed that the sun would hit me bright and early. No wonder it went unclaimed until then.

"I'm over by the garden," Ernie said, "and Nipper goes right by the—"

"Yes or no?"

"Like I was saying, no."

"Then this corner is mine to sleep."

"No problem," Ernie said. "Don't matter to me. I don't mind the company personally. I've been in the pound plenty of times—"

"You've been locked up?" I said as my ears shot up.

"Yeah. Why?"

"What for?"

"Nothing major. Otherwise I wouldn't be here."

"That's what they all say."

"*They?*"

"I've seen your type a million times before. In and out of the pound, causing trouble. It's never your fault, right? You're always catching a bad case or something. The powers that be have it out for you or some line of bull. You may be out now, but I haven't met someone who never went back. They always go back. Just a matter of when."

"Not me," Ernie said. "You won't catch me locked up ever again. Not even here in the yard."

"If you say so."

"I'm just trying to be friendly here. Strike up some convers— Wait a second. Nipper was right about you. Hey, Nipper."

Nipper was peeking from around the tool shed in the opposite corner of the yard like I hadn't known he'd been there the entire time.

"You say something, Ernie?" Nipper said, his voice bouncing off the cheap aluminum.

"Yeah," Ernie said as he backed away from me without breaking eye contact. "I can't believe I missed it."

When he was far enough from me, Ernie turned and ran off to go behind the tool shed with Nipper. Ernie's tail thumped off the side of the shed over and over. I ignored the annoying back-and-forth slaps of bone on sheet metal, thud-thud-thud-thud. I didn't care what they were saying about me. I just wanted to rest. I closed my eyes and stopped listening to everything. Sleep did not come calling. Instead, it was Ernie once more. This time, Nipper came out of hiding and was with him.

"Wake up," Nipper said.

"We need to ask you something," Ernie said.

"I'm awake, and I'm done answering questions. Just leave me alone."

"Let me get something straight," Nipper said. "This is my yard, our yard, me and Ernie. As far as we know, you ain't supposed to be here, so just make it easy on everyone here and cooperate, got it?"

Now this was just getting funny, but not ha-ha funny. This was funny like when you have someone cuffed and sitting on a curb and they swear up and down that they have nothing on them, then you take one sniff from three feet away and, wait a second, there's the bag of contraband that they're about to claim belongs to their friend. It's annoying, but there's enough desperate humor floating around to stop you from grabbing an arm and swinging it out of socket.

"Are you a cop?" Ernie said.

"He don't look like a cop," Nipper said. "Too small. I bet he's not."

"He's bigger than you."

"I don't think so," Nipper said.

"Yes I am," I said.

"Who asked you?" Nipper said, grunting. "Just answer him."

"What happened to your leg?" Ernie said. "Are you hiding out? Can we help?"

"I'm not helping," Nipper said. "I bet he was crying over his boo-boo."

"Could you two just leave me alone? I want to rest."

"I don't know where you come from," Nipper said, "but around here, you don't give the orders, we do. For the last time, why don't you just answer Ernie's questions?"

"Well then," I said, propping my legs under me, "since we've gotten to the point of 'for the last time,' I'm going to play my hand too. *For the last time*, I suggest you leave me alone."

"Not good eno—"

I was on him. I drove my shoulder into his chest. At the risk of ruining the impending drama, I didn't bite him nor was I planning to. I could have. His neck was there for the taking. Surprisingly, Nipper had some quickness to him and was able to brace himself on his hind legs and absorb the initial impact. I got an arm around his side and wrestled him to the ground and put him on his back.

"Let 'em go," Ernie shouted.

"I told you to leave me alone," I said as Nipper tried to push me off with his legs, but I circled around so that he was just kicking the air. "I'm not going to hurt you."

"Little help here, Ernie!" Nipper said as Ernie took off barking toward the house. "Hey, where are you going? We're supposed to be a team."

When I heard the door open, I let off and backed away while Nipper still squirmed with his eyes closed and kicked at an imaginary boogeyman.

"What the hell is wrong with you, huh?" Officer Hart said as he yanked me up in the air by my nape and yelled in my face. He'd never been so aggressive with me in the past; he never had to lay a hand on me. I couldn't even look at him. I broke the first rule of being a cop. I lost my cool. He was still holding me up, the veins pumping in his forearms, the disappointment barely concealed behind his eyes. He waited for me to somehow answer for myself. In the meantime, my leg couldn't support my body, and I slipped out of his grip.

"Is he okay?" Mrs. Hart said.

"He's fine. It's just his leg."

"I'm talking about Nipper."

They must've thought I mauled him, which couldn't have been farther from the truth. Officer Hart gave Nipper a once over, a pat down, and let him go. Nipper ran around to the side of the house with Ernie behind him.

"Not a scratch on him," Officer Hart said.

"Are you sure?"

"I'm positive. No bite marks. No scratches. Didn't even pull out any fur."

"Looks like Nipper held his own," she said, with some misguided pride sneaking into her indignation.

"A month ago he wouldn't have."

*Aw, come on. Give me some credit, would you? Let's not get ahead of ourselves.*

"Is this going to work with him here? I know he was your partner, but Nipper has been a part of the family since he was a puppy."

"He'll be fine, honey. It's his first day in the yard. I figured something like this would happen. New dog in a new environment and someone always has to try to be the big shot. They're establishing who the alpha is."

"I figured Ernie would've been the one to challenge him."

"Ernie's not stupid."

"And neither is Nipper," Mrs. Hart said. "He knows the commands I taught him."

"That's not what I mean."

"Fine. I'm glad none of them are hurt, but there has to be some punishment for him."

"Honey—"

"No, I don't want to hear it. He attacked Nipper and that's one thing. Maybe Nipper started it, I don't know, but he has to learn that this isn't downtown at midnight and he can't just pin down whoever he wants. What if he does it to Simon?"

Damn. You can't argue with that. With humans, the trump card is always the kids. No matter what the topic at paw is, when someone lays down the *kid* line, pack your bags and leave the argument with whatever dignity you have left. People will always put their children ahead of common sense. Not just women and moms or just men and dads. Not this type or that type. Everyone does it.

Evidence I've found has been used to send crooks away for life. They trust my judgment when lives are on the line, but what's the first thing they do when I'm at a school or in the Fourth of July parade? The leash. And why? Because some kid might get scared, or, worse, some kid's parent might get scared. As well they should, right? After all, it's because I'm on the damn leash. It's a sign to them that even a trained police dog can't be trusted, but take me off the leash, and they think I'm waiting for the moment when no one's looking so I can embark on a child-eating rampage. It's like cops who have tattoos. They can't show them because it looks bad to the kids, but how bad can they be? The guy with them turned out to be a cop.

"Give him a chance to adjust," Officer Hart said.

"Put him in time out until he calms down."

"He's fine. Look at him."

She didn't answer. She barely looked at me. Officer Hart did the only thing he could. He grabbed me by the collar and led me across the yard.

"Let's go, buddy," he said, leading me away from her. "It's just for a few minutes. I promise."

We turned the corner of the house away from her, and Officer Hart let me go, but I knew to keep alongside him. Nipper and Ernie followed behind us at a safe distance.

"He let go of him," Nipper said. "Is he crazy? What's going–"

"Nipper, shut up," Ernie said. "If he wanted to hurt you, he would have."

"If I wanted to hurt him, I would have too. I just didn't want to get in trouble."

I walked across the backyard next to Officer Hart, and we stopped at a chain-link door that connected the edge of the garage to the backyard fence.

The garage was to the far southeast corner of the yard and stood alone from the house. Between the rear wall of the garage and the fence there was a little area just big enough to put in, as was the case for the Hart family, five garbage bins. There was also enough room for me to fit in there too.

I went in without a fight. Officer Hart closed me in, and I wondered why this little area with the garbage bins was blocked off from the rest of the yard and with a latching chain-link fence, no less. Overkill, I'd say. Why do people in the suburbs take so many precautions just to protect their garbage?

Officer Hart pressed three fingers in through the chain link to give me a scratch. I lay down and stared up at him. You want to give me a scratch, maybe you should have come in here with me, you know, your partner, or otherwise just let me out.

"All right, buddy," Officer Hart said as I turned my head away from him. He got the hint. "Can't say I don't understand because I do. I'll let you out in a few minutes. When I have to go sleep on the couch, it's for the whole night."

"Now what?" I said as Ernie decided it was his turn to visit me, the moment after Officer Hart returned inside his house.

"Sorry," Ernie said. "Personally, I think you got a bum rap. Like you were saying, it's usually someone else's fault when you get locked up. It's the truth."

"Just keep your friend in line so this doesn't happen again," I said.

"It's not my job to take care of him."

"Spoken like a true stray," I said. "Keep looking out for number one."

"I was just trying to be friendly and apologize for how Nipper behaved, but if you want to be a jerk to me, that's fine. Whatever. I'm Ernie, by the way. If we're going to live together, we might as well know our names."

"Fritz."

"See you when you get out, Fritz."

"Fritz?" Nipper said, galloping over but keeping his distance from my side of the chain link. "Is that his name?"

"Leave him alone, Nipper."

"What kind of name is Fritz anyway? Sounds like Spritzer."

"Oh yeah, and nothing funny rhymes with *Nipper*, right?" Ernie said.

"Funny name or not," Nipper said, "you're a dog like the rest of us."

"I'm not just a dog."

"Could have fooled me."

"I'm a cop, *and* I'm a dog. There's no 'used to be' anywhere in that sentence."

"And look who's locked up?" Nipper said. "Not me. Not Ernie. This is our yard, and I'm the sheriff."

Satisfied with himself, Nipper walked away, and Ernie went with him.

Then finally, finally, finally, finally, finally, I was finally left alone. Finally.

## Chapter Seven – The Hunt

The imagery was not lost on me. On one side you had neatly arranged trash bins that were scuffed up on the corners. A smidgen of lettering peeled here and there, but enough were visible to determine where the glass and plastic went versus where they dumped the rest of the trash. Then there was me. Three feet away, next to the recyclables, trying to sleep.

I don't know for sure if that's a metaphor. Regardless, the symbolism was spread awfully thick. Or was I just depressed? Maybe I would've thought that a bird flying in the air was something more than just a gliding rat looking for another power line to plop down on. Good thing there wasn't a breeze because I would've attributed that to a higher power nudging me against the wall. But garbage and me? I got it. I flattened my chin on the ground and had a direct view into the garage through a mesh vent near the clothes dryer.

The little clean dog from inside, Missy, shot into the garage like a bowling ball of fluff. She disappeared out of my sight under a pile of camping supplies and behind some paint cans. *Strange*, I thought. That's something you'd expect a cat to do, running and hiding from nothing.

"I will exterminate the alien race," a high-pitched metallic voice said, from outside the garage. A four-foot robot covered head to toe in hard, toy plastic slammed the garage door open and stomped inside. The plastic covering did little to contain the same smell of wet feet that gagged me in The Intimidator.

Simon had shiny shell leggings slipped on over his pants. Down the side of the shell leggings it read "The Mini-Destroyer!!!" A Sam Browne gun belt hung loose around his waist and his shoulder. His chest plate was designed to look like a warped bodybuilder. No curves on these muscles, just hard right turns.

He carried a futuristic rifle that was connected to the Sam Browne by one of those squiggly cords you see hooked up to a CB radio. Futuristic human weapons are not among my areas of expertise, but I doubt as time goes on that handheld weapons get bigger. Small, sleek, and fast does it for me anytime.

Simon's face was shielded by a mask that was decorative but functionally laughable. A huge cut-out in the front of it offered his nose and mouth plenty of room and, thus, no protection at all. Above the nose were two giant fluorescent bug eyes. The mask itself was held to his head only by a thick elastic band that wrapped taut around the back of his skull, leaving a horizontal part in his matted hair. It too was connected to a sagging battery pack on the Sam Browne next to a tiny speaker.

"You can't hide from The Destroyer," Simon shouted from the mask and popping the speaker. "If you show yourself, I'll make it painless."

He toppled over a stack of boxes near the dryer, spilling Christmas ornaments all over the floor, several of them snapping on impact.

"What was that?" Mrs. Hart said from inside the house.

"Nothing," Simon said, lifting his mask and sounding like the child terror he was. He haphazardly kicked a few of the smaller shards of Christmas cheer out of the way under the washer and dryer. "Just playing with Missy."

"Be careful in the garage, okay?"

"Jeez, I'm fine," Simon said as he lowered the mask and whispered to his prey. "Look what you made me do. Don't make The Destroyer angry, you space monster."

The hunt continued as Simon poked through the garage. He picked up a basketball and threw it up against the wall, echoing a plastic *tiiiing*. Now he was giving me a headache. He got down on his belly and crawled across the floor trying to get a better line of sight, his chest plate scratching on the concrete. Frustrated by the lack of a living target in range, Simon jumped to his feet and fired his rifle at will while spinning in a circle. And it sounded real. Automatic weapon real. Not space-age laser fake. This was rat-a-tat-tat-tat rapid fire. If I hadn't been watching with my own eyes, I would've thought we needed backup from the SWAT team.

"Simon!" Mrs. Hart said.

"What?"

"What did I tell you about that thing?"

"I don't know."

"What did I say about shooting that indoors?"

"I don't remember."

*"What did I say?"*

"I'm not indoors, mom."

"You're in the garage."

"That doesn't count."

"What did I say?"

"Don't," Simon said, having tasted defeat in this game of generational wits.

"And what are you doing?"

"I was just playing."

"Playing's over. Come inside."

"I thought I *was already* inside," Simon said, zinging his mom.

"Don't get smart with me! Come inside, and take off Destroyer, and clean your room."

Simon was defeated worse than anything the nastiest space monster could do to him. He dropped his gun and slouched out of the garage as the rifle dragged behind him on the cord, ricocheting off the ground with each step.

What kind of game was this anyway? Hunting? The whole point was to get something to eat, so if you weren't born with the tools required to catch something, maybe you're being told you're not supposed to catch it and that it's not on your menu. Look at me; I can eat anything I catch. Chicken? Easy. A cat? In my sleep. A pig? Give me a break. Don't take this the wrong way, but there's not a human out there that, if I really wanted to, well, you can see where I'm taking this, so let's move on.

The point is you'll never see me take on a bear and nor would I want to; the required abilities to do so were distributed to other animals, not dogs. While I'm thinking about hunting and eating, you people do realize that cooking is a luxury, right? I've had cooked steak. I'll admit that it's a slab of paradise. But you know what? If I had that, with no seasoning, and had to tear it off the bone on my own, it would still be double delicious. I don't think the fat guy hovering over the barbeque could make the same claim.

My third year on the force I was brought along on a weekend hunting trip in the woods with some other officers. Initially, I thought it was a sting operation where I was going to lead the charge through the bush. Nope. They put a ridiculous shiny bright tarp over me that made me stick out like a guilty perp in a lineup with a nervous twitch in his leg; the more you try and stop it, the more you can't control it.

When the first deer went down in one shot, I realized that the trip to the woods had nothing to do with the job. The guys told me to go check the buck, and I did. I wish I hadn't. His eyes were still open. Probably had no idea what even happened. A quick flash of *what's that smell,* and that's all she wrote.

There was something not right about it. Like Simon, this was done, presumably, in the name of fun. They cheered and scratched me and scooped up the buck and carried him back to camp. These were officers who would lay down their lives for any of us on that trip. We all made careers out of risking our lives and putting ourselves in positions where bad things can happen at any moment. On that walk back to the camp, I felt like we let ourselves and that buck down. But what do I know about what makes humans tick? Brains and brawn, that's enough to get you what you need. Anything else is cheating.

Before long, Simon's scent vanished, and Missy's nose reappeared from underneath a blanket. She sniffed the pieces of broken ornaments and tiptoed across the cold garage floor, stopping every few feet just to be sure no one was waiting for her. I felt bad watching her. I wanted to tell her, *Hey kid, it's okay, don't pant it,* but I suspected that the sudden entry of my voice onto the scene would have done more harm than good. I stared at her until she felt me looking. She looked up from the remains of the jagged pieces of what used to be Santa, and she calmly caught my eyes.

I want to tell you that she inhaled a gasp, but quickly found comfort and warmth in my steely grin and a reassurance in my chiseled jaw that I was, despite the circumstances of our first meeting, firmly on her side and that with one wink I calmed her down and a bond was forged between us as two canines, each in a desperate situation all our own. But no, her fur puffed out, and she flew out of the garage quicker than she flew in, stomping all over Rudolph's nose.

When you're that small, everyone's a dog hunter, even a dog locked up in a cage. Locked up in a cage. And there I was trying to act like I wasn't talking about me the whole time.

## CHAPTER EIGHT – THIS IS HAPPENING RIGHT NOW

I'm in a long hallway. There are no windows, but I know I'm on the top floor. I can hear the echo from below, under the warping wood, as I step on each plank. I feel the splinters falling off the underside of the floor with every step, and I don't hear them bounce off anything beneath them. The only thing behind me is the feeling of a squeezing vice, as if my head is going to cave in if I look back. There's no way out but forward.

Each step is deliberate. I keep my head low, and something clangs off the ground. My badge. *My badge?* I have a lanyard dangling loose around my neck with my dull badge duct-taped to it. I'm in a dark, dirty, dusty wooden hallway with doors, paintings, ceiling fans, and spider webs. My nose can't register a smell. Another sniff. Nothing. Not even the intentional smell of nothing that fills hospital walls.

Stop second-guessing yourself. Each pause with every step makes me wonder if I should keep going. The only light is what's around me. The light moves with me. I don't get any closer to the end, and total darkness is still just a turn of the neck away. The parallel ceiling and floor extend ahead into eternity. There's a cacophony of doors to my left and right like a hotel hallway as I creep ahead to somewhere. The doors don't mirror each other like they do even in the sleaziest of motels. They are all askew from the opposing door. They aren't numbered; am I going forward or back?

"Come in, Eagle," a voice scratches the silence. Is it coming from one of the doors? Which one? The voice sways above me like a cheap chandelier. "Come in, Eagle. Do you copy?"

"Hello?" I say, slicing the echo and knowing that I can't be *Eagle.*

"Eagle, come in. Have you reached the lair?"

"Who is this?"

"Who is *this?*"

"Are you talking to me?" I say.

Silence. Then the crack of a radio. "Depends."

"On what? Don't play games with me."

"Eagle, come in."

"Am I supposed to be Eagle?"

"Only if you come in."

"What if I don't?" I stop, and I want my answer before I take another step. I'm going to focus on where this sound is coming from, which door, around which corner that I can't see. I'm waiting. As soon as I get my sound, I'm sprinting as fast as I can.

I spring-load my posture an inch off the ground. I swing my neck to get that damn badge out of my way, and I see that my injured leg is shaved bare. Now I'm cold. I'm freezing, and my leg is shivering. My posture unwinds as I sit down and wait.

"Eagle, do you come in?"

"This is Eagle," I say, not believing it.

"Very good, Eagle. We had trouble contacting you. Is everything okay? Are you code four?"

"I have no idea what you're talking about. I have no fur on my leg."

"No fur? What are we supposed to do about that?"

"Who's we?"

"This is base, Eagle. Do you copy?"

"Yes."

"Eagle, proper communication protocol is to state *affirmative.* Do you copy?"

"Affirmative," I confirm.

"What's your twenty?"

"I'm in a hallway."

"More specific on your twenty?"

"I'm in a long, dark hallway with no numbers on the doors. All I need is a psychopath with a chainsaw to complete this nightmare."

"Please don't offer unnecessary and disruptive details, Eagle. You're not in a comedy club. We need a status update on the operation."

"Can you refresh me on my objectives up here?"

"Just keep moving."

"That's it? That's the operation, to keep moving?"

"Chief's orders."

"Which way do I go?"

"Same way you're going. From this point maintain radio—"

"I'm not even on the radio. You are."

Then, as crystal clear as could be, like a recording studio with no echo, bass, treble, or reverberation, "Listen, Fritz. You're quite literally on your last leg with us. If you screw this case up, there's no coming back. Ever. Or should we just stop wasting time and get Nitro on the scene for you?"

"Negative." I say.

"Maintain radio silence."

There's a scream ahead, and I'm running down this treadmill hallway. I don't know how close I am to the scream as it engulfs everything around me. I run as hard as I can toward the eye of the scream. The hallway seems to be running too, racing me. It's winning. I barely get anywhere when my leg pleads with me to stop. Once your body argues with you, there's nothing you can do. It has to be trained to keep its mouth shut because a body isn't a democracy, it's a dictatorship. Your brain is the supreme leader. Everything else is a subject. I cave in to the revolt in my leg and jog to the side of the hallway. The scream becomes focused on the door next to me, a door superficially indistinguishable from the others. It's flat, no number, no peephole, no key hole, and a dull square handle. This door, unlike every other door, is cracked open.

I nudge my nose inside to get a scent. The trick is to not expect what scent to find. Take in whatever comes. It's a technique that often takes a turn for the unexpected quickly, but at least you find something. My nose is still not working, and I'm not hearing a thing, so I do the next best thing. I bark as loud as I can. The half-naked lady in the room screams again. Someone else in the room darts into a bathroom, pulling the blanket behind him.

"I heard screaming," I say. "Is everything okay in here?"

"Get out of here."

The lights are off. Even with the door now wide open, I can't see a thing in here.

"Are you hurt?"

"I'm going to call the police." she says.

"No need. I am the police."

"You?" she says as she laughs in my face. I want to maul her. "The police?"

"That's right, ma'am."

"Hey John," she turns, shouting to the man in the bathroom, "this dog here says he's the police."

"Oh, that's funny," John says from the bathroom.

"You should see him. His face is turning grey. He's got to be twenty years old."

"Oh, that's funny."

"And I haven't even told you about his leg. There's nothing on it. No fur, nothing."

"Oh, that's funny."

"Do you need assistance?" I say, trying to keep my voice steady with moderate success.

"We're doing fine in here. What about you? You sure you're okay? How about we help you?"

"I'm fine, ma'am."

"Oh, that's funny."

"There's nothing funny about it, sir. I'm just trying to do my job, and you're not making it any easier. I heard a scream, and I'm investigating."

"We don't want you or your investigating," she says.

"Oh, that's fun—"

"Shut up, John. And you, dog, I think you need to go home."

I back out and decide to not take a report on this incident. It's handled at the scene. I'm still in the hallway, and nothing has changed. Endless walls and limited light are in abundance.

There's smoke seeping out of the bottom of that door over there. It's faint and thin, but it's definitely smoke. It's swirling through some light shining out between the door and the floor. The smoke could be poison. Could be incense. Could be in my head. A muted bass line trickles behind the smoke as it escapes. One-two, one-two-three. One-two, one-two-three. I approach the door and hear several voices from inside. They're laughing and yelling at each other like friends do when they watch sports on TV. Like when someone calls you a "dirty scumbag" when they have no other way to say they love you like their brother.

I press my ear against the door. Only every third word or so is clear. I'm hesitating. I should lower my head and plough through this cheap door and tackle the first man I see and remove the meat from his arm. I wait for what I know isn't coming : a sign to tell me what I should do.

"Hey, is that pizza guy gonna be here soon?" I hear from inside.

"Maybe he's lost," says another.

"Take a look."

The door opens, and I cower as a mammoth police officer stands above me. He looks over my unseen head down the hallway. I look up and see bits of a chewed, moist cigar nesting in his moustache. He's oblivious to my entire being.

"He ain't out here," he says, throwing the door shut. I stop it from closing all the way with my paw. The door tries its best to smash the tiny bones in my paw. Tiny? Says who? Where did that come from?

The door opens with little resistance. I push my way inside and immediately notice the wallpaper. It looks like chipped bowling lanes, and it's peeling at the top and bottom.

A poker game is in full swing toward the back of the room at a circular table. Five cops from GCPD are huddled around the table. Baxter, Peters, Donaldson, McMichael, and Nitro. Nitro's leaning back in his chair with his feet propped up on the table. They're drinking, smoking, gambling, and staring at each other across the table.

"What're you holding, Baxter?" Nitro demands.

"I called you, hombre," bald, sweating Baxter says.

"Three queens," Nitro declares, flicking his cigar and tossing his cards across the table. Baxter holds his cards up eye level but curves them in his palm so no one can see them. He squints, and his foot taps. Defeat dances across his face as he folds, mucking his hand into a pot of chips and cash. "I knew you had nothing. You fellas can watch my back any night of the week on patrol, but at the poker table, you're a bunch of schoolgirls. You should be ashamed of yourselves."

Nitro scoops up his newly won chips and moolah with a sweep of his arm while exhaling a perfect "O" of cigar smoke.

"Hey, don't insult little girls," Peters, sitting clockwise of Baxter, snorts.

"I'm talking about you too, bro," Nitro says.

"Aw, come on, bro."

They laugh the patented collective laugh cops do when they passively wrestle for power in the guise of teasing each other. I don't laugh.

"Why don't you take it easy on us then, huh Nitro?" McMichael says.

"Take it easy? Are you nuts? With the new promotion, I got a lifestyle to maintain here. Now that I'm top dog, I gotta look and act the part. And acting the part means I can't let a bunch of sob stories ruin my run at the table. You remind me of the guy I took this job from in the first place. He was a big time crybaby—"

"Hey, whatever happened to that guy anyway?" Donaldson says.

"Who knows?" Nitro says. "And who cares? Your deal, Bax." Baxter snaps the cards between his knuckles and fires them across the cops of the round table. "Hey, you smell that? Smells like a wet rag in here."

"I didn't think Baxter was cooking his family recipe."

More laughs. Not as many from Baxter.

"It's definitely not anything that's cooking," Nitro says. "It's more like something is rotting. I think it's...yup, I know that smell. All too well. Three o'clock, gentlemen."

They all turn my way.

"What's going on in here?" I say.

"Just a couple of cops hanging out," Nitro says.

"I got a call that there was a criminal in here."

"No you didn't."

"Yes, I did, Nitro."

"You poor, poor, old dog. See, here's the thing, now point those ears and listen tight. You ready? In the world of law enforcement, only actual cops are the ones who receive and answer distress calls. And last time I checked, you're not a cop anymore. Therefore, if my math serves right, and I'm only up a few thousand here, so I'd say it's serving me pretty well at the moment, I'd say that means that it's outright impossible for you to be answering a call from anyone. Got it?"

"Nit–"

"Got it?"

"Just let–"

"Got it?"

"I think–"

"I'm asking you if you got what I'm saying, Fritz? Because I'm trying to play poker here with actual cops. Something that you don't know anything about anymore." I'm not talking. Neither is Nitro. Neither are any of the men in the smoky room. I turn back to the door. "You were going to say something?"

"Nothing."

"Nothing? You interrupted me three times for nothing?"

I push out a breath and force myself to speak. "I got a ca... I got word that there's possibly a criminal on the premises, so I'm investigating."

"Oh," Nitro says, with a soft sincerity, "I wish you would've just said that to begin with. There is a criminal nearby, and he's been dealing to himself from the bottom of the deck all night, haven't ya, Baxter?"

I shrink as the cops explode at the table. Even Baxter thinks it's funny while he peeks at the cards during the laughter. Donaldson waves his feet uncontrollably under the table like a baby waiting for a bottle. McMichael howls back in his chair to the point where he goes back on two legs and nearly topples over. Peters' laugh devolves into a lurching, hacking, doubled-over cough as he hammerfists his chest.

"Time to disappear, Fritz," Nitro says. "By the way, I like what you're doing with your leg. Very chic, the whole shaved look. So ironic and post-modern."

I'm back walking down the hallway in the same direction as before. The noise from the poker game evaporates, and I find myself facing the wall at the end of the hallway; it's an old brick wall. I feel a warm, damp breeze on the back of my head. I'm scared.

"Nowhere to go, cop," a guttural growl says from behind me. It's Clay. He's so much bigger than me now and his face hangs low toward the ground. He's a monster, and I'm shrinking in front of him. I can't go anywhere. I want to hide. I want to cry. I want to submit. Clay is the size of a car, and his breathing is a revving engine. I'm a broken flute. "What're you doing here?"

"I'm on a call. I heard a scream."

"I'll bet you did. A scream, you say?"

On cue, the scream jangles off the walls again and stops dead at the brick wall. Scamper is behind Fritz, and, while his body is the same, what his body is in is like something out of a comic book. He's sitting in the control center of a humanoid robot. The Super Destroyer.

"You gonna arrest us, copper?" Scamper says, through a walkie-talkie.

"He don't have the guts, do you?" Clay says.

"You're under arrest," I say.

"No we're not."

"Clay, you heard him. He sounds serious."

"I think I've decided to resist arrest," Clay says. "Is that all right with you, cop?"

"I would advise you against it."

"You would, would you? Or what?"

"Be careful Clay. He's liable to slap the cuffs on you," Scamper says as his exoskeleton twirls a two-by-four with its hands. "Oh, and what's this? Looks as if I have a weapon now."

"I don't need a weapon," Clay says. "All he has to do is put those cuffs on me."

"Watch out for them cuffs, Clay," Scamper says.

"They don't have cuffs that I can't break," Clay says, getting even bigger until I can't see him or Scamper anymore. He's all black. The wheezing in his chest is still right in front of me. There are no doors now. No wallpaper. The hallway is gone. No ceiling. The floor beneath me is gone. I can't hear the woman with John or Nitro and the poker game. "The cuffs, Fritz. The cuffs. Just slap those cuffs on our wrists."

"I don't have any cuffs," I scream.

## CHAPTER NINE – EVERYONE PRETENDS THEY'RE SOMETHING SOMETIMES

"Just put on the cuffs, will you, Nipper?" Ernie said.

"I'm trying," Nipper said. "If you would just stay still."

"I am standing still. Your mouth is shaky."

"It is not," Nipper said. "You're gonna still help me with my uniform when we're done, right?"

"Yeah. It's a costume, though. Not an actual one."

"Don't ruin this for me. As far as I'm concerned, it's a uniform. That's what I want it to be, so that's what it is. I don't care what you or anyone says. Today, as far as you're concerned, you respect the uniform."

"Whatever, Nipper. Just don't drool all over my cuffs."

"I can't do it!" I said, out of nowhere. In case it wasn't clear, I had been dreaming. Nipper and Ernie froze, Ernie with his hind leg up in the air like he was about to leave a mark and Nipper with Ernie's pants in his mouth–hold that thought on the pants, I'll get back to those in a moment.

My legs involuntarily kicked as I jolted awake. Perhaps it's better to say that my legs tried their best in rapid succession to relieve themselves from the restraining confines of my hip sockets. In the process, one of them found its way into the corner of one of the garbage bins. As I shook the cobwebs out of my eyes, last week's newspapers, including a damp one on top, toppled over me.

To hear Nipper retell the story, my arms flailed like I was "playing an invisible, oh, what do they call those things, Ernie? Where you have a paddle-like thing and there's a string with those rubber balls that I choked on that one time. You know the thing that Simon tries to do but can't ever hit the ball more than twice? Well, anyway, just imagine Fritz had two of those things going while he knocked the trash over on his head."

"Are you okay?" Ernie said, pulling his leg from Nipper's mouth.

"Ow, Ernie. Watch my teeth."

I brushed off the newspapers and remembered where I was, why I was there, and wondered what Ernie was doing in a pair of tailored wool pants with a square cut out in the rear for his tail. Ernie came up to the chain-link fence and poked his nose through.

"Am I still dreaming?" I said. "Why are you wearing pants?"

"It's Halloween," Ernie said.

"Why were they in Nipper's mouth?" I said.

"We're going to the dog park."

"Did I sleep all night?" I said.

"The whole way through. Even when the people in the condos down the street were up screaming at each other. I love when that happens. I can yell back, and I don't get in trouble."

"I thought this guy was supposed to be smart," Nipper said, under his breath.

"Wait," I said. "So, what's going on?"

"We're getting dressed up and going to the dog park with the other dogs," Ernie said. "You're going too."

"I doubt it," Nipper said. "He doesn't have a costume."

"Let me ask you something," I said to Ernie. "You ever hear of a dog named Clay? A big Rott."

"You could've just said 'Rott.' Big sort of comes with that. Clay? Nah. Never heard of him."

"Nope."

"You're not lying to me?" I said. "Never? He runs with a little Jack Russell terrier named Scamper. Squeaky voice. Too much energy for his own good."

"Sounds like every Jack Russell I ever met. Sorry, can't help you. Why do you want to know about these two anyway? I've been off the streets for a while, but I'll ask around today."

"I didn't say anything about asking around about them."

"Ernie," Nipper said, "get back over here, or I'm not going to fix your cuffs, and you'll look like a fool at the park."

"My appointment beckons," Ernie said.

Ernie sat down by Nipper, who resumed tugging at Ernie's pant leg. What he was trying to accomplish was beyond me, but that didn't stop him from hovering back and forth around Ernie like one of those office fans that makes a lot of noise and blows a lot of air but couldn't cool an igloo.

"So," I said to Nipper, "you're a German seamstress instead of a German shepherd, is that it? I bet your mommy and daddy are real proud of their boy."

That one stung him, and it made me feel good. Sometimes happiness can only come at someone else's expense. I didn't feel bad about it.

"Leave him alone," Ernie said. "Besides, Nipper ain't even a full German shepherd, so–"

"Ernie," Nipper said.

"What? You're not. So what?"

Nipper batted Ernie's foot away from his face and took a step toward me and said, "Yeah, well, I'm not the one who they had to lock up, so there you go."

Officer and Mrs. Hart unlocked the side door from their house and joined us in the yard. They had matching robes, hers more worn than his, his smelled worse. Their slippers didn't match; neither did their coffee cups.

"I can't believe you left him in there all night," she said.

"He was sleeping, and I didn't want to disturb him," Officer Hart said. "He didn't sleep at all the last few days at the department. Plus, I thought we needed to keep them separated until they get used to each other."

"Yeah, but all night?"

"Isn't that what you wanted me to do? And if you actually would look instead of jumping at me, I unlatched the gate, so if he wanted to get out, he could have."

She drank her coffee in lieu of answering. Officer Hart pulled open the already-opened door and officially let me out of the garbage hold.

"We got a surprise for you, buddy," Officer Hart said, turning to Mrs. Hart. "Do you want me to get it?"

"I guess that means I'll just do it," she said.

"That's not what I said."

"If you were going to get it for him, you would have already brought it out without asking me if I want you to get it. Of course that's what I wanted; it's why we came out here in the first place. But don't worry, I'll go do it."

She set her coffee cup down on the ground and went back inside.

"It's a whole 'nother world out here, buddy," Officer Hart said. Ernie crept over and sniffed at her cup. He took a lick and spit it back out right away. "Come on, Ernie. Get away from there."

*You're telling me.*

"Nipper," Officer Hart said as Nipper, who stood with Ernie a few feet away, lowered his nose toward us. "Come here. I mean it, Nipper. Come here."

"Go on," Ernie whispered as Officer Hart slapped his leg three times. Nipper took a few steps forward. I took a seat and Nipper stopped a few feet away. Officer Hart left my side and split the difference between us; he squatted all the way down, first tucking in his robe.

"Now listen, guys, we all have to get along here. Trust me, I wouldn't have brought Fritz home with us if I didn't think you two would become friends, got it, Nipper?" Officer Hart did what all humans do: waited until he imagined the answer he wanted from us. "And Fritz, you gotta understand that this is Nipper's home too. He doesn't know you just like you don't know him. Until yesterday, all he knew was that it was him and Ernie, so cut him some slack." He didn't wait for an imagined response from me. I listened to Officer Hart, and he knew it. "Now you two sniff each other and be done with it for good."

My nostrils opened, and I leaned in. Not too much, mind you. I wasn't going to look desperate and be the one to apologize. Nipper did as well. Not too close either. Good for him. I thought Nipper might have some gumption after all.

It was the first time I got a really good whiff of him. Nipper had been in that backyard for a long time, longer than Ernie. His scent was safe. It was non-threatening. It was pleasant enough. It was sterile. He ate the same food every day. He drank from the same water bowl, from the same side of the bowl. There was nothing extraordinary about Nipper's scent unless its complete lack of distinguishable scent was to be taken as something of note.

"Truce?" I said, through the side of my mouth.

"Huh?"

"Are we square?"

"Sure. I guess," Nipper said.

"Okay, that's enough," Officer Hart said, lightly tugging us apart and letting us go.

"Surprise, Fritz," Mrs. Hart said as she rejoined us with a bulging paper grocery bag.

Mrs. Hart dropped the bag and picked up her coffee cup. She wiped the area where Ernie licked and had left evidence of his fur.

"Thanks," she said as she wiped away Ernie's wet chin fur from her cup.

The cement absorbed the bag's contents as they splashed out. It looked like a pile of rags from where I was standing. Mrs. Hart kicked over whatever was in the bag toward Officer Hart.

"Don't take it out on the dogs," Officer Hart said as she scooped up the bag and tucked back in the linen that had burst out. She sat down next to me on the concrete. "Aren't you cold?"

"No," Mrs. Hart said, arranging the bag's contents in front of me.

"Wait a second," Nipper said. "Now wait just one stinking second here."

"Hold on, Nipper," Ernie said.

"I told you this wasn't a good idea," Officer Hart said, petting an increasingly upset Nipper.

"Why? Because I came up with it?"

"Look what it's doing to Nipper. He already tried it on. He thinks it's his."

"He's fine," Mrs. Hart said, clearly not looking at Nipper. He wasn't fine. By the way his eyes were aching and pleading, the poor dog's heart was zeroed in on what Mrs. Hart was digging through.

"He's too big, honey," Officer Hart said.

"No, he's not."

"He's bigger than Nipper. He's thicker."

She smothered me with the contents of the bag. She wrapped things around my waist, tucked my arms and legs into dark sleeves, and adjusted my collar. She tugged my tail through a hole in what I assumed were pants that I was now snuggled into.

"That's not right, man," Ernie said.

"See, it fits," Mrs. Hart said, stepping away from me. Then I saw what she'd done to me. Tight felt pants that were essentially chaps now covered my back and hind legs. Ridiculous. A long-sleeved shirt with stars and meaningless stripes below a flimsy shirt collar and fuzz balls glued down the front that were supposed to be buttons. I felt something bounce against my side and saw a plastic baton wavering from a thin nylon belt that was connected across my back by Velcro.

Even the smell of the outfit made me sick. The chemically treated plastic, the cheap dye coating the fiber, and the dusty felt that must've been sealed away in the bag for months. I could only imagine how idiotic I looked. A fake cop outfit for a real dog. What was I, some sort of joke now? A show pony? Some human fantasy to represent something I never was in the first place? I never had to wear a toy costume to know what I was.

No. I bit at those sleeves and tried to shake those pants off, but the more I shook, which wasn't very hard considering my leg, the more they stuck to me like when a human without a sense of humor rubs a balloon against you. Detective

McConomy tried that move on me once in my rookie year. Key word being *once*.

"He don't even want it," Nipper said.

"It's not his fault," Ernie said.

"Stop taking his side, Ernie," Nipper said.

Mrs. Hart bent down and held my head in some attempt to relax me. She tried to balance a cop hat on my head. I knocked it off, and she came back again with an elastic strap that was supposed to rest under my chin. I fought it and tilted my nose up and away from her while making a concerted effort to not show any teeth. I had to suck in my cheeks just to make sure no fangs accidentally frightened her.

The only things I saw were her eyes. For years I've heard people, cops mainly, apply a lot of attributes to human eyes. They're globular balls in the head. Sometimes the middle part gets big in the dark, and sometimes it shrinks. That's it. You can't see fear in them. You can only smell fear. Here's a tip for you humans. When you get scared, you emit a foul odor intended to scare off your predators. It's meant to trick them into thinking you'd make for a rotten, disgusting meal. That's fear. Naturally, humans are unaware that this stench comes from their pores. More often than not, it's drenched away in the deep end of your sweat. I assume it still works on some predators, but we dogs have been around you so much and for so long, eh, we're used to it.

Fear also has a distinct sound too. It's basic, but it's unique. Too many heartbeats and too many rapid breaths exploding over one another and there you go, pussy cat.

But those eyes? They aren't windows to anything. The only thing I get out of looking into a set of eyes is figuring out what you're looking at. And if you should be looking at me, I'm going to stare back until I've figured out why. Plus, eyes have a limited range of motion and are easily injured. If they were so important for survival, they wouldn't be so vulnerable.

The lines that surrounded Mrs. Hart's eyes? Those were a whole other story. Now we have a conversation going on because there's actually something tangible there. You don't see her lines at first; it's not until you get up real close that you see that she has more than you thought she might. They were faint that morning, but the nature of lines is that once those creases take hold, they don't go away. Her lines were fine and soft, and on a man they wouldn't be given a second glance. Something I've gathered about adult human females is that once they start to age they aren't treated with the same respect. The lines around her eyes looked like me.

I stopped fighting and put on the stupid hat. Dressed up like a phony cop.

Ernie the sailor.

And whatever they decided Nipper was going to be.

Simon appeared with a box of junk.

This is what they called a holiday.

## CHAPTER TEN – THE UNVEILING

Counting the stoplights, it took us twenty-seven minutes to reach Williamson Park from the Hart residence. The park was named to honor Grand City's third mayor, Millard Williamson, who served one term in the early days of Grand City from 1932–1936. He lost his reelection bid, abandoned politics altogether, and opened a resort hotel in southern Mexico.

The ride was quiet, awkward, tense, and no eye contact was made. The air conditioning was too loud, and the talk radio station was barely audible. Mrs. Hart drove and Officer Hart angled himself away from her toward his side window with his arms folded and chewed gum with his mouth open. Missy was perched in Officer Hart's arms. She wore a pair of wings and a flimsy shiny ring made to look like it was hovering over her head.

"Could you keep your mouth shut if you're going to do that?" Mrs. Hart said. Officer Hart rolled down his window and spit the gum out. I watched it stick to the asphalt. Missy tried to poke her head through the window to get some air. Her wings and the head ring were blown off into the back seat with Simon. She looked relieved. "That's great. One more thing I have to do again."

"I'll fix her costume," Officer Hart said as he pressed the button to roll the window back up. He held the button down after the window was all the way up until the side of the door buzzed. "Weren't you supposed to take the car in to get the noise fixed during the week?"

"I was busy."

"Then so am I."

Ernie circled the cramped back of the car and tried to get the best view of every lane change, turn, and stop that we made. I lay still, afraid to move for fear of tearing my get-up. As long as I stood, the clothes fit okay. As soon as I sat down they stretched in ways that they weren't designed to. If they ripped, Mrs. Hart would think I tore it. Nipper, poor jerk, was curled up in the back corner. I didn't look at him with what that kid did to him with the contents of that box. He was most definitely dressed in a manner unbecoming a canine. I've never been one to stare at car wrecks. Either help out or don't. Just don't slow down and stare. Everyone was in their own little world. Simon played a video game on his TV screen, his world being the only one that seemed habitable.

Seven individual planets on a collision course toward the collective unknown. Oooh, that's a good one.

"Aw, the sweet smell of the dog park," Ernie said as Officer Hart opened the back door of the Intimidator. "These are the days we live for, fellas."

He leapt down and jogged around the parking lot until Officer Hart yelled at him to get back here before he got himself killed. I gingerly stood on the tailgate. Jumping down would have been the end of that costume.

"Come here," Officer Hart said, wrapping his arms around my torso. "Nice and easy on your leg."

My leg. Maybe it wasn't the costume I was concerned about. Officer Hart scooped me up and lowered me to the ground. I heard him cringe as he bent his back to set me down. I felt bad and gave him a lick. He shouldn't have had to hurt himself just to get my hunk of junk out of the Intimidator.

"Make sure they don't get hit by a car," Mrs. Hart said, carrying Missy away to a picnic table where the other women sat.

Nipper didn't budge. He stayed in the corner of the Intimidator with his head down and his tail curled under him.

"Nipper, get out," Officer Hart said, slapping the side of the car. "I can't leave you in the car, so you're coming out one way or the other."

"It's not that bad Nipper," Ernie said.

"Easy for you to say."

"I've seen worse-looking mutts when I was on the streets."

"How much time did you do on the streets?" I said.

"Three-and-a-half years," Ernie said, too proud. "But then I was *rescued*. Before that, me and Saucy were doing just fine."

"Could you do something, Ernie?" Nipper said. "Everyone's gonna laugh at me."

"No more than usual—"

"Not funny, Ernie."

"Okay, you guys, stop barking," Officer Hart said, leaning into the car and grabbing Nipper by his collar. He tugged Nipper toward the light of the parking lot. Nipper did his best to anchor his rear end to the floor of the car, but his costume robbed him of any chafing friction.

Now I've been saying costume, but the word doesn't truly describe what Simon did to Nipper. Over the course of my career I've seen a good share of ridiculous costumes. The junkie in a spider-webbed tutu with bunny ears who made a decent claim for belonging to either gender. The woman in a caveman outfit after a high-speed pursuit; she assured us she was evading the ensuing apocalypse and not the police. The guy who doused himself in chocolate syrup and barricaded himself in his closet with the lights off. They wouldn't let me at that guy. We once even jammed up a derelict Santa Claus for begging next to the freeway off-ramp. Nipper's costume was one for the books alongside those.

Let me start from the back and work toward the front of this disaster. Christmas tree streamer was tightly coiled around his tail and tied off around his leg. The mast for a plastic, toy-sized Canadian flag was tucked and taped into the tail coil as the flag punctuated Nipper's every wag. Both legs were adorned with superhero socks that were kept taut with doubled-up rubber bands. I shouldn't fail to mention that the socks did not match. The right leg featured a caped muscleman. The left was brighter and depicted a female Viking swinging from a rope and shooting a laser.

His lower torso was surrounded by cardboard, with old cereal box covers taped up the sides, evidence pointing one to conclude that the Hart family had no problem indulging Simon's sugar cravings. Simon left several messages in between the box covers like "I Love Nipper!" and "Nipper is the meanest most tough dog!!!" A saddle, too small for anyone to sit on, was taped to the top of the box. *Happy Birthday* wrapping paper was taped around Nipper's forearms. At least both arms matched.

A gaudy necklace hung from his neck, one I suspect came from Mrs. Hart's early collection. I wondered what Simon was doing with it. A skull-and-bones eye patch obscured his right eye while the capstone of Nipper's Halloween nightmare was secured to his head: a dreadlocked hat specially woven for dogs so that the ears could stick out. The result resembled a cross between an elf, an alien, and the smoking guy on a lot of bumper stickers. When it's added to the rest of what Nipper had, it was a nuclear explosion of embarrassment.

I felt a yank at my side as Simon removed the handcuffs off me.

"Earrings," he said, draping the loops over Nipper's ears.

Nipper shook off the toy handcuffs, and Officer Hart told Simon that Nipper had enough costume on him before he tried again. Officer Hart led Simon away from Nipper by the hand and walked ahead of us toward the park. Nipper stayed behind Ernie and me.

"You have to understand," Ernie said, "he's upset because since he's not a pure breed like you, I'm assuming you're one at least, so Nipper couldn't ever be a cop." Wanting to do something when everyone has told you that you can't? Maybe Nipper and I had something in common after all. I was no closer to being a cop that day than he was, costumed or otherwise. "Hey, don't worry about it, Nipper, I think you look cool."

"So, what do you do here?" I said. I'd never been to a bona fide dog park. I've been to regular parks before, who hasn't, but I always thought the idea of a park just for dogs was nonsense. They have the same stuff as the other parks. The other parks are less crowded too.

"You do whatever you want, man. Up to you. Just don't mark on the front gate. No one likes that. There's plenty of room in the back."

"Hadn't crossed my mind, Ernie," I said.

"Oh, well yeah. I mean, *you* wouldn't, but some of the breeds who show up here—"

"What's happening, big Ernie?" Godzilla said, interrupting at one o'clock. Godzilla being a beagle in a costume that cost far too much money. "The big E. Easy E. My main man E up in the park."

"Hi, Gringo. How you doing?"

"Ah, you know. Just surviving. Making the most of the holiday. You like my digs?"

"First class," Ernie said.

"I know it. Sailor outfit's looking sharp too."

"Have you seen Saucy, Gringo?"

"Nah. But then again, it's tough to see in this." Godzilla left to wreak havoc elsewhere but not before making a crack about Nipper's tail being a stiffy.

"Like I was saying," Ernie said, "some real low-class mutts around here, you know what I mean?"

"I know what you mean," I said.

"Hey, you know what?" Ernie said, stopping and turning to me. "You never know, maybe someone here knows about those two dogs you were looking for, uh, Scamper and what was the other one?"

"Clay."

"Clay. That's it. Might be worth investigating. Let me know if I can help. Anyway, make haste, like they say. We only get so much time here, so I gotta run and find Saucy."

Ernie disappeared into the hoard of costumed dogs. The cat calls were really starting to pick up as Nipper made his way into the park.

"Love it or leave it, Canuck!" said a cowboy-dressed yellow lab.

"Awww, Simon says Nipper is the most meanest," said a cocker spaniel, dressed like a swashbuckler. "I best not be messing with him."

"Make no mistake Nipper," said a Great Dane in a lazy basketball jersey, "I think your costume is the most ridiculous, most stupid thing I've ever seen, but you got guts. Or you left your brains in the garbage can you got that costume from."

"That's enough," I said. "Leave him alone."

"Who's the new guy, Nipper? What's his problem?"

"Nothing," was all Nipper could force out.

"Well, tell him to lighten up. We're just having some fun. A little teasing never killed anyone."

"Nipper," I said, "if it means anything, I'm sorry."

"Just leave me alone. You wouldn't understand."

You can't talk with someone who doesn't want to talk. If they've committed a crime, you do what you have to do to get them blabbing, but it was a nice day out, so I left Nipper to his fate.

As I waded through the crowd of dogs, all doing everything in their power to soil their outfits, I started to feel like myself again. I was in charge here even if none of them knew it yet. The costume actually helped me fit in. That feeling of being part of the group again allowed me to walk with a head higher than it'd been since before the night with Nitro and the buffalo heads and the greatest-hits video. I was a dog again. Even better, I felt like a cop again. Ernie was right. It was time to make these mutts talk.

I cornered a full-sized French poodle in foofy military regalia by a tree. He sat in front of me with his chin up and his paw resting inside his coat against his chest.

"I don't have to answer you or your questions, monsieur," he sneered as he took his paw out of his jacket. I watched the shadows of the tree tap dance across his face with his crooked mouth trying to keep up.

"Watch it," I said. "Slow. Let me see your paw. Don't you try to pull anything out on me. Keep your paws where I can see them, Frenchie."

"Frenchie?"

"You heard me."

"You Americans. Hmmpft, I never!"

"Clay or Scamper? What do you know? You're not going anywhere until I get an answer. No more wine and cheese for you at the pound where you're headed."

"Aren't you getting a little carried away here?" he said, suddenly dropping his accent completely. "I get it. You're a cop, but take it easy, buster. It's just Halloween."

"You're right," I said. "I'm sorry. You're free to go, sir."

"I know."

A good cop had to readjust to his setting. If I was going to get anywhere, I had to play it cool and remember that I was dealing with the pampered suburbanites. These weren't the con artists and hustlers I'd wrangled throughout my career. I had to ease into things. You got more with honey than you did with vinegar. It was time to get sticky.

I looked around for a dog who looked like he knew something. A football hit me in the back of the head. It was a real football with points on the end. Not the kind Detective Hernandez and Sergeant Rodriguez watched on their lunch breaks.

"Gee, sorry mister," a mutt with a football helmet too large on his head and mud smeared in his fur said as he ran up to me. "That didn't hurt ya, did it?"

"What's your name?" I said, standing in front of his ball.

"I just want my ball, officer."

"Your name?"

"You can play if you want? We need a ref. A cop would be a good ref."

"I want your name or you and your buddies don't get your ball back."

"Buddies? I'm playing by myself. Just me, Mr. Mac Nugget Head."

"You just said you needed a ref."

"Who did?"

"You did."

"Oh. Maybe. Well, since you bring it up, we could start a game if you want to be the referee."

"Does your head bounce around a lot in that helmet?"

"Sure does," he said, laughing. "Kinda gives me a headache, but then it's like I don't feel anything after a while. I can't figure it out. My humans think it's funny."

"I bet."

"So, can I have my ball?"

"Do you know a Rottweiler that goes by Clay?"

"Hmmmm, no, but I know a chow named Chuck over there."

"Does Chuck know Clay?"

"I don't know. They both start with the same letter, so maybe."

"Do you know anything?"

"Can't help you there, officer."

"Here." I nudged his ball over to him. He tried to catch it in his mouth, but it bounced off his facemask. This cycle of the helmet bobbling side to side with rhythmic thuds repeated as I watched this most interesting creature off.

I saw a crew of pugs acting suspicious and went code five on them. I watched them sniff each other for an extended period and decided to make contact. Ernie intercepted me with another dog close beside him.

"Hey Fritz, this is my friend Saucy. She's from the streets too, like me. We go way back." Her eyes were different shades and she was part border collie. I want to say there was some dachshund tossed in there too.

"Nice to meet you," I said. "If you'll excuse me–"

"I don't live on the streets anymore," Saucy said. "I have a nice yard, and I don't miss the good old days as much as Ernie does."

"What do you think of her costume, Fritz?"

"Ernie, that's rude. Don't put him on the spot."

"It's fine," I said. "Looks nice."

"She's a nurse."

"I see that, Ernie."

"She wanted to be a sailor like me. That was our plan, but her owner wouldn't go for it."

"I'm sure Fritz doesn't want to hear my life story, Ernie."

"Just trying to introduce my best pal," Ernie said.

"I thought Nipper was your best pal?"

"He is, Saucy, but you're my best girl pal."

"Speaking of Nipper," I said, "is he okay? This whole costume thing seems to be bothering him more than it should. It's just an outfit. Who cares what any of these hounds think?"

"It's not that, man."

"It's not that he cares about what these hounds think of him," Saucy said. "He cares what one *hound* thinks of him."

"And not just any hound," Ernie said.

"Well, who is he?" I asked.

"It's not a *he*."

"It's a she," Saucy said. "My yard mate, Scarlet. She's the prettiest dog you've ever seen. At least that's what everyone, literally everyone, says. I don't know, maybe they're right. I think I see it. But Nipper, like every other tongue-dragging mutt in here, he's got it bad for her."

I've never been one to bite when dogs fish for compliments, but, Ernie, she teed that one right up for you. I gave him a moment to tell her he thought she was pretty. His face remained idle.

"So what's the problem?" I said.

"Easy for you to say," Saucy said. "You look like a cop."

"He is a cop," Ernie said.

"Oh yeah? Here in Grand?"

"This is just a costume. I was a cop. If it were up to me, I'd let Nipper have it."

"It wouldn't even help," Ernie said. "Nipper's been stuck on her for years, but she won't give him the time of day. He's tried everything. Every line in the book. He's sang to her. He tried poetry. I helped with it. Something like wait, wait, okay, your eyes are a pleasant surprise like a half-eaten cheeseburger in a garbage bag, and your voice is the fries; when you pass me your scent sticks with me like a fresh piece of meat that I want to devour. Your legs are—"

"We get it, Ernie," Saucy said. "And who could ever figure out why that didn't work."

"It's art. It's not for everyone, okay? Besides, those were my words anyway, and they were meant for... Here we go."

"What?" I said, my ears tingling up.

"There's Nipper," Ernie said. "He's going for it. He's going to talk to her."

On the other end of the park Nipper took small steps in a direct line toward a dog who had to be Scarlet. The word *perfect* gets tossed around nearly as much as *genius* does, but I'd be a stone-cold liar if I said Scarlet was a tad short of being anything less than a, yes, perfect feminine canine specimen. Purebred Siberian husky. I was quite positive she wasn't pulling any sleds, though she had the hips for it. There was just enough trace of wolf in her face that was as intimidating as it was mysteriously magnetic. She had curves where it counted and a striking jaw line that said *yeah, mister I'm talking to you. You know all of that attention you have for the rest of the world that you like to spread here and there, yeah, that. It's mine, and you don't have a say in the matter.* Poor Nipper.

"Let's get a good seat," Ernie said.

"If he's going to talk to her," Saucy said, "give him his respect."

"Respect? Look what he's wearing. Besides, we're both going to hear about it, so let's get the real story with no spin."

For no good reason, I followed Ernie and Saucy behind nearby bushes where we interrupted some Yorkies eating rotten mushrooms out of the ground. I shooed them off, and we hunched down as Nipper made his final approach toward the unsuspecting Scarlet.

"What is he supposed to be anyway?" Saucy said.

Neither of us could answer.

Scarlet was looking up into the sun with her eyes closed and her neck tilted up toward the light. Her costume was simple and fitting: a tiara. Nipper walked around in a nervous circle like he was debating what to say when Scarlet whipped her tail up and caught Nipper in the jaw.

"Excuse me," Scarlet said. "I'm trying to get optimum sun on my tai... Lord, look at you, honey."

"Hi Scarlet," Nipper said, staring at the ground.

"My, my, my. Well, it is Halloween, isn't it."

"Nice princess outfit," Nipper said.

"Honey, I'm the queen. Don't you forget that."

"Oh yeah."

"I say sweetie, you could be Petrucio's dog with the way you're dressed."

"What's a Petrucio?"

"Oh dear, that's Shakespeare, honey."

"What's Shakespeare? Some new toy?"

"Toy? A toy? No, it is not a toy. It's poetry."

"Oh. I know poetry. Remember my poem?"

"How could one forget, Nipper? Now what can I do for you this fine day? But make it quick. The sun is unobstructed right now."

"I was wondering if you wouldn't mind," Nipper said, "if you weren't busy... Or if you were, that's fine too, just let me know otherwise I totally understand and in fact-but-if-you're-not-which-would-be-great-if-you-were-able-to-and-it-would-be-great-because-I-would-do-whatever-you-wanted—"

I couldn't watch that anymore. I'd seen some grisly things out on patrol, but watching Nipper flounder like that was too much. He looked moments away from speaking in tongues.

"Hey Fritz," Ernie said as I came out from behind the bushes, "he'll see you. Where you going?"

I had better things to do than watch this latest episode of *Barks of our Lives*. I was in the midst of an investigation. I scanned the park for those pugs. As a breed, they always seemed to know something, though they played dumb at every opportunity. If I couldn't find them I for sure wanted to have a chat with the mushroom-eating Yorkies.

"Oh my," I heard from nearby, "now who is that wonderful hunk of dog sashaying away from me? 'Scuse me, Nipper Dipper. You hold that thought of yours."

"Okay," Nipper said, remembering to again exhale.

"Where do you think you're disappearing to?" Scarlet said as a pair of paws trotted up to me from the side, and a warm breath of air found its way into my ear. "Well, aren't you going to introduce yourself, or am I the only one with any manners in this here park?"

"I'm Fritz."

"Fritz. A rugged name for a rugged dog, I'm sure. Now here I was afraid I was just going to have to call you darling." Her eyes were surrounded by smoky fur that faded perfectly into glistening white across her back.

"Fritz will do."

"It sure will, sugar."

"May I help you, ma'am?"

"I've never seen you here before. Maybe I can help you get to know the surroundings."

"Okay," I said, feeling like I was getting somewhere. "Do you know any dogs that go by Clay or Scamper?"

"Oh, now I know plenty of dogs, Fritz. But how about we just talk about you and me."

"Clay is a large Rottweiler and Scamper is his sidekick, one of those Jack Russells. Know 'um?"

"If it'll keep you talking to me, of course I know them. Now how about I show you a few of the more quiet areas of the park?"

"Where can I find them?"

"Over by that tree in the corner where no one's looking, that'd be good place to start."

"I'm talking about Clay and Scamper."

"Still on that, are you? Have I said how much I like a dog in uniform?"

"No."

"Well then let me be the first to say how much I do."

"Thank you. Now, can you help me?"

"Of course I'll help, but don't you think about playing hard to get with me. I'll answer anything you want, but not here."

She sniffed my nose as close as she could without our noses touching and left.

"Where?" I said, yelling after her, wanting to follow but feeling paralyzed.

She answered me with her hips. They bounced up and down and swayed to and fro. I stood there like a lump. A lump who was having a hole seared through him by the laser eyes of a dog a few yards away dressed like a lollipop junkyard.

## Chapter Eleven – On the Other Side of Town

Since my departure, Nitro had the Grand City kennel all to himself. My bed was gone. My bowl was gone. My scent was washed away.

I pictured the overbred dope alone in my kennel late at night, thinking no one was watching him. I imagined that they took the opportunity to knock the kennel down and completely rebuild it for Nitro as one of those projects they use leftover budget money on. I was sure that it had wall-to-wall insulation and a heating system. I was sure it had soft light. I was sure the barks didn't echo for minutes in there. I was sure it had multiple windows. I was sure it was ventilated and didn't trap in unwanted smells. I was sure it had a life-like human dummy hanging from the ceiling with bungee rope. One that Nitro could tackle and attack like it was the real thing. I was positive Nitro gave the dummy a ridiculous nickname too, something like "Chewy."

I pictured him living it up in there with all the perks I never had. A working speaker mounted into the ceiling. They'd turn on the radio for him, and he'd romp around hyping himself up for a chase.

"You got this brother," he'd tell himself as he slobbered and salivated at the thought of tackling some scumbag and taking a clean bite off a sweaty forearm. "You're the dog. You're the envy of the canine race. No one holds a candle to you, Nitro.

Get some, Nitro. That's it. Oh, dog, you're getting a medal for
this one. Here comes the news, you're getting that camera time.
Nitro, the hero, coming to you live at eleven o'clock from the
crime scene. No fear. All action. All Nitro. All the time."

Nitro was in better shape than I was or ever had been. I
knew that when we worked together. He was lean and
muscular. The veins on his arms and hind legs were like ropes.
He was faster than me too, but what did you expect? Now they
have bio-engineered food for every stage of your life from puppy
to adult to mature. Me? I just got food. Big fifty-pound plain
sacks of grub were just fine for Fritz. Food that made the same
sounds twice a day as they poured it into my bowl. Clang-clang-
clang-clang-clomp-clomp-clomp. That's it. There was nothing
for my skeletal health or my digestive tract or my circulatory
system or for muscle density or to promote strong teeth. I got
knuckle-sized clumps of dry food sprinkled with what people
think a chicken smells like. Year after year after year.

If I wanted to strengthen my bite, I had to get creative and
deal with whatever I had to work with. If that meant I had to
chew on a spare two-by-four that one of the other cops gave me
after they remodeled their home, then I destroyed that thing
until you could pick a lock with it. Toss me an old crowbar and
in six months you'd be left with tin foil. I didn't get tennis balls
to chew on; I sharpened my enamel on steel wool wrapped
together with rubber bands.

When I ran, it was on flat ground or up a hill. Sometimes
they'd take us to where the firemen trained, and we could run
the stairs. That made the Dalmatians throw a piss fit. Now
they have a whole obstacle course at the academy for the dogs
with ropes, tires, netting, hurdles, bushes, and forts to climb
through.

Instead, I was now curled up in the backyard of the Hart
residence after a day of playing make-believe while
entertaining my insomnia with a view of the stars and power
lines.

It's wasn't my place to say what's fair and what wasn't in
the world, but I couldn't help the way I felt. If I had the
advantages Nitro had, or if I had the great fortune of his year

of birth, then maybe I would've been in the kennel with Nitro the night when Clay and Scamper showed up looking for me.

What I know is that there was a crash outside at the kennel when there shouldn't have been anyone out there. What Nitro was doing at the time was anyone's guess (he later claimed "nothing much"). Since I'm the one unraveling this yarn, I'm going to speculate that he was training to a corny song like what they play at the police banquets when all the officers are too drunk to walk straight, something like "Kung Fu Fighting."

"Ni-TRO was fast as lighting," he sang as I imagined him taking a flying leap across the kennel. Knowing Clay and Scamper, they didn't just go up and tip their hand with an outright disturbance. They wouldn't have gone without a proper plan, one that surely would have included some recon. Clay would have forced Scamper to squat down so Clay could stand on his shoulders to get a good peek in through a window, unbeknownst to the training buffoon.

Clay got a good look inside with his empty eyes and didn't see me. Instead, he saw what would appear to be a rhythmic dance routine. Then the breath from his nostrils fogged up the window in a half-circle. That's when Scamper's legs gave, and Clay crumbled to the ground.

That had to be the crash that Nitro told me he heard. Clay, disgusted by his partner's lack of sustainable lifting strength, improvised and sent Scamper and his cramping body to the door while Clay took cover out of sight.

"Can I help you?" Nitro said, opening the door to a grimacing Scamper.

"Umm, yessir," Scamper said, hopping on three legs. "I was here to see if you've mailed in your census form for this year and if not–"

"Census was last year."

"Well, you know how slow the government can be. We can't help–"

"What was that noise?" Nitro said.

"Noise? What noise? I didn't hear anything," Scamper said, too quickly for a seasoned cop not to raise an eye.

"It sounded like something fell. Like a thud."

Nitro took a look around. Clay held his breath in the shadows and squinted his eyes to abduct all reflection from them.

"It was me," Scamper said, reeling Nitro's waning attention back in to him. "I'm scared is all. I don't really work for the census. I just needed a reason to knock on the door."

"Don't be silly, you're at the police station. What can I do for you? I'm Nitro, the new guy in town."

"What happened to the other one? That's who we're, I, me! That's who *I'm* after. I mean, looking for."

"Fritz?" Nitro said, spitting out of the side of his mouth. "Figures."

"That's his name?"

"I thought you knew him?"

"Just by reputation only. They say he was the best, right?"

"They may have said that at one time, but I'm the best now. How can I help?"

"You can tell us where to find Fritz."

"Who's us?"

"Me. Sorry. Me. I just mean me. So, where is he?"

"He got old and retired somewhere out in the suburbs, pal. Look, you want help, you got Nitro. It's my kennel now. Fritz can't help you anymore. What do you want with a beat-up old-timer like him anyway?"

"He's retired and beat up now, you say?"

"Last time I saw him. You sure I can't find a way to help you?"

"Well, I just wanted to tell him thanks. You see, he saved me and a friend of mine. I guess it was right before he retired, and we just wanted to return the favor if we could. I guess you can't help us."

Scamper turned his back to Nitro, stood up straight, and walked away. Nitro had to feel a pang in his chest; was it rejection, or was it something else? Ineptitude? Suspicion?

"He's living with Officer Hart at his house off of Sycamore," Nitro said, trying to be of service somehow. "If that helps you at all."

Nitro waited by the door for a thank you that wasn't going to come. He returned to the kennel and his funk jams. He didn't run around the kennel, and he didn't practice on Chewy. He sat there and wished for the day when I was no longer around.

While he sat there, I can only hope that before Nitro joined me that night in a late-night double date with the insomnia twins that he noticed the hulking shadow that emerged from nowhere. The shadow that caught up to Scamper and engulfed him before both sets of footsteps vanished into the night's echo. I want to think he did.

## CHAPTER TWELVE – A MILD DISTRACTION

While Nitro wondered if that Jack Russell had told him the truth, I was in the Hart's backyard with my eyes zeroed in up toward the sky. Stars can make excellent company in short doses. Their constant blank stares taunted me, like they knew the world's secrets and would love to tell them to me. I was just too far away. I wished that I was consumed with finding a way to track down Clay and Scamper. I wished that backyard had seen the last of Fritz. I wished that Nitro's kennel was going to be mine again. I wished my leg didn't scare me.

The truth was... Truth was... Those hips. Scarlet and her hips walked for miles and were no closer to getting out of my mind as when they began their jaunt hours ago. And not just those hips, that voice. Like a tipsy songbird caroling like no one was watching. Every note massaged the part of the spine that even the most limber of stretches will never reach. I tried to focus on Clay, but she kept creeping into the foreground.

Ernie had it on good word that we were being taken to the dog beach in the morning. He also advised that Saucy and Scarlet would be there. My plan was to see what she knew about Clay or if she knew anyone who did. I had to focus on that. She seemed like the type who knew a lot of dogs. But the more I pictured her in my mind, the more I wanted to talk to her about anything besides police work.

Maybe this would be okay after all, I thought. Maybe I was overreacting to losing my job; maybe it was time to reinvent myself. I could be a lover. I could be a playboy like Ricky in Internal Affairs. Scarlet wasn't a potential informant, no, she was a new start for me. A new Fritz who wasn't consumed by the past. A Fritz uninterested in a quest to recapture something lost. I could be a dog who might be able to track down something new. Something I hadn't had since the salad days of my career. A future. Hours passed, and the stars held their ground. If I wasn't going to sleep, no one was.

"Ernie," I said to the snoring heap out cold on his back leaning into the stucco with his arms extended over his head. "Ernie. Ernie. Get up. Hey."

"I lost my collar," Ernie said, half-awake, "I'm licensed, don't worry."

"Ernie."

"Look it's a public alley, anyone can rest here, pal."

I bopped him a little with my paw. It took three bops until he saw my face staring down at him. His eyelids dribbled and he squirmed like a poked balloon until he eventually landed on most of his paws.

"What're you doing?" he said, yawning. "You don't do that to someone who's sleeping. You made me lick the wall."

"You wouldn't get up."

"I know. That's the point. You look terrible. Have you slept?" I shook my head. "Aw, come on. Is something wrong? Stupid question, of course something's wrong. Spill it."

"I don't know what you're talking about."

"I'm gonna go get some water to get the taste of paint and dirt out of my mouth, and when I return, you're gonna tell me what's eating at you. If, at that point, you still don't know what I'm talking about, I'm going back to bed, and if you wake me up again, I'm gonna bark until they come out and scream at us because if I'm gonna be miserable, we all are."

Ernie stumbled to his water bowl, took a few sips, started back, thought twice, got some food, a few more sips, and then sat down against the wall.

"You were saying?"

I didn't know what to say.

"So?"

I didn't know how to say it.

"Last call."

I didn't know if I even *wanted* to say it.

"Fine. If my eyes open again before—"

"Okay. Wait. Give me a second."

"Fritz. Listen, clearly you've been up all night with whatever it is. The last thing you need is more time with it, so just spit it out. First thing that comes out. Open your mouth, and let's go already."

"It's just that... I think that... The thing is—"

Ernie slapped me.

"A. That's for waking me up. B. I don't want to hear an ill-prepared speech, and C. I'm still basically asleep, and oh my god, I just slapped a cop. Dogs have been put away for less. I mean, you have to understand that when a dog needs his sleep and he doesn't get it that said dog, who may or may not be me, otherwise yours truly, is prone to do something that he doesn't mean and instantly regrets it and hopes that it's something that can be forgotten about in no time. In fact, if I keep talking and you just stay still and don't make a sound, I'll never know if you're even mad at me, and I think that I actually prefer it that way—"

I slapped Ernie back.

"We're even," I said. Ernie nodded. "I need your help. You're sure they're taking us to the beach?"

"That's what Saucy said. Her person was talking to our people, so it seems to be the case. Usually that's how it works."

"What should I do?"

"You woke me up for that? Easy. You run, you get wet, you get dirty, you eat stuff buried in the sand, and then you get a bath when we get home. Was that really something that couldn't wait?"

"I'm talking about with Scarlet."

"I knew it. Me and Saucy saw the way you were looking at her. She does that to everyone, but unlike everyone else, she did it to you on purpose."

"She didn't do anything to me."

"Oh yeah? You were saying that you haven't slept yet. And why is that, Fritz?"

"It could be a lot of things. I'm still trying to relate to life here after my career was ripped from me by those dogs."

"Okay. I'll give you that, but you slept fine until last night. You sure it's not something else, huh?"

Of course it was something else. I used to look down on guys who fawned over a female. Have some self-respect, am I right?

"Fine," I said. "It's her. It's her, so what? I was going to only ask her about Clay because she claimed she knew something. In fact, I'm pretty sure she's lying to me, but I don't care. I want to get my brain screwed back on, but I can't shake her from it. Why does that happen?"

"Couldn't tell you, my friend."

"Well, what do you do with Saucy?"

"Saucy? What are you talking about?"

"Isn't she your girlfriend?"

"No. No-no-no-no-no-no-no," Ernie said, wagging his head so fast that his whole body convulsed and the tags on his collar jangled like a car alarm. "We're just friends. Never even thought of her that way and if I know her, she's never thought of me that way. But don't worry, I can help. I know my way around a thing or two."

"Good. Believe it or not, most females I've ever been around are ones I've arrested."

"You've never had a lady friend or anything?"

"I've always been too busy with work."

"I'm going to take care of you," Ernie said. "Just go along with me and don't wake Nipper."

Ernie stretched his legs out and turned away from me. He took some deep breaths and wiggled his jaw loose. He pranced around me, puckering his lips and winking his eye.

"Hiya boys," Ernie said, in his highest octave. "It's me, Scarlet, you know, the prettiest dog, I do say, in the whole widest world of ours. Mmm-hmmm, well hello there, Fritzie, you big piece of hunk."

"Umm, hello?"

"Is that there a question or a declarative statement?"

"The latter."

"Ladder? Honey, you don't have to do any climbing to see me."

"No. Not ladder. Latter. Lat-ter. There's a difference. One means–"

"Sounds the same to me."

"They're two different words."

"You calling me stupid?"

"No, Ernie."

"Ernie? My lordy, let's not talk about that rascal."

"Fine," I said, knowing this exercise would accomplish nothing. I was never a fan of role-playing or simulations because they're a waste of time. There's no substitute for real-life practical experience. That's where you learned to react on your toes. But Ernie meant well.

"Now, I have it on excellent authority that there's something you wanted to tell me? No one's around, baby cakes, let's hear it."

"Scarlet, I just wanted to tell you that–"

"You like the way my eyes reflect the splendor of the moonlight?"

"No. Hadn't occurred to me."

"The way I don't even have one piece of fur that's out of place?"

"I'm sorry. Most females I encounter are criminals."

"So, I'm a criminal?"

"No. Um, unless being so pretty is a crime, okay?"

"You dogs are all alike!"

"We're done with this, Ernie."

"I said don't talk about him." *Scarlet* slapped me again. Harder than Ernie did before. "That'll teach you to treat a lady with some- Oh no, I did it again. I'm so sorry, Fritz."

"Thanks for trying, Ernie," I said, licking the inside of my mouth, "but it looks like I'm on my own."

"Sorry. Can I go back to bed then? I don't want to hit you again."

"Go back to sleep," I said.

Ernie dropped where he was and was snoring within moments. I went over against the wall, took a seat, and tried to calculate how much self-respect I just tossed by the wayside.

"Don't change a thing," Nipper said. "Hey, you want help, why don't you go find a love doc, all right?"

"What'd you say, Nipper?" I said as my ears shot up, and I suddenly felt wide awake.

"What? I'm tired. I don't feel like arguing."

"No. What did you just say? Please."

"I said if you want help, why don't you go to a love doc? You gonna make fun of my joke now? Go ahead."

"I'm not going to make fun of you. The doc. Of course. Nipper, that's it. You're right. The dock. I gotta go to the dock! I don't know why I couldn't remember. They said the dock. Nipper, can you hear me?" He turned his body away from me. "I gotta find the dock. That's the last thing they said. That's where I'll find them."

Who cared about sleeping? I was up on my feet patrolling the yard. I looked up at those last few remaining stars. Now I was doing the taunting. I figured out their little riddle, and come the following night, they were going back to what they did best. They watched over me as I slept. But for the rest of that spectacular night, I didn't close my eyes. It was glorious.

The docks sliced out from the coastline above the horizon. The dog beach was relatively new to Grand City and had arrived fast on the heels of a news report that detailed the pollution levels of the local beach water. Code Orange. The water approached a hazardous level thanks to the waste and pollution from the port.

The residents were concerned about the effects on the children (what else is new?) who swam too close to the bad water. In a packed chamber, the city council voted unanimously to dedicate a half-mile buffer zone of coast between the docks and the rest of Grand City State Beach. A week later, I was at the ribbon-cutting ceremony for *Grand City Dog Beach*.

A volunteer now charges two dollars for parking plus another fifty cents per dog to visit the beach on the weekends. During the work week, there's no charge beyond the parking. Dogs from neighboring cities are charged seventy-five cents. Locals rule.

The docks have always been the backdrop for most of the crime in Grand City. There's the petty stuff that happens downtown and the squabbles in the gated neighborhoods, but the big stuff, the stuff they make movies about, those crimes are the lifeblood of the docks. To have a successful local importing and exporting industry, you need a bunch of men willing to work long, tough hours in lousy conditions. You think the guys willing to take those jobs are going to listen to a suit and tie with a piece of paper from the local college that says *Business Management?* Not a chance. You needed even tougher guys from a different school to handle those types of workers.

The type of organizations needed to make the docks run smooth are the same types who strike deals with foreign companies to import the types of *goods* that don't make it to the shelves at the mall. A lot of money came in and out of the docks. The police didn't spend as much time out there as we should have. That's where Clay was. That's where I had to go. I couldn't just make a run for it right then. Mrs. Hart would've seen me, and after a few phone calls to Officer Hart, I'd be in custody. I needed a plan.

"Are you listening to me?" Scarlet said as we walked together down the sand a few hours later at the beach. The other dogs chased Frisbees (led by Ernie), dug holes (Ernie again), got yelled at for eating from the trash (take a wild guess), or were stuck on a leash and on a blanket with Mrs. Hart (Missy).

"Yeah," I lied.

"That settles it then, sugar."

Ahead of us, Ernie and Saucy took turns trying to bite the waves as they crashed into the shore. Ernie attempted a style that saw him take a running, barking sprint from the shore as the wave approached. He leapt as his feet hit the water and fired off a crapshoot of bites. His head smacked the top of the wave, which sent him tail over skull. Then he ran back to Saucy and Nipper to explain that he meant to do it that way.

"Would you stop staring off at those ships?" Scarlet said. "All you need to be focused on is right here next to you."

"I'm not staring at the ships," I said. "I'm staring at the docks."

"There can't be anything worth looking at over there."

"That's where I'm going."

"Well, you'll just have to schedule that in between our dates because I'm not going to join you over there."

"You weren't invited."

"Excuse me? Do you know who you're talking to? I'm invited everywhere you go."

"Says who?"

"Says you. You just said I'm your number one. I'm the belle of your ball. That means that when you go somewhere, I automatically have a spot next to you. Of course, I can decide what engagements I want to attend. I may change my mind and say I'm coming to the docks with you."

"That's not happening."

"If I say so, it is."

You're not supposed to get mad at females or children. They embed that into your brain in training. If you do happen to get mad at either one, you bury it until it goes away. I was not going to stand there on that beach with the docks just a few minutes away and let her, let anyone, tell me that they're going to stop me from giving Clay his receipt.

"Let me explain something to you," I said. "I think you're pretty. Under normal circumstances, I'd explore the weird feelings you gave me, but I can't and I won't until I right some wrongs that have been done to me. I'm not some dog from the park who you can just snap into obedience. I'm a cop. It's who I am. It's what I do. So, do me a favor and save the power plays and the blinking eyes for someone else. If it's any consolation, I was close to giving up, and you could've had me, but I wouldn't have respected myself, and neither would you."

I turned and walked away from her. Away from the docks. She knew not to follow. What was I going to do? Change everything about me because Scarlet gave me a furtive glance? Clay hid back behind my eyes. Instead of seeing myself curled up with Scarlet, I saw Clay on my throat. I had to shake him off before I could ever think about anything else.

## Chapter Thirteen – The Ballads of Chucho and Lincoln

"Ernie, you smell putrid," Nipper said, back at the house.

"You mean it smells like I had a good time," Ernie said.

"No, because I stink too, and I had a lousy time."

"Well, whose fault is that, Nipper? You know, it's getting old, this pity me act you have going on."

"Ernie, they're still laughing at me over the whole Halloween fiasco. The last thing I wanted to do was make a fool of myself by trying to eat the waves."

"I didn't make a fool of myself if that's what you're trying to say. Me and Saucy had a great time. Besides, we were biting the waves, not eating them. *That* would have been dumb."

Officer Hart came into the yard, grabbed Ernie by his collar, and dragged him to the front yard. He didn't say anything and pulled at Ernie harder than I thought appropriate.

"She still likes you," Nipper said. "Now she thinks you're playing hard to get. Thanks to that move, she only likes you more. So yeah, thanks."

The door from the garage opened, and Ernie darted back in, still wet. He shook off the leftover water and scratched himself along the stucco on the side of the house.

"You're still wet, Ernie," Nipper said. "That was a fast bath."

"A bath? Sheesh, I got hosed off with the high-pressure nozzle. That stings, man. He dumped a bunch of soap on me and blasted it off without even scrubbing me down. Then he yells in at her something about not taking us to the beach if she didn't plan on cleaning us up. Then she screams something about at least him noticing that she did something while he was at work. Then he says that the neighbors were watching, which they weren't, and to be quiet. He says, 'sorry, Ernie, you're done' and then doesn't even towel me off. That's my favorite part of the whole thing."

"Nipper, get over here. Let's go," Officer Hart said, with the door to the garage wide open. Nipper took plenty of extra steps on his way and incurred the wrath of more Officer Hart shouts and swears. Mrs. Hart yelled to not yell at us. He answered her with a holler. She responded with a bellow. He with a roar, which was answered by a screech, which culminated in a whisper, a "what," and a "nothing." Officer Hart seized Nipper's collar out of the silence and yanked him into the human abyss.

"What do you think is up with them?" Ernie said.

"Who knows?" I said.

"I thought you were a detective. Do some investigating."

"There's nothing to investigate. There's no crime. It's not against the law to be upset at someone."

"But, what's the story, you know? Let's get some dirt."

"Let me tell you another story, Ernie. Before I was on the force there was a dog named Lincoln who was there for six years. He was tough, durable, a quiet dog, and a serviceable officer. And before Lincoln there was Hammer, and Hammer is who this story is about.

"Hammer was a natural. He took to the job like no one had before, human or canine. His instincts were the sharpest anyone had ever seen; he could think half a dozen steps ahead of any criminal. You hear too many times that someone is born for something, and while most of the time it's not true, Hammer was a born cop. Not born to *be* one. He came out of the womb an officer. He was respected and was poised for a long and successful career on the force.

"Then he disappeared from the kennel one morning. When his partner went to get him all he found was an empty food bowl. Hammer was a ghost. The third shift cleaning crew claimed they saw Hammer in the kennel on their rounds and that the door was closed.

"Grand City spent thousands of dollars and man hours trying to find Hammer. The search made national news. A few dozen citizens spent every weekend for six weeks combing every alley, underpass, park, and dark corner they could. They all turned up the same thing. Nothing. There were rumors he was kidnapped, but there was never any ransom offered. Besides, if half the stories about Hammer were true, you'd need an elephant rifle to knock him out. The fact that his body never turned up convinced a lot of us that Hammer was still alive somewhere. He had to be; he was Hammer.

"No matter who you are, eventually life will go on with or without you. While, officially, Grand City left the Hammer file open, they just stopped trying to find him. They kept his picture up on the wall and made T-shirts for him that still saw the light of day once in a while when I started out.

"It's my second year on the force, and we get a call on a pursuit headed toward Grand City. Officer Hart radioed that we're nearby, and we join in. We spent forty-five minutes on and off the freeway until this guy crashed into a parked motor home. Then, the driver foot bailed and tried to huff it toward an apartment complex. That was my cue. Officer Hart let me out, and I did what I do. The old sprint, leap, takedown, and bite routine until the officers with the cuffs caught up. The runner was a three-striker who didn't want to go back for good. When the day comes that these yahoos can outrun me, they're free to go anywhere they want.

"Within minutes there were plenty of eyes and hands on scene, but I caught the prying gaze of an onlooker more in tune with my height and build. He was on the other side of a chain-link fence separating the scene from a neighboring tow yard.

"'Good work, officer,' he told me as I approached the fence.

"'Who are you?' I said.

"'I'm no one, pal. Just a dog on the wrong side of a fence.'

"'You got a name?'

"'Yeah I do. What happened to Lincoln? He retire?'

"It was him. Hammer. He'd been there a few years and didn't miss the force since walking away. Which is exactly what he did. He jimmied the kennel door open that night and never looked back. He was years removed from the chiseled dog in the help-missing posters. His fur had faded, and the skin around his mouth and neck hung in boredom. His whiskers drooped as did his ears.

"The day he left for good he'd been on a traffic stop on the side of the freeway during rush hour. Nothing special; expired tags and a speeding ticket. While he sat in the backseat of the unit, waiting for his partner to clear the stop, Hammer heard an outburst of horns and saw a semi truck, clearly not paying attention, barreling straight at him. Hammer watched it first weave into the shoulder toward the squad car then jerk back into traffic moments before it would've plowed into the squad car.

"A breath away from death will give anyone a fresh look on life. Hammer's new outlook was DOA. He said in that moment that he learned how powerless he was and always had been. There was nothing he was able to control. He took it as a warning. He was a good cop, a good partner, and a good dog. At that moment in the squad car, none of it mattered. One random occurrence and the lights could go out for good. Once that dam broke in his mind, Hammer was never going to go back to pretending that any of those things, the accolades, the good deeds, meant anything if they could all go away in the snap of the finger. He couldn't control if he lived or died. So what was there to care about?

"He said the only peace he found was one where he removed all order from his life. He didn't feel bad for leaving the other cops behind. He wandered up and down the coast and found his way into that lot where he slept all day and watched the place at night. They fed him. They called him Chucho. They left him alone.

"He had a life where a swerving truck could be the end, so he made sure that there would be no more swerving trucks."

"Wow," Ernie said. I'm not sure he got the point of the story, but he seemed impressed by it. I'm not sure I got the point of the story either. I'd been thinking a lot about Hammer. I didn't want to be another Hammer. I was not going to be a Chucho.

The door to the yard opened, and Nipper was let back in, still dripping wet. He shook himself as dry as he could. Officer Hart was more wet than before. Looked like Nipper put up a fight.

"Fritz, come here." It was my turn for the treatment. I met Officer Hart at the door, and I saw how tired he was. His face was puffy, and his shoulders hung low. He looked me over and scratched my chest. I wondered how I looked to him. "You're fine, Fritz."

Officer Hart shut the door. I sat down and kept my eyes on the door. This whole life-in-the-backyard thing was not going to work.

"Oh, come on," Nipper said. "That is not fair at all. Why doesn't he get a torture bath like we did? What, am I surprised at this point? Figures."

"I guess he don't need one," Ernie said, while, more diplomatically, he matched Nipper's tone.

"Yeah, well, something stinks around here."

The two of them dispersed to different spots in the yard. Nipper to the food bowl. Ernie to the opposing wall. I joined Nipper at the food bowl. He turned his body away from me to shield the food.

"You want to get out of here?" I said.

"I want to eat," Nipper said, between bites.

"I'm not stopping you, Nipper. Just hear me out. I'm not saying I'm leaving forever, but there's something I need to do. I need help."

"Yeah, good luck with that," Nipper said.

"I could use your help."

"Like I said, good luck with that one."

"Nipper–"

"What do you want from me?" Nipper said, looking up as food fell from his mouth. "You show up, Ernie likes you, you get my costume at the park. Scarlet likes you, and I'm left on the sidelines as the big punch line. I'm tired of being the joke, and with you around here I might as well be invisible, so do me a favor and don't rub it in my face and just let me be. Is that too much to ask of the super dog?"

"Why don't you come with me? I could use some backup."

"Did you just hear what I said? Even if I knew where you were going, and why, and how, and on the miniscule chance that I wanted to go with you, I'm not going to be some dog's rhythm section."

"You wouldn't be my rhythm section. It would be like our own patrol unit."

"I don't think so, Fritz."

"Let me try to explain to you, Nipper. Before I was on the force, they had a dog named Lincoln. Before Lincoln, there was a dog named Hammer. Hammer was everything you could ask for in an officer, to the letter, but this story is about Lincoln, the dog who had to follow Hammer. For reasons beyond his control, Lincoln spent the first weeks of his tenure trying to find the dog that he replaced. Can you imagine what that does to someone mentally? You want to do the best job you can, but you know that your reward is going to be a one-way ticket to a demotion at best. At worst, he'd get moved to another department and all because he proved he was a capable officer.

"The memories of Hammer could never get far enough behind him. Everyone had a Hammer story, the time he did this extraordinary thing or the other time when he did something unbelievably brave. So Lincoln chose to do what he thought he was supposed to do: be like Hammer. He started taking risks on the job, he'd jump off things, he'd run harder than he should, and he'd make stupid choices to go for the glory. The result was that he went from being a highly skilled officer to someone who was accident prone, who got hurt, and who endangered people. So, sure, he earned a reputation as Hammer had, but it wasn't the one he was seeking. Had he just been the best Lincoln he could, they would've forgotten about Hammer—"

"I get it," Nipper said.

"I'm not finished," I said.

"Be yourself, and don't try to be anyone else. I got it. Contrary to what you may think, I'm not stupid. And your little moral, it's easier said than done."

"Ernie's gonna come with me."

"Sure he is," Nipper said, looking past me to Ernie. "Ernie, are you going with Fritz?"

"I don't know," Ernie said. "Where're we going, Fritz?"

"We're escaping to solve a case. You in?"

"What case?" Nipper said.

"The one I was on before I got sent here."

"Aren't the police already working on it?" Nipper said.

"Maybe. But I'm not. That's the point. I'm going to get Clay. He and Scamper put me here, and they don't get to say where I spend the rest of my life. I do. So I'm going out there, and I'm bringing them down. You want to come, Ernie?"

"Okay, sure. Sounds fun."

"Fun?" Nipper said.

"Yeah," Ernie said. "Doesn't it?"

"Told ya, Nipper. I could use a smart dog out there with me, especially if Ernie's all I got so far."

Finally, I got a grin out of him.

Later, it was quiet inside and outside the Hart house. My eyes closed while my brain worked up a plan. Ernie was asleep, sprawled out on his back against the stucco. Nipper was wide awake. He approached Ernie and sat next to him. Nipper got up and paced around and sat next to Ernie again. Got up, walked, sat, and got up, all driving me nuts. *Oh, just wake him up already*. He sat one more time and gently pawed at Ernie.

"Hey," Nipper said, whispering. He sat still for at least a minute before pawing Ernie's arm. "Hey," he said again, now pawing at Ernie's shoulder.

Ernie's eyes finally creaked open. He blinked a few times until he realized it was Nipper now disturbing him. This time, he didn't startle and remained on his back. "What is it, Nipper? This is happening too many times."

"Umm, did you need me for something?"

"I need ten hours where no one bothers me. That's what I need from you right now."

"Oh, I thought I heard you say my name."

"Nope. I was dreaming of being at a sausage factory."

"Cool."

"You weren't there. It was me and all the smoked sausages that, well, that I could dream of."

"You sure you didn't call for me?" Nipper said.

"Positive, Nipper. Maybe it was Fritz."

"No. He's sleeping, but hey, since you're up already, do you have a minute?"

Ernie rolled over to his side and rubbed the side of his face with his arms. He wasn't sleeping, but I'm not convinced he was awake either. "What's up, buddy?"

"You're really gonna go with him?"

"Sure. Why not? It's been boring here anyway for too long. The people have been acting strange too. We'll come back."

"Aren't you scared? I mean, these are bad dogs that he's going after. Look what they did to his leg. He can barely run anymore."

"He's still a cop, and I know my way around the streets pretty good. It's where I'm from. Don't get me wrong, I like it here, but out there is my home too."

"Why does he want to get these dogs? I don't see the big deal. He's safe here."

"Nipper, don't you understand? As bad as you don't want him to be here, he doesn't want to be here even more. If I can help him get what he wants, maybe we all get what we want."

"Everyone seems to like him. The people. The dogs at the park. Scarlet. You."

"You stop right there. Ever since I've been here, it was Nipper and Ernie. You're my buddy, and nothing's going to change that. What's wrong with you, Nipper? This is our chance to have an adventure. Nipper and Ernie—"

"And Fritz."

"Yeah. And Fritz. Yes, we *could* do it without you, but the thing is, I can't do it without you, so that's it. I'm just gonna wake up Fritz and tell him, sorry pal, you're on your own. You know he's gonna be miserable, which is going to make you miserable, which is going to make me miserable."

"Wait," Nipper said as Ernie committed to his ruse by getting up on his feet, which for Ernie to stand at that late of an hour said something about his ability as a salesman, "you think I should go with you guys?"

"I think you should come with us," Ernie said, getting ever closer to me.

"Hold on. Don't wake him up, Ernie. I'm gonna go. Now, uh, you don't worry. Just go get some sleep, okay? I'm gonna go. Wait a second; he's got a plan for this thing, right?"

"Oh yeah, he's got it all figured out. Don't worry about it."

"I'm not worried, Ernie. I sleep like a puppy."

Nipper disappeared into the sanctity of his corner of the yard. Call me corny, but I opened my eyes in hopes of enjoying a moment with Ernie where we made eye contact. I hoped to share a synchronized head nod like a scene from a movie where the heroes acknowledge that a seemingly chaotic scene went exactly the way they planned it to. But no, Ernie was already back up against the stucco racing to catch up with his snores.

Instead, it was the scene in the movie where the hero was lulled into a false sense of security. He thought the foolproof plan he had devised was on the verge of being seamlessly rolled into action while his two mortal enemies were perched in the child's fort one yard over spying on him and the two other dogs. The tiny one wanted to attack at that very moment, but the other one, the bigger and craftier one, he did not expect two other dogs. He'd been around long enough to know that it was the wise dog who regrouped and devised a better plan.

The large dog, while frustrated, was satisfied enough to know that his prey would be there when he returned. The hero fell asleep.

## CHAPTER FOURTEEN – A ROUTINE

**08:00 Hours** – I'd been up for an hour. Breakfast was eaten, washed down, and digested. I ate lighter than I had in years and upped my water intake with a goal of increased endurance and mobility. I woke the boys. Ernie put up a hassle (as always), but Nipper took to the new schedule and structure better than I thought he would. Nipper had been eating my leftover share of chow to help bulk him up some. Ernie's portions remained constant.

**08:20 Hours** – Morning exercise. Nipper worked on a body-weight routine that consisted of a lot of squats, lunges, and free jumps. I jogged laps around the yard with him as long as my leg could hold. We still didn't talk much, but we didn't argue either. Ernie was on an all-sprint routine; one end of the yard and back. And again. And again.

I reminded them that the dogs we were going after would not show them any mercy. They did their damndest to put me on the shelf for good. We needed to be as lean, as mean, and as tough as our bodies would let us be.

**08:45 Hours** – Cool-down session. I made sure Nipper stretched his hips well and showed him some simple moves. Ernie complained about the stretching, saying he never needed to stretch after a run before.

"Be quiet and get it over with," Nipper said.

**09:00–11:00 Hours** – We waited to see if today would be the day they took us back to the dog park. Another bust. This marked three weeks of remaining in the yard.

**11:20 Hours** – Simon came into the yard to play. He gave Nipper and Ernie treats. I'm offered some, but I decline. He dropped one in front of me, the foulest smelling of the handful. I sniffed it and walked away. Ernie gobbled it up. Simon tossed a tennis ball across the yard. Ernie's surprised at how much quicker he can retrieve it. I didn't play with the child.

**11:25 Hours** – Simon got bored and went back inside. I explained to the boys that lunch will have to wait an hour due to the extra treats they ate. Ernie protested, as expected.

**11:30 Hours** - Officer Hart made an appearance. He led me out of the backyard and into the front seat of The Intimidator. Before I left, I reminded Ernie about the added wait time on lunch.

"I know, Fritz," he said.

I didn't believe him.

I rode in the front seat of The Intimidator with Officer Hart. He listened to talk radio. AM 680 – The Home of Grand City Conservative Talk. Miles Shumer returned from commercial break with breaking news on a Senator. Their staffer broke into the campaign offices of their opponent with the aim of making it look as if the opponent misappropriated funds on a recent trip overseas... I can't even pretend to understand what that meant.

Miles screamed through the speakers. The pitch hurt the fur on the tips of my ears. I don't understand why people get so mad about this stuff. If everything went their way, they'd have nothing to talk about and would be out of business.

Officer Hart's phone vibrated, and he turned down the radio. Not low enough for me.

"Hello," he said. "I'm sorry. I wasn't aware that I had to check in with you every time I came and went."

Ten seconds at a red light. Officer Hart closed his eyes for five of them.

"Dear, is it okay with you? Do I have your written express permission to go for a ride with the dog in The Intimidator?"

Three seconds.

"Of course Fritz is with me. What did you think, he ran away? Police dogs don't do that." *Good to know. Moving on.* "Yes, he's in the back."

Officer Hart reached down to scratch the top of my head and kept his one free elbow on the steering wheel. Miles took a phone call, a concerned citizen on line one.

"I don't know where we're going," Officer Hart said as he stopped scratching me and returned his hand to the wheel. His free foot bounced up and down on its heel next to the brake pedal. "Out. Does it matter? I have no idea when we're going to come back. Before dinner, okay?"

Miles gave the name of a website to the concerned caller where they could read more information with charts and detailed figures. He further disclaimed that the website was in fact associated with his law firm but that the information came from unbiased research.

"I don't know how many times I have to apologize," Officer Hart said. "I don't even know how you've turned this so that it's me who's doing the apologizing to begin with. What do you think? You think I'm feeling fantastic over it?"

Miles segued into a news story that ended as an advertisement for an online identity-theft prevention service; only a few hundred dollars annually.

"I have to drive. I'm gonna go," Officer Hart said, folding his phone shut and tossing it over his shoulder in the back seat. "If you want to try eating it, I wouldn't stop you, Fritz."

I just looked at him.

**13:00 Hours** – Lunch at a Mexican fast-food place. We went into the drive through. I hung out the window and breathed in what Grand City used to smell like for me. I smelled the tar of asphalt, the cherry lipstick on the cigarette butts tossed on the sidewalk, the stagnant water in the gutter, the exhaust from the cars as they passed by.

I smelled every single ingredient inside the restaurant. The black beans, the grilled veggies, the buckets and buckets of pork, the fresh carne asada, and the newly chopped chicken. The steel of the butcher knife roared through my nose.

We paid and parked and waited until they brought us a tray of food. Officer Hart let me out of The Intimidator with no leash. We sat down at the end of a long, hard plastic bench that was carved up with gang logos and covered with the remains of peeled stickers. I sat next to him on the ground. He gave me a plate of mini-burritos.

"I won't tell if you won't tell," Officer Hart said. I wanted to eat the food. I didn't want to be rude, but the key to any fitness routine is a steady diet. I used to absolutely love human food, but I knew it would feel like I swallowed a brick for the next week. I politely lay down and turned my head away from the food. Officer Hart rubbed my back. "You feeling okay, buddy? How's that rear wheel of yours doing?"

I turned back and half-heartedly licked at the guacamole on the plate.

"Alright, well, don't eat it if you don't want it. I'm sure Nitro'll gulp it down."

Nitro?

**13:24 Hours** – The Intimidator rolled into the Grand City PD parking lot, and we parked a few spots away from the squad cars and SWAT vans. I saw the K-9 unit with my face still painted on the side. It now read "Nitro!" under my face. I wanted to be anywhere else. My head felt heavy, and I took deep breaths. If I was going to feel like this I should have had one of those burritos.

"Let's go say hi," Officer Hart said. I didn't budge. What were my choices? Go inside and be paraded through the halls and offices like an ancient relic, a token of the old days, and a reminder that this too will happen to all of them someday? Or did I sit there in the car waiting for someone to pull up and see my mug in the window and then what? "Come on. Everyone wants to say hi. They miss you." I hopped down out of the car and my leg buckled. "Whoa, not so fast, Fritz."

**13:28 Hours** – So far, so good. We hadn't passed anyone of note in the hallways of the department; some rookies, a dispatcher, a records clerk. We turned the corner, and there was Nitro with his partner, Officer Richards, who took over the K-9 role with Nitro. Officer Hart was offered the spot, but he took a transfer to auto theft instead.

"What're you doing here?" Nitro said.

"I came with him," I said. "I didn't know we were coming. If I did, I wouldn't have got in the car."

Officer Hart and Richards talked about last night's basketball game.

"You expect me to believe that?" Nitro said, leaning in and smelling my face. "Must be nice spending time at the beach."

"Not as much as you'd think."

"Couldn't stay away, could you? Can't say I don't understand. It is a bit rare for the old timers to come back. Makes the rest of us feel uncomfortable, to be honest. To see you all beaten up, hobbling, struggling just to stand up. I feel like I should ask if you need any help like I would any other victim in need."

"You know what it is, Nitro. It must be so hard for you to wake up every morning knowing without any doubt that even if that day is the best day of your career, it'll never be half as good as any regular day that I had."

"You keep talking about yourself in the past tense," Nitro said as he snarled and showed his teeth with his eyes focused on mine, "and I'll be glad to help you get there."

"I dare you," I said, putting the side of my face next to his and pushing his away.

"Hey, hey, hey," Officer Richards said. "Nitro, down."

Nitro sat submissively next to Richards. I stayed on my feet and stood behind Officer Hart.

"Did you see what happened?" Officer Hart said.

"No," Officer Richards said. "But I've read that when you have two alphas who've been apart for a while and then you bring them back together without any type of, uh, this guy called it pre-scenting, that sometimes they'll fight."

I don't care what he'd heard or read; it was pretty simple. I wasn't letting Nitro, or any dog, disrespect me. Ever again. Officer Hart and Richards made a quick farewell and took the two of us away from each other. Richards yelled after something about meeting for a beer and a bite for the next game.

"What's wrong, Fritz?" Officer Hart said as we went up a flight of stairs. "You know better than that, but I can't say I blame you. I wouldn't take that dog's crap either."

I'd never spent much time on the top floor of the department. It looked like any other top floor of an office building – desks, phones, vending machines, and bathrooms. Officer Hart took me inside the empty auto theft office where desks were scattered along the walls. Officer Hart's was in the front corner, closest to the door, and offered the least privacy.

"I was hoping some of the guys would be here so you could say hi," Officer Hart said as he sat down, shuffled through some files, and took notes. He grabbed a handful of bone-shaped biscuits from an oversized coffee cup on top of his computer and dropped them down for me. They were stale, but they were the same ones Officer Hart always had in supply for me. I ate them.

**15:53 Hours** – Back in the Intimidator on our way home. Miles Shumer wrapped up his broadcast with a warning for all of us to stay vigilant, remain informed, and keep our families safe until we met again next time. Officer Hart graciously didn't wait for the next host to take to the airwaves. He replaced the tinny auto-square commercial with a CD. Even if it was country music, I'd take it.

I watched Officer Hart as he drove; his elbow pressed up against the side window, propping his head up. He looked over at me and maneuvered a deadpan smile with nothing behind it. Just scrunched lips and a brief nostril exhale.

"We'll be home soon," he said.

*Don't hurry on account of me.*

Another few minutes of an increasingly bumpy ride took us to an area of Grand City that was primarily comprised of run-down, post-World War II apartments. We stopped on the side of the road, and Officer Hart lowered his hat, put on his sunglasses, and slouched down in his seat.

**16:09 Hours** – We continued to sit in silence until a nondescript sedan pulled into the front driveway of the Chez Petey's Apartments on the opposite side of the street from us. It stopped in front of a closed garage. Classic rock music came from the open windows of the sedan. Loud enough to justify a car stop. The rear window of the car was covered with decals advertising a home yoga service and an eight-hundred number. Officer Hart set his unflinching gaze on the man who emerged from the car. Caucasian, in his thirties, six foot, a hundred and seventy, long hair. He wore jeans and a shirt with a design that looked like a paint can vomited all over it. Visible tattoos on his forearms.

The man popped his trunk and hooked several bags of groceries to one arm and a box of books under the other. He tried to close his trunk with both hands full but finally set down the box of books to slam it shut after four unsuccessful tries. Moron. He scooped up the box and walked to the metal gate next to the call box a few feet away from his car. Officer Hart continued to watch this non-show.

The subject tried to fish his keys out of his pocket, but too many plastic bags hanging off his wrist prevented any success. He set the bags on the ground and got his keys. He turned back to his car, aimed the keys at the car, and set the alarm. Even I know that it's totally unnecessary to point and shoot those things; just hit the button and let the magic work.

He unlocked the gate to the complex and kept it open by sticking his hips between the end of the door and the doorjamb while he strung the grocery bags up along his wrist again. He backed into the palm tree-lined courtyard of Chez Petey's and disappeared into the complex.

Officer Hart's fist squeezed the steering the wheel so hard that veins came up for air up and down his arm. He reached beyond me into the glove box, grabbed a pen, and took some notes on a spiral pad. He quickly flung the pen back into the glove box and slid the notepad into his back pocket. We stayed across the street from the apartments for a few more minutes while Officer Hart slowed down his breathing. We left with him mumbling, I think to me, something about needing to see what the *bastard* looked like. I always hated working a surveillance.

**16:43 Hours** – We returned home, and Officer Hart led me back into the yard.

"Were you at the park?" Nipper said.

I shook my head.

"We were afraid you took off without us," Ernie said.

"I wouldn't do that," I said. "Let's just keep up the routine so that we're ready when the moment comes."

"Where'd you guys go?" Ernie said. "Did he take you to the hospital? Are you okay?"

"You tell me," I said. "What does my scent tell you?"

"Uh, well, you spent some time in the car with Officer Hart," Ernie said.

"How do you know?"

"I can smell the front seat on you. At first I thought it was a potato chip, but no, it was too dull. I picked up on the car deodorizer too. I don't smell medicine, so I don't think you went to the doctor."

"Very good," I said.

"You cheated on the diet," Nipper said as he took in my scent. "With Mexican food."

"I didn't cheat, but good pick up on the food. Officer Hart ate some."

"We did," Ernie said. "I mean, we did a little."

"I'll admit it," Nipper said. "We waited to eat, but not as long as you wanted.

"It's okay," I said.

"What did you guys do?" Ernie said.

"I'll skip the details, but we did a whole lot of nothing. We drove around the old spots we used to patrol. A big waste of time if you ask me. But at least tomorrow is a new day."

"Who's the other dog you saw?" Nipper said.

"That's Nitro you're picking up. He's the one who took my job."

"Are we going after him too?" Ernie said. I shook my head. "Is he going to help us?"

"Not a chance," I said.

## CHAPTER FIFTEEN – OF THINGS CONCERNING UGLY LITTLE BUGS

Plenty of time passed before we found ourselves at the dog park again. Long days that led to long nights and long nights that led to waning support for my plan. There were plenty of false alarms, the most frustrating one was when Mrs. Hart took us with her to the store to buy our specialty food. Ernie suffered an adrenaline dump in the toy aisle which only further convinced Mrs. Hart that he needed a high-protein diet. On the way back home, she unknowingly tortured us by driving by the park.

"Stop the car!" Ernie said.

"Pull over," I said.

"Shut up," Mrs. Hart said, yelling back at us. "We can't go to the park without Missy."

But we did finally return to the park. By the time we did it was colder, and there were fewer dogs out than before. Mrs. Hart led us into the park and took Missy to a nearby picnic table to join the other women, who were pouring fruit juices into their champagne. Once we were in, I had to keep Ernie focused and stopped him on three separate occasions from running off to play with the other mutts. Nipper stayed a few feet behind me and kept his nose to the ground. I hoped he was where he needed to be mentally. Distractions aside, we were in the park and that meant one thing. The plan was in action.

Ernie assured me during training that he could dig a large hole and that he could dig it quickly. He couldn't show me there in the yard because in his first week with the Harts, he dug, in his own words, a *heroic hole*, for no other reason beyond a case of the locked-up blues. When Officer Hart came home and saw what Ernie had done to his yard, he filled the hole with water and dunked Ernie's head in it. That was the last hole Ernie dug, in that yard or otherwise. The first stage of our plan required a mound, which required dirt, which required a quick digger. Ernie met the charge gloriously.

"Where'd you learn to dig like that?" I said.

"Where I learned everything," Ernie said, his arms coated in dirt, "the streets. Food doesn't dig itself from a dumpster when you're hungry." Ernie licked a patch of dirt off his nose.

I helped him pack the dirt into a tight mound a foot high and just over a foot away from the rear fence. It looked like a freshly sealed volcano.

"Looks good," I said. Ernie, waist deep into his hole, continued to create rainbow showers of dirt. "Ernie, you don't have to dig anymore. We got it."

"Are you sure?" he said, from the hole.

"Yep. You gotta stop. We can't draw attention." Ernie sighed and reemerged from the hole. "Keep your eye on the prize, Ernie. We're almost there. Now it's Nipper's turn. How is he?"

"He's nervous. How did you think he was?"

"Where is he?"

"See the dog over there going around the tree in circles, talking to himself? That's him."

"Can you talk to him?"

"He's gonna do it. He has to."

"No," I said. "He doesn't have to. He doesn't have to do anything. For this to work we need a distraction. If he doesn't want to do it, we're sunk. Give him a confidence boost, can you?"

"I'll try. Hey, where are you going?"

"I need to do a quick foot patrol to make sure there's nothing that's going to get in our way. I need to check on her and make sure she's not planning on loading us back up in the car too soon."

I walked the perimeter of the park and everything seemed within the ordinary. No one, human nor canine, had any idea that our plan was in motion.

"Heck of some weather we're having, don't ya think?" a striped dog said, having joined me on my walk.

"Hadn't noticed."

"It's colder than it was last week, that's for sure." I ignored him and kept looking for anything unusual. "Well, at least it's Friday, right? I hear people say it all the time. Seems like something everyone agrees on."

"Get away from me."

Minutes later, a wiry greyhound crept up to me in a whisper.

"Hey, what's the haps with you?" he said.

"Who are you?"

"Shadow. You hear about the hubbub going on?"

"What do you know?"

"I was asking if you know anything. Any gossip?"

"You trying to tell me something? Because if you are and you know something, you better tell me now."

"Huh? No, I was seeing if you knew any hot tips on who's dating who around here, any of that stuff?"

"Get away from me."

I'd never had time for small talk or yip yap about a dog's personal life and wasn't about to start caring while I made my rounds. I stopped at the front of the park by the main gate and sat with my back against the fence and my ears turned toward Mrs. Hart and her friends.

"I really like our truck," a raspy-voiced woman said, "but have any of you driven one of those hybrids?"

"I hear they're quiet," a high-pitched lady said.

"Oh, well that won't work," Mrs. Hart said. "Any noise that distracts me from my passengers is a welcomed one."

The rest laughed along in agreement. Even Missy, who sat on top of the table, cheered along with the ladies. They quickly cooed and shushed her.

"You can get them in SUV sizes now," raspy said.

"Do any of you really believe in that global warming stuff?" Mrs. Hart said. Some of them did; some didn't. They all agreed that pollution and littering were bad, but as raspy said, cigarettes stunk up your car, so it was easier to just toss them. "Well, I'm happy with the Intimidator, so I'm not really concerned about if it pollutes or not. They wouldn't be so popular if they were that bad."

"Are you still, you know, taking advantage of the leg room in the back?" high-pitched said.

"Very smooth, Donna," raspy said. "Way to ease into it. Well, so are you?"

"We're taking a break," Mrs. Hart said. The ladies exhaled their collective disappointment. "Hey, hey, hey, don't worry. Like I said, I'm happy with the Intimidator and have no plans to trade in its...extended fringe benefits anytime soon. Just letting things cool off."

"You didn't say anything about him being French," raspy said.

"Fringe, Karla. Fringe. Two different things, honey."

"Maybe that's just what I wanted to hear. There's something about that accent that gets me."

"Sounds like someone needs a refill then. And for the record, he's Italian."

"Even better," high-pitched said. "Or should I say even worse?"

A hyperactive cheer came from the table.

"I'm loving this," Missy said, barking over the women.

"Missy," said high-pitched. "She knocked over my mimosa."

"Sorry. Come here, Missy," Mrs. Hart said. Missy was removed from the table and placed underneath it. She should have been in the dog park with the rest of us to begin with instead of being sequestered under a table, locked in between crisscrossed pairs of human legs. Missy twisted herself out of Mrs. Hart's arms and plopped to the ground. While she appeared trapped, she headed toward the one broken link in the chain of human legs. All she had to do was squeeze below that one low-hanging table support...

Satisfied that I'd surveyed the entire park and that all was ready, I returned to the packed mound where Ernie was doing an awful job reassuring Nipper.

"Just pretend like you're in a movie," Ernie said. "I heard them say it when we were watching TV with Simon one time."

"But they were already in a movie, Ernie. So what are you trying to get at?"

"Stop," I said. "Both of you."

"They're going to laugh at me," Nipper said.

"That's the point," I said. "We want them focusing on you."

"I don't want them focusing on me."

"Fine. I'll do it," Ernie said.

"You can't."

"Why not?" Nipper said. "If he wants to, it's fine by me."

"It won't work," I said.

"You trying to say Ernie can't do it?" Nipper said.

"They don't respect you, Nipper," I said. "Okay? That's why it has to be you. They'll laugh at you. They'd only laugh *with* Ernie because they'd think he was trying to be funny. You'll distract them. That's what we want. It has to be you. I don't know what else you want me to say."

"They don't respect me?" Nipper said, looking more hurt than I had expected.

"No, that's not true at all–"

"No, Ernie," I said. "They don't. Not yet, but I promise you, when you return here, they'll be singing your praises. The sea of dogs will part when you cross."

"You promise?"

"I do," I said.

"Why should I trust you?" Nipper said.

"You don't have to trust me, Nipper. Trust the plan. That's what matters to me, getting out. Not making a fool out of you." He started to waver; his body argued with what his brain asked of him. With each eye twitch and sharp pang in his chest, Nipper's body crafted a formidable argument. I didn't blame him. If the positions were reversed, I wouldn't do it. I'd tell whoever was in charge that they, along with their half-brained operation, could shove it. "It takes a lot of guts to put yourself out there. You got my respect."

"Let's just get this over with then," he said, finally.

The three of us walked in silence across the dog park in a triangle formation with me at the apex. I saw all the other dogs playing, running, and lounging. That was all their life was. All it was ever going to be. Moments of nothing. How did they manage to get up each day? As we walked to the starting point, I knew this world of the sheltered and confined wasn't mine. If it was my fate to end up here, it was going to be on my terms or not at all. I wasn't ready to be sentenced to a backyard with an off chance of parole. I certainly wasn't going to let a dog like Clay determine where I was going to spend my life. And if I'd reached a point where I couldn't stop a dog like Clay from determining where I went, then I wasn't coming back.

All that mattered was that I got out. If Ernie could make it out behind me, I'd take him. He looked like he knew his way around an alley or two. If things got tricky he would be a loyal back up. If Nipper was able to get out before things calmed down or before anyone noticed, I'd take him too, but I wasn't going to wait around for him. If he didn't come, then he didn't come. If he did make it out, I'd probably have to lose him along the way and hope that he got home safe. I didn't think Nipper was cut out for this. He was cut out to be another dog at the park. He was safe there.

"This is it," I said. "Everyone know the plan?"

"Let's do this. See you on the other side, Nipper," Ernie said. Nipper nodded and walked to where the other dogs congregated near the water fountain. He began to ask for their attention. "Between you and me, you could've given him something less embarrassing to do.'

"Yes, I could have," I said, "but we need a distraction that allows us to escape with no one noticing. He'll be fine, and he'll end up with a boost of confidence that you and I both know he desperately needs."

"I'm just saying–"

"I get it, Ernie. We're going to wait for the signal, and I'm gonna go. Once I'm clear, it's your turn, and then Nipper is going to be right behind us. They'll be too busy laughing that no one will notice we're all gone."

Nipper had interjected himself into conversations, interrupted enough fetching runs, and annoyed enough dogs to where they'd stopped and turned their attention to him. They formed a half-circle of unamused mean mugs around him.

"Thank you all for stopping what you were doing," Nipper said, taking in a gulp. "I've gathered you all because I have a special treat for you. Feel free to take a seat and get comfortable."

No one moved. Any tails that had been wagging, even slightly, had stopped.

"Come on, Nipper, what's the big deal?" someone chirped from the crowd, a sentiment echoed by others.

"I brought you all here for one reason—" Nipper said.

"Are you trying to sell us some junk?"

"You better not be trying to do any preaching to us."

"Listen," Nipper said. "The sooner you stop interrupting me, the sooner I can get this over with... Like I was saying, some of you may or may not know that I've long fancied myself as a dog with a sense of high culture and have always been a bit of song-and-dance dog—"

"Not once."

"Nope. Never heard that one."

"Well, it's true," Nipper said. "I've been working on something, and I want to share."

Nipper lowered his head and turned back at Ernie and me. I nodded. Ernie couldn't look at him out of, what I assumed, pity. Maybe Ernie just wanted to be able to look Nipper in the eye in the future. Nipper circled in place for a few orbits and exhaled a deep breath.

"The tension is killing us, Nipper. Let's go."

Nipper snapped his head up to the sky with a showman's flair and bounced up and down on his two back paws. His tail whipped side to side like a snakebite.

"I've thrown away my toys, even my drum and train," Nipper sung, no louder than a muffled hum. "I wanna make some noise, with real live aeroplanes."

The other dogs made various versions of the stupid head-crooked-sideways, ears-half-pointing-out, tongue-frozen look that humans like to edit to music on the Internet. Stereotypes exist for a reason. The dogs watching Nipper did not get it. This was going to be a monumental failure.

"He's dying out there," Ernie said.

"Let him finish the verse," I said while stretching my leg again to make sure it was loose enough to get me through.

"Someday I'm going to fly. I'll be a pilot too," Nipper sung, having mined some vocal confidence from an unknown source. "And when I do, how would you like to be my crew-ew-ew-ew."

For the critics among us, Nipper may have held that last note too long, but he looked to be enjoying the added vibrato on the "ew" sound as his throat dribbled. He puffed out his chest and pointed his mouth to the sky like a lonely wolf seeking comfort in the night air. The other dogs snapped out of their stupor and saw Nipper for what I wanted him to truly be at that moment: a blithering fool.

"On the good ship lollipop!" Nipper belted. And cue the explosion. Howls of laughter engulfed Nipper as he really got into the show, prancing like a flea between the rolling canines. "It's a sweet trip to a candy shop, where bon-bons play, on the sunny beach of Peppermint Bay. Lemonade stands everywhere. Crackerjack bands fill the air. And there you are, happy landing on a chocolate bar."

"He did it," Ernie said, more embarrassed than impressed while Nipper crooned, dashing and sashaying circles around the convulsing dogs.

"I'm clear," I said. "Wait until I'm over, and then you take off."

"What about Nip–" I was gone, trying to keep as much weight off my leg as possible. I sprinted forward toward the mound. Nipper's song became a blur, and the only thing in focus was the quickly approaching launch pad. I smelled the other side of the fence. It was a sharper, sweeter, more dense and far more powerful scent than the fertilized dog park. Nipper was still going strong. The other dogs piled up on each other as they convulsed in laughter. A quick glance at the humans proved that no one was watching yet. I turned to Ernie, who was lowered down like a compressed spring. Then his eyes shot open wide in surprise. My head snapped back forward. The plan was suddenly in immediate danger. Scarlet was steps ahead of me sitting in front of the mound.

I veered out of the way and tumbled over on my side, with most of the impact landing on my good side, but it still felt like a knife was shoved through my hip socket.

"What are you doing?" I yelled at her. "Are you stupid? You want to get us both hurt?"

"Oh now," Scarlet said. "You wouldn't dare hurt me. I knew you'd move."

"Get out of the way. Do it now."

"No."

"Scarlet, I'm warning you. Get out of my way."

"Or what? You gonna bite me?"

"Scarlet—"

"I want to apologize to you."

"Fine. Apology accepted. Now get out of here."

"Don't you even want to know what for?"

"Not really because I don't care." I snarled and tried to push her away. If I retraced a few paces, I could still make the jump. She snapped and showed me her teeth with enough of a flash of what I took as pure insanity in her eyes that I stopped.

"Do that again and I'll scream," she said.

"Fine. What do you want? This is a really bad time."

"A bad time?" she said, looking around and seeing the mound. "Oh, I see what's going on here."

"And what would that be?"

"You're trying to avoid me?"

"You could put it that way."

"No one avoids me when I don't want them to."

"Are you done?" I said. Ernie started to walk over toward us. "Stay in your position, Ernie. That's an order."

"Don't lose focus, sugar. You keep your eyes and nose on me, hot stuff." At that moment, she was the ugliest dog I'd ever seen in my life. Her curves were blocky, her lips razors, her legs tree stumps, her voice barbed wire, her fur steel wool.

"Don't you be thinking too hard now. It's not a flattering look on you."

"What?"

"You ever hear of poetry, hmm? Just so you know, I like to have poetry recited in my ear by a warm, soothing, masculine voice. And it so happens you have one of those voi–"

"Shut up!" I screamed in her face. And then the park was too quiet. Nipper had stopped singing. He sat in the center of a pack of dogs, some on the verge of collapsing while others just tried to catch their breath. He gave me the coldest stare I'd ever seen from a non-criminal. "Show's over. Leave me alone."

I walked away from her to nowhere as Nipper absorbed the realization that he was forever stationed as the fool of this canine world.

"What happened?" Ernie said, catching up with me.

"What does it look like? We didn't make it."

"We can still do it. Let's go."

"We can't. We needed a distraction so that none of the other dogs would notice we were leaving because if they noticed, then the humans would, and that would've been it for our escape. Does that not make it crystal clear for you?"

"Hey, don't take it out on me."

"Didn't you see her coming? You could have warned me."

"I was watching Nipper. He was getting good."

"It wasn't your job to watch Nipper!" I said. We stopped at the fence I should've been on the other side of. "Your job was to be ready to move."

"I don't need this. See you at home, Fritz."

I stared through this thinnest of borders that separated me from the rest of my life. A rusted chain-link fence with too many marks from too many other dogs. This is what kept me in that world. Woven strings of metal no thicker than my teeth and there was nothing I could do about it. I looked up at the birds who could come and go as they pleased, the squirrels perched in the trees free to roam, and Ernie says he'll see me at home? He'll see me at *his* home.

I didn't have a home. I had a place where I could eat, sleep, and have some semblance of company, but I didn't con myself into believing that was my home. I didn't know if one was out there or if I ever had one. What I did know was that the only way to find out was to get over that fence and not have to worry about being chased by a manic human in a car.

"Looks like your little plan went exactly as you wanted," Nipper said, having appeared next to me at the fence. He too stared at the other side of the fence. He sounded reserved and resigned like a hostage who knew they weren't going to be rescued. "It makes sense, actually. Smart move on your part to be honest. Get me to cement my status as public spectacle while you simultaneously woo the one dog I've ever loved."

"You love Scarlet?" I said.

"Yeah– I guess– I guess... I don't know. Who cares?"

"My plan was for me to be on the other side of this fence."

"Sure it was."

"It is. Or it was. I want to be gone. I have something I need to do."

"Just you, huh?" Nipper said.

"Us." Then neither of us said anything. Maybe he expected an apology. Whether Nipper would have believed it or not, I felt as miserable and as hopeless as he did.

A bug shimmied up the chain link in front of me. He paused every few steps to wiggle the feelers on the side of his head while he hung upside down by doing nothing more than standing on his feet. Further proof that life isn't fair. I say he, but it very well could have been a she. Who can tell the difference with these things? They all look the same. It's not like with another dog where you look at one and say *oh, that's clearly a female.*

It stopped what it was doing and perched up on two of its eight back legs and looked me up and down like it had any right to pass judgment on me. There he was right in my face with his wiggling tentacles and beady eyes that looked like soccer balls and a set of wings that looked more for decoration than anything else. It opened its mouth and showed me a set of teeth that looked like they couldn't get the better of a single strand of my fur. I stuck my nose up to it, and the little jerk leaned its head toward me. I shot a double blast of exhaust from my nose and blew it away.

"They should just make it a wall, you know?" Nipper said, continuing to look forward. "That way no one can see you over there."

"That's not a bad idea."

"Yeah..."

"Yeah."

"Yeah."

"I'm not interested in her," I said, "for the record."

"I don't care."

"Sure you do."

"Yeah, I do. You know how mad I am at you?"

"I have a pretty good idea," I said.

"I'm probably not going to forgive you for this. But hey, it's not like there's anything I can do about it, you know?"

"I wanted it to work too," I said. And wouldn't you know, that little bug returned and scurried right in front of my face. He ran by on the exact same stretch of link I blew him off of. This time he didn't stop to gawk at me. He kept his head down and quickly passed. But of all the many paths up those links that he could've avoided me with, he chose the same one. I laughed to myself and let him pass. I had to.

"Get a load of this," Nipper said.

"I know. Bug's got guts if nothing else. Or is it just stupid?"

"Bug? Huh? Turn around. Looks like someone's trying to break *in*."

Over on the other side of the park near the front gate, Missy was in the midst of plowing through a hole she'd dug under the fence, a hole that could rival any of Ernie's best work, speaking in terms of pound-for-pound, obviously. Her fur was dulled with mud. I suspected she tried to look that way on purpose, a welcomed addition to the dog park congregation.

"C'mon Missy, almost there," I shouted at her, wanting something to go right for at least one dog today. She was halfway into the dog park. Her tail looked like hummingbird wings while she dug. A couple of the other dogs saw what she was doing and started to encourage her too. Ernie, who was now chasing Saucy around, was the most obnoxious of the group. "Keep digging! Get under that fence! Come on, Nipper. Let her hear it."

Nipper looked like he was trying very hard to stay quiet for fear of shortchanging his righteous anger with me.

Like a seedling sprouting up from the soil, Missy's nose pushed its way through the dirt on the other side of the fence. The rest of her miniscule body wasn't far behind. She emerged on our side to an eruption of cheers and barks from the other dogs at the park. In that moment, Nipper's performance debacle was forgotten. Missy grabbed the first stick she could fit into her mouth and was off and running. She was out of control. Missy's legs flew through the air like a bronco as she flung the dried twig like she'd been zapped by a taser.

"Misssssssy!" Mrs. Hart said, exploding up from the humans' bench. "Get back here!" If my years in the field taught me anything, it was that shouting a demand to stop-and-return at a recently escaped individual is the most ineffective choice one can make in a crisis situation. It never works.

Mrs. Hart got her legs momentarily caught as she tried to stand up from the table. She bobbled up and down like a broken "s." Her friends made minimal attempts to help her or, at the very least, get out of her way. Instead, they looked bothered by the sudden outburst. Mrs. Hart frantically circled halfway in each direction before placing her glass on the table and trying to slip her feet into her sandals. Her right foot slid in without an issue, but it took four attempts with some help from her hands to get the left one on. She took a slight jog toward the dog park as Missy ran with the speed and direction of a balloon with a hole in it.

Mrs. Hart abandoned her sandals as she approached the mud and dirt adjoining the fence to the dog park. She flung the door open and went after Missy. The door quickly snapped back but had been thrown open so hard that it didn't secure back into place. A nosy Pomeranian, a redundancy if ever there was one, stuck his head between the gate and fence.

"It looks like fate is on our side today, my friends," he announced. He, along with a following St. Bernard, were the first two to push their way out of the park. They also were the first ones to send the remaining humans into a sudden pursuit of their escaping dogs.

"The gate," raspy screamed. "Close it!"

"They're getting out!" high-pitched said.

I stood back with Nipper as the chaos of humans and dogs splashed in and out of the park.

"Now there's a distraction," Nipper said. "Can't plan that."

"Yea–" I started to say. "Let's go. Right now, Nipper."

"Huh?"

"Looks like we have a second chance."

"I don't know about–"

"If you haven't noticed, everyone is occupied at the moment, and everyone is focusing on the front of the park. We have an open window here, but we have to go right now."

"Where's Ernie?"

"I don't know. Get to the spot and wait for me. I'll get Ernie."

"What if you can't find him?"

"Then it'll be just you and me. Go." Nipper took off toward our starting point. I found Ernie and Saucy scratching themselves on some freshly trimmed bushes away from the other dogs.

"Hey Fritz," Ernie said. "You always get a better scratch after they cut the branches."

"Ernie, we're leaving."

"Aw, we just got here," Saucy said.

"Right now," I said.

"I don't want to go... You're not talking about home, are you?"

"No," I said. "You see all that commotion at the front of the park? We've got thirty seconds to do what we came here to do, and we have to do it now."

"I don't know," Ernie said. "I'm hanging out with Saucy now."

"Fine. Me and Nipper are gone."

"Where are you going?" Saucy said.

"Don't worry about it," I said.

"Hey," Ernie said, "don't talk to her like that. It's top secret, Saucy."

"You need to decide right now if you're coming, Ernie. We're going with or without you."

Ernie hesitated. I rejoined Nipper at the launching site. Dogs were still running around the parking lot. The St. Bernard who led the charge jumped into the back of a pickup truck that didn't belong to him and marked it for himself.

"Where's Ernie?" Nipper said.

"He's not coming."

"What? We have to—"

"He's not coming. On three, it's you and me. Ready?" Nipper nodded. "One... Two... Three." We took off. Nipper got out several steps in front of me. I had blocked out the pain on my previous escape attempt, but I felt it on that one with every stride as my leg jammed into the hard earth. "When you hit the mound, push off with your hind legs. Once you get clear, take cover behind the bathrooms eastbound and wait for me."

"Which way is east?"

"You see those bathrooms?"

"Yeah," Nipper said.

"That's east. I'll be right behind you. Don't look back, and don't stop. We're approaching—" Up ahead at the dirt mound, a trio of pugs were taking turns sliding down the mound and didn't see us coming. Giggling little goofballs grunting and snorting as they bowled themselves down the mound to get themselves dizzy.

"Pugs!" Nipper said, shouting back.

"I see them. Keep going."

"What if they won't?"

"Keep going. They'll move."

Nipper yelled at the dogs to scram, but they remained in place, happily oblivious to the impending collision as they danced in a tribal circle atop the mound.

The pugs didn't see Nipper until he was a step away from the mound. Even then, their reaction was a muddled "huh, wha?" while Nipper took his jump a step early and flew over their heads. The pugs watched with a stunned and oddly harmonic "whoa" as Nipper took flight inches from their heads. Nipper landed clear of the fence on the other side to a chorus of "awesome" in triplicate from the pugs. It wasn't until they saw me following behind that they snapped back into living amongst the residents of this planet.

They all screamed versions of "Run!" and ran into each other like only cartoon characters would.

"Move!" I said. I knew that if I stopped I wasn't getting another chance at this. Nipper cleared the jump with plenty of room to spare and took cover around the corner by the restroom. One pug managed to tumble off the mound as I stutter-stepped on my approach. The sudden adjustment made my leg feel like it was whipped. I lost all strength in it. I pushed off as close as I could to the top of the mound with my one good leg. I wasn't going to have the distance Nipper had. A little bit of luck would need to go a long way. I was mid-flight at five-and-a-half feet over the bushes that outlined the fence and was already making my descent. I turned toward the fence to create some extra momentum as my arms and head cleared the top of the fence. I tucked my head toward my chest and rolled through the air as my torso and legs finally cleared the fence. The top of the chain link snagged the end of my tail. That stung. A graceful landing was not had as the wind was bludgeoned out of me upon impact with the ground. I saw threads of my fur still in the clutches of the top prongs of the fence where it snagged me.

"Are you okay?" Nipper said from around the corner. I couldn't immediately get back to my feet. "You need help?"

"Keep your cover," I said as I shook my head while enough air came back for me to get up. I couldn't bend my leg at all but was able to drag myself over to join Nipper. "Did anyone see us?"

"I don't think so. What about Ernie?"

"He made his choice. He wanted to stay at the park."

"Let's give him a minute."

"He's not coming, Nipper. He said so himself. I gave him a chance and said we were leaving, but he stayed. I'm sorry. I wish he was here, but it's you and me."

"I don't know about this. You look hurt."

"I'm fine," I lied. "What's done is done. We made it. The hard part is over."

"I wish I could believe that."

"My leg is fine. I didn't expect those pugs—"

"That's not what I meant. The hard part. Somehow I think we're only just getting started."

"We should get going," I said, heading off into the wooded area that surrounded the dog park as Nipper remained planted behind the bathroom. "We gotta disappear. Nipper, we can't let them find us. It's time to go."

I continued into the trees away from the cement bike path that surrounded the restroom. Nipper's footsteps quickly caught up to me.

"Wait!" Ernie said, having just rounded the corner from behind the restrooms. "You guys aren't leaving without me."

"Ernie," Nipper said, running back to greet him. "What happened? Fritz said you were going to stay."

"I wanted to stay and play with Saucy. But I also wanted to go with you guys, so here I am. Where's Fritz?"

"I'm over here. We need to stop wasting time."

"Ernie," Saucy said, sticking her nose through the fence. She had pushed her way through the thick bushes on the dog-park side of the chain link. "Are you going to be okay?"

"We'll be fine, Saucy," Ernie said, poking his head around the corner. "We got a cop with us. What could go wrong?"

"Then can I come?"

"No," I said, loud enough for just Ernie to hear.

"Not this time," Ernie said, looking over his shoulder at me.

"When are you going to be back?" Saucy said.

"I don't know. Um, not too long I think."

"Just be careful."

"I will, Saucy. You don't have to remind me."

"I'll miss you," she said.

"Oh... Uh... Yeah... I'll uh, uh, me too. Gotta go."

Ernie ducked his head, and he and Nipper joined me. Before we vanished into the woods, I looked back and saw Saucy sitting against the fence with her paw up resting on one of the links and her tail curled up under her. Behind her, off in the distance, most of the dogs had been corralled back into the park with a few stragglers being led back into their cars with treats. Mrs. Hart had caught Missy and was carrying her back to the Intimidator with her arms extended and her nose up, keeping Missy as far away from her chest as possible. Missy panted and kicked her legs like she was in a race.

That bug was gone, and so was I.

"Thanks Missy," I said.

# CHAPTER SIXTEEN – WHAT'S MORALITY WHEN IT'S TIME TO EAT?

The three of us found cover in the remnants of an old campground near the nature center a few hundred yards away from the dog park. An area "closed for the season" according to the posted sign. You could smell all the other animals in the vicinity – rabbits, squirrels, some snakes, all of which told me that we weren't going to encounter many humans, if any at all, around here.

"Now what?" Nipper said as we rested under a fallen tree whose branches served as a makeshift cover.

"We wait," I said.

"What are we waiting for?" Ernie said. "I thought we were in a hurry."

"They're out looking for us right now," I said. "We have to lay low until it gets dark. They're probably checking the route between here and the police station, thinking that's where I'll go. We have to stay off the streets for a few hours."

"You think they know we're gone?" Ernie said.

"By now, they must," I said. "I'm sure that Mrs. Hart wanted to leave as soon as she got Missy back in the car and when she went back to find us . . . oops."

I felt bad for Officer Hart. I hoped that he wouldn't take the news of my escape as a personal affront or a commentary on our partnership. He might not understand, but part of me was convinced that he would only pretend to be upset at hearing the news. There might have been a chance that he wouldn't come looking for me. He'd go looking for Nipper and Ernie because he'd have to. If he knew they were with me, though, maybe he'd know that I had something up my sleeve.

"How's your leg feeling?" Nipper said.

"What's wrong with your leg?" Ernie said. "I mean, other than, you know."

"Nothing," I said. "It's fine."

"Fine? He crashed and burned over the jump."

"Leave it alone," I said.

"What happened?" Ernie said. "Are you okay?"

"He barely made it over the jump," Nipper said. I didn't appreciate how much Nipper clearly enjoyed explaining this. "When he landed he basically just bombed into the ground, and it took him forever to get up."

"You left out the part about the pugs," I said.

"Oh yeah," Nipper said, like it was the most obscure and insignificant of details. "There were a few pugs hanging around the mound—"

"Wait," Ernie said. "Pugs did that to you?"

"They were at the top of the jump," I said. "I didn't want to hurt them."

"Pugs can't hurt anything," Ernie said.

"I didn't have a problem with them," Nipper said.

"Have you made your point yet?" I said. "Or do you need more time?"

"What's my point?" Nipper said.

"What are you guys talking about?" Ernie said.

"I just wanted to know if he was okay," Nipper said. "Since we're this big team, or squad, or unit, or some other fancy cop term that us regular folks aren't privy to. Aren't we all one or something like that?"

"Change the subject," I said.

"What do you want to talk about?" Nipper said.

"Anyone hungry?" Ernie said as he quickly got up and made for the boarded-up, hand-painted snack shop near the campsite. It looked big enough to be semi-comfortable for one human to fit into. It was covered in stickers of every level of decay. The back door was padlocked shut. Ernie sniffed and marked around the converted shed while Nipper stood a few feet away and watched. I remained back under the cover. "I am."

"Is it open?" Nipper said.

"Does it look open to you?" Ernie said, clawing at a loose wooden plank until it was loose enough to jam his nose into. Ernie wiggled his whole stocky body and pushed his head into the space until the wood plank snapped off at the bottom. Once his head was inside, Ernie only needed another few wiggles to wrestle enough of the planks off for him to get into the stand. He returned with a mouthful of bags of chips, candy bars, bubblegum (god knows why), beef jerky, and water bottles. "Oh, here we go. Bingo."

"Anything good in there?" Nipper said.

"Are you kidding? Do you not see all this stuff?"

"We're not going to be here too long," I said as the two of them brought back enough for the three of us to hide out for a week. "Remember what it was like sprinting after you ate?"

"You never know," Ernie said. "Take what you can get. Now that we're out here, I don't know when I'm eating next."

"You do know that technically what you two just did is a felony in Grand City?"

"What's a felony?" Ernie said.

"It's a crime."

"Why not just say crime?" Nipper said.

"Because there's different types of crimes, and a felony is the worst."

"Getting food isn't a crime," Ernie said. "I have to eat."

"Stealing it is," I said.

"Who'd we steal it from?" Ernie said, tearing into a stick of beef jerky, wrapper and all. "I don't see anyone around here."

"I didn't do anything," Nipper said, spitting out his hard candy and quickly burying the wrapper.

"You went with Ernie to do it," I said. "You watched him, and it's clear you were acting as his lookout and accomplice–"

"I did not."

"Did you stop him?" I said.

"No."

"That's all a lawyer would need to send you up the river alongside Ernie. Aiding and abetting. That's a felony too."

"Then you did the same thing," Nipper argued.

"Nope. I stayed here, and, as you so clearly illustrated, I'm nursing an injury, so I couldn't be of much help or serve as a capable lookout."

"Whatever," Ernie said. "No wags off my tail."

"You don't care that we could get in trouble?" Nipper said.

"Nope," Ernie said. "Not in the slightest. Mainly because it's impossible. The worst that can ever happen is that some fat man comes yelling 'Get out of here, you mutt' at you. Sometimes they try and throw something at you, but they never come close. You don't go to the pound for getting some food. The only sure way to go to the pound is to bite someone. Even if it's just another dog they take you. What I don't get is that, and maybe Fritz can help me here on this one, if you bite a cat, and I'm talking some scraggly, mangled-eared, psycho cat. You bite one of those, and why wouldn't you, you can still be hauled off to the pound. Why is that?"

"Because you can't hurt another living thing," I said. "Even if they might deserve it."

"Hold on," Nipper said. "Isn't that what you want to do to this Clay dog?"

"Yep."

"You're risking going to the pound?" Nipper said.

"You asked if I wanted to. Of course I *want* to. I can't get the image of me squeezing on his neck and thrashing him until he goes limp out of my mind, but I won't do that. I'm a cop. I'm putting *him* in the pound."

"You guys want some jerky?" Ernie asked, obliviously changing the subject. "Looks like I got teriyaki, um, some barbeque, Cajun, but I'm almost done with that already."

"Not me," I said. "Maybe he wants some of the spoils? His share of the loot?"

Ernie flung a bag of the teriyaki over Nipper's way. Nipper took multiple sniffs and inhaled the savory aroma.

"Not hungry anymore," Nipper said. He batted the food back over Ernie's way.

"More for me then. Your loss, Nipper. We're not getting popped for this so-called heist. He's only busting your chops."

"How do you plan on doing this?" Nipper said.

"I'm going to down the jerky and the chips," Ernie said, "that's for sure. If there's still any room left in my stomach, I'm gonna see what damage I can do to that candy and maybe the popcorn."

"I'm talking to him, Ernie. How exactly do you plan on putting Clay in the pound when, now hear me out and don't go all crazy on me, but I know you say you're a cop, and that's cool, but you know, technically, you're not."

"Yes I am," I said.

"Okay, I understand what you're saying," Nipper said, "but you're not. I know, maybe there's something I don't get because we're not as smart as you, but if you're still a cop, why were you put in our backyard?"

"Nipper," Ernie said, while a cord of jerky dangled from the corner of his mouth, "let it go."

"What? He says he needs us, but as he's made perfectly clear, you and I aren't cops, so it stands to reason that if he is still truly a cop, then he wouldn't need us. He could just call in for backup. But no, here we are helping him without even knowing what the actual plan is yet. So, does that make me and Ernie cops now?"

"Neither of you are," I said, much more excited than I'd let on. I wanted to take to the streets that moment and start shaking down all my contacts for information. I wanted to chase and hunt and bite and tear and tackle and snarl and squint my eyes in fury and smell fear and pin anything down on its back and scream in its face. I wanted to abandon my years of training and be raw, mean, ruthless, and not care about the damage I caused, not worry if I made it back in one piece because, why not, Nipper was right. "And neither am I."

"Thank you for admitting it," Nipper said.

But I was going to continue to act like one.

"Let me ask you something," I said. "What are you?"

"Huh?" Nipper said.

"What are you?" I said. "Easy question, right?"

"What kind of question is that, Fritz?"

"You tell me."

"The two of are going to make my head explode," Ernie said as he enjoyed some grape taffy. "Would one of you just answer a question? This is why I tried changing the subject to food."

"Well?" I said.

"What *am* I?" Nipper said.

"What did I just say to you two?" Ernie said. "Oh no, now I'm doing it."

"Anytime, Nipper," I said, "Don't worry, I'm not trying to trick you."

"I guess I'm a dog," Nipper said.

"You guess?"

"What is going on?" Ernie said. "Now I can't stop. Did we eat candy laced with something? There it is again. I should just stop talking, shouldn't I?" I nodded at Ernie. "Thank you."

"Yeah, I'm a dog," Nipper said.

"And what does that entail?" I said.

"I don't know. Just being a dog."

"What's it mean to be a dog?"

"I have no idea," Nipper said.

"Sure you do. Don't think about it. What does it mean to be a dog?"

"It doesn't mean anything. I'm just a dog. I didn't choose to be one. Not to say I don't like it. I love it and wouldn't want to be anything else—"

"I'd want to fly," Ernie said. "Just to try it, you know."

"I chose to be a cop," I said.

"No you didn't," Nipper said. Now I was mad. This dog had the nerve to sit there with his lazy hips draped over to the side and his floppy ears and his soft tail and he tells me what I did or did not choose. "You didn't choose. They chose you. The people. They chose you to be a cop, and then they chose when you weren't one. They choose for all of us. For you. For me. For Ernie. They decide what we do. They decide how we live. They decide where we live and who with. I'm not complaining, Ernie, relax. What we eat? They choose. Where we sleep? That too. You have no control over anything in your life. Not a thing. You want to sleep? Not if they decide they want to play, and by play, they mean annoying you to the point to where you want to tear their fingers off, but you can't do that either, because they say otherwise. So, don't sit there and lecture me anymore about what's right and wrong and how you're on a different level than the two of us. You're no different than me or Ernie or anyone else. They just chose to make you a police dog, so congratulations, but don't go running around holding it over our heads like it's some sort of achievement on your part. You were in the right place at the right time. That's it. You know what, I don't want to talk about this anymore. Let me know when you decide that it's time for us to go, okay?"

I didn't agree with Nipper, but I didn't think he was necessarily wrong. This was something that had clearly brewed inside him for a very long time; the way his voice cracked said as much as his words did. That wasn't just meant for my ears. It definitely wasn't meant for Ernie. Maybe it was meant for the world? For everyone and everything. Maybe the words got caught up in the wind and got swept away to a place where something else could hear them and make sense of them. Something like that is possible. Why not? Different things hear different sounds. Officer Hart had this whistle that he would blow as hard as he could. You could see the veins in his neck burst, and extra spittle would shoot from the corners of his mouth as he blew this thing. He closed his eyes so tight that the edges of his face wrinkled like a wadded-up piece of paper. That whistle sounded like a million needles jammed into your ear, not just scratching around the tip, I mean as if they were hammered in to where all you could do was lay down, curl up, and hope that the pain went away. You couldn't even get your paw up there to rub yourself; it paralyzed you. Your brain goes into panic mode, and you become a quivering mass of agony. And then the officers just stood there and asked if they could hear anything. They never did.

If we can hear that whistle that people can't, something out there could've heard Nipper. Who knows, they might have been able to do something about it if they saw fit. All Nipper could do was put it out there and see if anyone was listening to him.

I figured out what was getting to Nipper. He'd been a dog-park dog his entire life. Even when he was free at the park, there were still fences around him. They were just farther away from the fences he was used to. There was comfort in that. He knew exactly what his world was and where his world ended. If you got comfortable within those parameters, then all of a sudden, when there were no more fences, it made sense Nipper felt that way. I was scared too.

"You're one of those 'the bowl is always half empty' kind of dogs, aren't you?" Ernie said. "We gotta change that."

## CHAPTER SEVENTEEN – SOUTH SIDE, GRAND CITY

Once the sun had sufficiently set low enough, the three of us split from the park. The only people who saw us leave were a few joggers who couldn't be bothered by a few dogs sneaking alongside the running path. I led the way out of the park and through the side streets of Grand City.

"How mad do you think he'll be at her?" Ernie said, lagging behind, weighed down by his sugar consumption at the park. It seemed like a good idea at the time, right Ernie?

"Very," Nipper said.

"She's gonna catch the blame for our escape. I don't feel bad. I don't think I do. It's not like they ever expressly told us that we couldn't jump over the fence. Should we feel bad?"

"I don't," I said.

"Missy's probably going to get some heat," Ernie said. "I'm proud of her. Good for her, though. That's torture, what they do to her. Hey, I got an idea. I think when we go home, I'm going to fake a limp for a few days. I bet they don't yell at us if they think we got hurt. What do you think?"

"I think I wish I could be inside your brain, Ernie," Nipper said. "I'd always be amused. I don't know where you get this stuff."

"I don't know either," Ernie said. "I just start talking. Ugh, my stomach. But yeah, he's going to yell at her."

"There was nothing she could have done to stop us," I said, crouching behind a mailbox. "We're here, boys."

South Side, Grand City. Every big city has their version of "South Side." Whether it's called Downtown, The West End, or Northern Heights, it's all the same. Other times, the area has a nickname based on whoever lives there, like Chihuahua-ville, Daschund-place, or Shih-Tzu Town. Point is, it's where you found the dirtbags.

In Grand City, it's South Side. It's the part of town not on the same vitamin regimen that the suburban tracks were on. It's where the city planner hid a trash dump the size of a high school in the middle of a maze of low-rent apartments and parks within a square-mile city block. From sun up until a few hours after sun down, swarms of dumpsters converged on South Side with fresh (figuratively speaking) deliveries for the dump. The outlining streets have your typical strip-mall fare of comic book shops, video stores with four-for-a-dollar deals, a boxing gym, a few rub-and-tug parlors, and an upstart church that took over a vacant trio of stores that included a sandwich joint, an outdoor garden-supply shop, and a family-owned computer-fixit place.

Other than being a majority of dirtbags, the people weren't any different in South Side. The back seat of a squad car didn't care if you're from South Side, Industry Park, the suburbs, or Grand City Harbor. The calls from South Side were the same as anywhere else in town – domestic squabbles, auto thefts, assaults, and burglaries.

South Side was never a part of anyone's regular patrol. There was a great Thai food place a block away from the unofficial South Side border, the intersection of Warrington and Parker. That was about as close as we'd get unless there was a call for service. Even a block away at Rudy's Thai Palace, the smell from that dump curled your nose with even a slight breeze from the west.

"Finally," Ernie said. "I don't know what happened to me. Sheesh. Why does it hurt more when you stop?"

"See that house," I said. "That's where we're going."

The house was across the street from us and still halfway down the block. It was surrounded an empty lot on either side and a drainage ditch adjacent to the backyard. A boarded-up two-story home right out of one of those TV shows where the little boy gets lost and the dog runs back to get help. Give me a break. And I'm supposed to believe that a collie does this? A collie? I haven't known a collie yet who would take two steps out of their way for anyone else, canine or otherwise. Have you? Exactly.

"Are we in South Side?" Ernie said. "Smells like South Side."

"That's the garbage dump," I said.

"Is that what that is? I always wondered. I haven't been here in forever."

"What's South Side?" Nipper said.

"Eh, don't worry about it," Ernie said.

An iron rod fence, a few inches higher than me, stretched around the house's perimeter. The front gate was padlocked shut. The second story of the home was overcrowded by a large oak tree in the front yard that caked most of the home in an unnatural shadow that magnified the night's darkness. The moon shined off the top of the tree, but none of that light made it to the house. The place looked empty, which was the point, of course. The first step to any successful hideout, and make no mistake, this place was a hideout, is that it couldn't look like anyone was there.

"This is where the investigation begins," I said.

"Investigation?" Nipper said. "I thought we were going to the docks, and I don't see any ships around here."

"We need to investigate first," I said. "We need to gather some intel. Now look, they probably have squirrels up in the tree watching out, but they can't see this far, so just stay low next to the cars on this side of the street. Let's go slow."

"Squirrels?" Nipper said.

"Yes," I said. "Hopefully they haven't seen us."

"How do you know?" Ernie said.

"Take a listen. What do you hear from that tree?"

"Nothing," Ernie said as he lurched forward, his head parallel to the chewed-up asphalt. "It's quiet."

"Wouldn't you expect to hear birds, bugs, cats, and rabbits?"

Ernie sniffed, keeping his head still, and then he snapped back to a wide-eyed realization. "I don't smell a thing on that tree."

"Exactly. What does that tell you?"

"There's no reason why that tree shouldn't be covered with freeloaders," Ernie said.

"Which tells you what?" I said.

"That someone wants it empty... Ah, I get it. You know what, though, I could probably leave a pretty good claim on that tree. There's a spot right over there that's begging to be marked."

"Why are they watching an empty house?" Nipper said.

"They're not watching the house. It's the basement they're guard–"

I stopped and took an embarrassing gasp of breath.

"What?" Ernie said. "Your leg?"

I shushed them both as two pit bulls with skulls the size of small televisions and the requisite neck muscles required to swivel those heads rounded the corner from Downston Ave. They walked down the middle of the street in our direction with their tongues out and their matching rusted chain collars scratching the air. One stopped with his nose up in the air and bewilderment hanging from his gaunt mouth.

"You smell that, Knox?" he said.

The other one, the wider of the two, stopped and scratched himself. They were a few yards away from us on the other side of the cars.

"What am I supposed to smell?" Knox said.

"*That.* You smell it?"

"I don't know, Gash. Just tell me what it is."

"It's a cop," Gash said. "The way his fur secretes that odor of *I'm put here for the sole sake of giving you a rough time.* I'd know that–"

"Oh, there it is," Knox said. "You're right. Unmistakable."

"Where's it coming from?"

"Were we followed?"

"I think I'd know if we were followed," Gash said. "Wouldn't you?"

"Well, yeah. Gimmie a break."

"So, was a cop following us?"

"I don't know. Stop pressuring me."

Ernie sat totally still. Nipper looked at me with eyes screaming at me to fix this. I quietly pried open the flap above the rear wheel that covered the gas tank with my paw. I bit the end of the gas cap and twisted it off as both pit bulls were directly on the other side of the car. As soon as the gas cap was off they both sniffed in rapid succession.

"That's gasoline," Knox said. "You idiot."

"There was a cop too," Gash said. "You smelled it, right?"

"I only smelled it because you said it was there. Not my fault you have the nose of a chow."

"Not cool," Gash said.

Their footsteps moved away from the car and down the street toward the abandoned house. Nipper took his first exhale in two minutes and Ernie...Ernie was gone.

"Knox? Gash?" I heard Ernie say.

"What's he doing?" Nipper mumbled.

"Who's that?" Knox said. They both turned back to face him.

"It's me," Ernie said.

"It's me, who?" Gash said.

"C'mon guys. Me. Ernie. From back in the day."

"I don't know no Ernie," Gash said, puffing his chest out.

"Get ready," I told Nipper.

"For what?" he said, turning *what* into a three syllable word.

"Sure you do," Ernie said, taking a few steps closer to the pit bulls. "Ernest Tubbs. Ernest T, Muscle Machine–"

"He's big, bad–" Knox said, like he was singing an ad jingle.

"–bad, dirty, and mean!" Gash said, joining in an extremely off-tune chorus with Knox.

"Yeah," Ernie said, in relief.

"Of course we remember you," Knox said. "We thought you were a goner. Didn't we, Gash?"

They surrounded Ernie, and the three spent a moment inhaling the scents of reminiscence with each other. When these two dogs stood next to cars in the dark, they didn't look so big, but under a streetlight next to Ernie they looked like they might have been part horse.

"What happened to you, Ernie? Everyone misses ya," Gash said.

"I got locked up. The pound." Both pits cringed in agony. "Did a six-month stretch." The cringing evolved into low groans as Knox and Gash contorted their faces into mush pots. "Then, I finally got paroled but ended up in the suburbs."

"Oh, that's even worse!" Gash said.

"The suburbs? Just gimmie the needle now, you know what I'm saying?"

"It's not *that* bad," Ernie said.

"Not that bad? Not that bad! Listen to this guy, Knox. Does he sound like the same Ernie we knew?"

"No way," Knox said. "They brainwashed you out there."

"No, really, it's not too bad." Ernie said.

"Oh yeah?" Gash said, looking down at Ernie. "Tell us then, if it's so bad, whatcha doing out here?"

"I don't know. Looking for one last adventure, I guess. Had that itch again."

"Well, look no further," Knox said. "Come with us. We can get the itch scratched again. No doubt."

"Where are we going?" Ernie said.

"The house," Gash said. "It's where it's at."

"But it's empty," Ernie said.

"Ernie," Gash said, "you have been away far too long. Welcome back, Mr. Tubbs. Our dog, Ernie T., is back. Time to celebrate."

They flanked Ernie and led him toward the house. I couldn't tell if they sounded like old friends Ernie hadn't seen in years who wanted to catch up or if they pegged him for a mark. I hoped Ernie could tell.

"We have to do something," Nipper said.

"It's okay," I said. "Calm down."

"Are you crazy? He's with them. Who knows what they're going to do to him. They're pit bulls."

"He seems to know them," I said.

"What are we going to do, Fritz?"

We watched Ernie follow Knox and Gash beyond the padlocked gate to an area of the fence where the bars were broken. Ernie hopped through while Knox had to help shove Gash and his muffler-sized legs through the opening. I lost sight of them as they went around the front of the house. One of them threw a hushed bark up toward the tree. They disappeared around the back of the house, and I lost their scent.

"We're going after them," I said. "Our turn, Nipper."

We emerged from behind the car and crossed the street to the house. We finagled our way through the mangled bars in the fence and through the alternately soggy mud and dried-hard dirt that masqueraded as a front lawn. A slab of concrete along the side of the house was inscribed with an expanding list of names, dates, and handprints in concrete from "Madam Lucille 6/4/29" all the way up to "D-Bone$Man PLAYA AUG '98." As we rounded the corner of the joint, Nipper looked up at the oak tree that hung over us like a hovering spaceship.

"Eyes forward," I said. "Don't worry about the lookouts."

"Hold it!" a voice said, booming from the narrows ahead of us to our left. A large shadow grew along the ground as it approached us, absorbing any remnants of the visible walkway. "Not another step. What are you doing here?"

"No trouble," I said. "Just looking for a good time."

"You came to the wrong place," the voice said.

"We both know that's not true," I said. "We just got out of the pound."

"Oh yeah?" the voice said. As quickly as the shadow expanded to a grotesque size and shape, it descended back to normal as a miniature pinscher appeared in front of us. He showed us his collection of teeth, most of which were unnaturally sharp. "How you hear about this place?"

"Everyone knows about it," I said. "This place alone is why half the dogs locked up don't give up hope. Someday they may get a chance to hang out here again."

"Wait a second," he said. "You're a German shepherd. Both of you."

"I'm only half—"

"Nipper. Quiet," I said. "Yeah, so? What of it? What, you don't cater to all breeds? I thought those days were long gone. Haven't we moved on as a species?"

"Everyone's scratch is good in here, don't insult me."

"What's your beef then?"

"My beef? You better watch that snout of yours."

"Tough talk," I said. "And from a pinscher, that's saying something. Well, a *mini* pinscher, that is."

"I know who you are," he said, with a spark of recognition.

"No you don't." I said.

"Sure I do," he said, with a cocky grin. The door dog took several brave steps forward. "You're that cop. Fritz, right?"

"And you are?"

"Someone who knows all too well of your handy work. Just released from the pound, he says." He looked us up and down and looked particularly unimpressed at Nipper. "Word was you had some replacement, but by the looks of this one, it seems they'll take anyone nowadays."

"Is he talking about me?" Nipper said.

"Yes," I said.

"Let me clear some things up," Nipper said.

"No need," the door dog said. "You know what, it would be my absolute pleasure to let the both of you in here tonight. A complete and total pleasure."

"That's mighty kind of you," I said. "But we were going in whether you gave us permission or not. Just to be clear."

"Then I'm glad clearer heads prevailed," the door dog said, walking over to a double doorway that led down toward a cellar. He pulled on a rope tied to one of the doors. Once the door thudded to the ground, he smiled with that mouth full of needles and stepped out of our way. "Many of our patrons will be excited to see you tonight, Fritz. Enjoy your evening, puppies. Welcome to The Dogcatcher's Net."

## Chapter Eighteen – Inside The Dogcatcher's Net

My hip popped with each step that I took down the stairs toward the cellar of the house. I wasn't in pain, but the rhythmic snaps from the socket did not instill me with a boost in confidence. The cascading roof that ran parallel to the descent of the steps was covered with framed fronts of dog-treat and biscuit boxes. The sides of the walls were plastered with taped-up and torn movie posters. Any poster that featured a K-9 officer was mangled in the same spot, the part where the dog was supposed to be.

"So what exactly is this place?" Nipper said at the bottom of the stairs. We stood in front of the closed door that separated us from the cellar.

"It's a dive," I said. "It's where dogs go when they don't want to be found."

"And how does this help us?"

"Because they all bring their secrets with them to this place."

"I see. Just, uh, what do you think is about to happen in here?"

"I have no idea," I said.

"Not even a faint one?"

"It's impossible to ever know these things. Could be nothing or it could be the end of the road for both of us. We could find Clay in there, and he could go quietly. Or, they figured out

Ernie was with us and are on the other side of this door waiting to ambush us. I doubt that's the case, but it's a possibility. Just play it cool. The only way to know is to go. Don't stare at anyone. Let me do all the talking. Stay close, but not too close."

"Sorry," Nipper said.

"And stop saying sorry. Just take a deep breath."

In what was just another step for me and a rite of passage for Nipper, we pushed the door open and stepped into *The Dogcatcher's Net*. You name the cliché and it was there in full force. A tepid and soggy cloud of smoke exhaled from countless lungs clung to a ceiling that was too low to be welcoming. Scratchy blues music snuck into the walls from a jukebox on its last breath of neon. A sign hung above it that said "If anyone else marks on the jukebox, so help me, you won't see tomorrow's sunrise! – Henry."

A gang of wolfhounds shot pool in the corner, no doubt running some hustle on the poor Labrador who slowly racked the balls for what was surely another forced round of nine-ball. You came in and wanted to blow off some steam, make some time disappear, and a pack of wolfhounds decided to take you for everything you had. And you thought they were sincere when they offered you a simple wager on a fair game of chance and skill played on the billiards table.

Mutts chewed on plastic darts off to the side. The degenerates sat in a row at the bar. Their heads drooped into bowls full of whatever concoction the bartender had whipped up for the night. The walls were covered with tacky-looking (mostly felt) paintings of humans from a different decade playing poker, driving in convertibles, lounging on the beach, farming, boxing, and so on.

And on cue, everything stopped on a dime before we could take that second step in. One of the wolfhounds stopped mid-stroke on his pool shot, the music skipped to a halt, the mutts spat out chewed pieces of darts, and the drunks somehow found the resolve to turn their heads from their bowls to face us in unison. I half-checked to see if anyone in the paintings turned.

"Don't move," I told Nipper.

"Wasn't planning to," Nipper said, under his teeth. I absorbed the sneers and muted snarls and quickly realized that no one was going to budge from whatever activity or inactivity they were engaged in to make trouble for us. Not that they didn't want to. Then, as quickly as everyone pointed their attention at the two of us, it went back to normal. It was as if we weren't there again. We made our way through the dump, having to nudge our way through dogs who either saw us and didn't care to move or were just too stupid drunk to know better. "Uh, Fritz?"

"Yeah?"

"You notice how it's like no one wants us here?"

"Uh huh," I said.

"Should we be concerned?"

"I wouldn't be. Half these dogs are more worried about going back to the pound than getting revenge on me for putting them there in the first place."

"So that means that—"

"Congratulations," I said, stopping. "Everyone in here thinks you're a cop. At one point or another, I've busted just about every creep in this place."

"That doesn't give me the reassurance I thought it would."

"Follow me." I led Nipper to the bar. The closer we got, the more the drinkers shifted away from us. Others, like the sheepdog spying on us through the fur covering his eyes, summoned the courage to keep their eyes covertly trained on us.

I pushed my face in next to a drunken Saluki at the bar. The greasiness of his fur and the odor that radiated off his skin told me this wasn't a one-off bender. The stench from whatever was in his bowl was enough to fold my teeth, but he lapped at it completely unaware of my face inches from his. The bartender, an increasingly annoyed boxer who aimed that annoyance my way, slammed his paw down in front of the drunk to get his attention.

"What?" the drunk said. "Okay, top me off, but that's it. I mean, maybe one more, but who's counting?"

"Where's Henry?" I said as the bartender gestured toward me. The drunk turned to me like he was on a broken axle, and his expression struggled to remain blank.

"I don't...Wait, what?" the drunk said.

"I need to see Henry."

"I'm not gonna be walking anywhere tonight. Believe me." I grabbed him by the nape of the neck and yanked him to the ground. I was rough, but he wouldn't remember that tomorrow anyway. I straddled him with my arms and repeated my demand. "Please tell the room to stop spinning first."

"You leave him alone," a female said as she exited the restroom and hollered across the bar in our direction, before stumbling toward us. I backed off, and the drunk spent precious moments trying to put his feet underneath him until he conceded defeat and gave his body to the floor. The female got in my face. Her breath left no doubts as to what she expelled moments prior. "Why don't you two creeps get out of here? No one wants you breeds here. He didn't do anything wrong–"

"I was just asking a question," I said. "He was being argumentative. Not my fault he slipped."

"Oh, don't you think you can go and interrupt me. I'm not afraid of you or the pound. And for the record, my litter daddy would never argue with anyone."

"That's right, baby doll," the drunk said. "You tell him."

"We're going to need a refill over here, bartender," I said as I leaned over and spilled the rest of the putrid contents of his bowl on the drunk. I made sure that some splashed on his litter momma. We walked away. I turned to Nipper as we surveyed. "There you go, Nipper. No one will mess with us the rest of the time we're here. Feel better?"

"That was for me?" Nipper said.

"For the most part," I said. It did feel good, though.

"What brings you 'ere, mate?" a low voice said, rumbling three feet away from me. The voice came from behind Knox and Gash, who were shoulder to shoulder directly ahead of me. Ernie was nowhere in the vicinity.

"Since when were you in the business of hiding behind goons?" I said.

"You better watch that tongue," Gash said.

"Or what?" I said. "You saying you aren't a goon?"

"He's got a point," Knox said. "I, for one, take not a small amount of pride in my goonery."

Henry pushed his way between the two pit bulls with a face and scent reminiscent of a chewed cigar and punching bag. His jutting underbite and features would've been comical if not for the extensive rap sheet that those deformities were associated with. Various stints in the pound on everything from gambling charges to assaults and robberies. Like other English bulldogs, Henry was built like a bowling ball welded onto a Buick. His right eye was permanently closed shut, the result of a rattlesnake bite, according to urban myth.

"I was looking for you," I said.

"Now why in the world would one as smart as yer'self go an' do something like that for?" Henry said.

"I thought you could help me."

"'elp you? Me? Me? 'elp you there, you say? You 'ear that gents, this bloke says... Oh, ah! 'elp me! 'elp me!" Henry clutched at his chest and feigned a heart attack for the amusement of the reprobates who surrounded our conversation. They yucked it up while Henry rolled his tongue from the side of his mouth and blew out to make the folds in his face flap. He continued until every last mutt had a chuckle. Henry caught his breath and looked at me, squinting his one good eye.

"You better be careful," I said. "With your level of apparent fitness, next time will probably be for real."

"If it is," Henry said, "I can only hope I got me an 'ero like you to step in and save me."

"Nah, I'll pass."

"You wouldn't save a sick dog, Fritz?"

"Depends on who has the sickness," I said.

"Brass tacks then, copper. You comin' after me club? Because if ya are, I ain't going down without no fight."

"I'm not interested in your club."

"So, what do you want? I'm clean. Ya got no business 'ere."

"Are one of your ears not working too? You heard what I said, and I'm not going to repeat myself."

"No need for personal insults," Henry said. "Because by the way yer bouncing of your back wheel, that's no position to talk from. You hafta understand, last time I saw you, I spent a year in th' pound, 'member mate?"

"Yeah. I 'member."

"That tone ain't gonna be winning you no friends round 'ere."

"I'm not on the force anymore," I said.

"Oooh," Henry said, looking Nipper over. "I bet that hurts to say. 'Ooo's this? The silent majority?"

"Well," Nipper said, "My name is Nipper—"

"He's my partner," I said.

"Partner, isn't he? You don't say. Knox, Gash, show these bums the door, will ya?"

"Wait, wait, wait," said Ernie, appearing through the crowd with half of a pool cue in his mouth. "What's going on, Henry? These guys are with me."

"Ernie," Henry said. "You know this bloke's a copper, ain't ya?"

"No he's not," Ernie said. "I mean, he ain't now, anyway."

"So yer not no bobby, is you?"

"That's what I've been trying to tell you," I said.

"And for the record," Nipper said, "I'm not one, nor have I ever—"

"Yeah, I can see that now," Henry said, then turning back to Ernie. "You can vouch for these two, can ya, Ern?"

"Of course, Henry," Ernie said. "You know me. I wouldn't bring you any problems."

"What should we do?" Knox said. Henry was one of these beasts who rumbled a growl as he thought. Knox and Gash were two of those beasts who got nervous when someone was thinking.

"It wouldn't be hard to tear their brains in," Gash said.

"Whoa," Ernie said. "Everyone needs to calm down."

"I'm just saying," Gash said. "Look, it's nothing personal, guys. If that's the direction Henry wants to take this, if he wants you out, then you're out. If he wants you gone to where you never come back then, you know, that's all I mean. But hey, it's Henry's call."

"So?" I said.

"Fine," Henry said.

"What does fine mean, Henry?" Knox said.

"It means you guys can go back to chasing each others' tails," I said.

"It's been six months since I even thought about chasing a ta–"

"Scram, Knox," Henry said, snorting. "You too Gash. Get out of 'ere. Go patrol the block again."

The two pit bulls resumed doing what they did best. They took orders from Henry. It made me wonder because those two could've ruined Henry without so much as a pant. They could've run Henry out of town, took over his club and whatever interests he may have elsewhere, but they were totally content to shut up when he spoke and act when he directed them.

"The help these days, huh?" I said.

"Ya got somethin' to say to me then," Henry said. "Mister used-ta-be-a-copper?"

"You got an office around here?"

"What sorta joint you think I 'ave? O'course I got me an office. Follow me. Just you."

"Don't look at me," Ernie said. "I have a game to get back to. You want to watch, Nipper?"

"Umm, no," Nipper said.

"Okay," Ernie said. "Suit yourself."

"Let's get this over wit'," Henry said as he led me away off the club floor. Ernie went in the opposite direction back to his game with a waiting Weimaraner. Nipper stayed put like a lump, smack dab in the center of the club. By the time Henry squeezed his way through the rubber flap marked "Private Office" at the bottom of the back door, no one noticed Nipper standing frozen, afraid to look at anything specific except the ground. I followed Henry through that flap.

"Tight squeeze there," I said.

"You play checkers?" Henry said.

"A blue blood like you," I said, "I imagined you for a chess player."

"Not a chance." Henry's office was a plain one with spots of character hidden throughout. An old striped couch hugged the wall nearest the door. A bookshelf across from me kept Henry's personal stash of hooch and treats. His tastes were uniquely un-British; no Earl Grey tea for this dog. It was all exotic mixes and liquors. A walk-in humidor was next to the bookshelf and was close to being depleted. A slow burning flame in the fireplace kept the room more comfortable than I expected. "A lot of blokes'll tell ya that chess is the game of the elite, the brains, a true sign of intelligence, but I think they is right wrong on that regard."

"Right wrong, huh?" I said. "That accent you're sporting cuts through my ears like a blender, a sure sign of class if ever there was one."

"It's supposed to be a war, this chess. That's what they say, right? But it's not how war is played. You do whatever it takes to win. No rules except last dog left standin' is the winner. Too many rules in chess. You gonna tell me that that a castle piece can't go one way even if it means that 'is side'll win the game? In a real game of life an' death, that castle piece would go wherever 'e 'ad to if it mean 'e was like to open 'is eyes the next morning, you see? Now checkers, that's the game for me and for any true dog. Any piece can win the game. There's no such thing as a king unless you earn it. You jump over enough blokes on yer way and yer a king. That speaks to me more than saying that one piece 'ere or there is a pawn and can't do nothin' about it, 'cept be fed to a slaughter. Besides all the philosophical reasons, it's supposed to be a game, and games are supposed to be fun, and who ever 'eard of anyone 'aving fun playing chess? I ain't ever seen none. You?"

"Can't say that I have."

"I always knew yer smart, even if you were a bobby." Henry said. "So what's yer business? Spill it. What do you want from me?"

"I thought we were playing checkers."

"Okay, then. It's yer funeral." Henry retrieved a warped and chipped checkerboard from inside the humidor. He dropped the board in front of me and returned to the humidor for a bag of checkers. "Keeps the wood fresh."

"Looks like it's doing a bang-up job to me," I said.

"And I'm getting to not be a fan of yer condescendin'-like tone. Smoke?"

"No thanks."

"C'mon. One won't kill ya."

"I don't smoke."

"Then yer liable to be at a severe disadvantage in the game," Henry said. "A good smoke'll clear yer 'ead. Now it's even easier for me to outplay ya."

"I'll take my chances," I said as Henry poured the pieces onto the board and arranged them in front of us with the same touch humans give to their babies, cradling each piece until it fit perfectly in the center of each square. He did my side first, then his with the same precision. He stood up and waddled over to the fire. He stuck his face and his long cigar into the flame, immediately blocking the heat with the width of his frame. "I wouldn't put my face that close to the flame just to smoke a compacted tube of dirt."

"You see this?" Henry said, exhaling a fresh puff of smoke with a laugh. "You see this 'ere face? You can't hurt this thing even if ya try. Least no flame could. If ya don't believe me, I be willing to lift up this eye patch of mine to prove me point."

"That won't be necessary," I said. "I have no doubt of nature not having the ability to do more damage to your face."

"Always the mouth on you, Fritz."

"What can I say, Henry? We have too much history for me to be anything less than honest with you. It comes from that bond created when one dog takes another dog off the streets when said dog has proven time and time again that he can't handle the responsibilities that come with freedom."

"You never proved nothing on me, Fritz. That's why I'm still 'ere."

"Maybe. Either way, like I said, I'm not here for you. I couldn't care less about your club or whatever racket you're running from here."

"That's left to be seen," Henry said.

"Why keep these pieces nice and clean and smooth just to subject them to this lousy board?"

"As long as yer pieces is clean and clear, you can win in any setting."

"Sounds deep, Henry."

"It is," Henry said. "And just to correct ya, Fritz, my friend, your face is right up next to the flame. Yer move."

"You know a dog named Clay?" I said, moving a corner piece out. Henry immediately responded by moving a center piece.

"Nope."

"He's a Rott. Big guy. Hangs around with a Jack Russell."

"Never 'eard of 'im."

"Never?"

"There an echo in 'ere?" Henry said, having claimed most of the center of the board already.

"I thought you knew every dog that had an operation in Grand City?"

"What sorta operation you mean?"

"I don't know yet. Something to do with the docks, but I guess you aren't the big timer you once were. My mistake. I guess we don't have to finish the game, do we?"

"Sit down, Fritz. Finish the game. It's yer move. What'd you say that name was?"

"Clay. And I'm not saying it again. Either you've heard of him or you haven't." I moved my back row out, bringing the corners out first.

"Oh yeah," Henry said as he scored the first jump. "Sounds familiar now. I 'aven't met him yet. You say 'e's new in town?"

"I didn't say anything other than his name, but yeah, I suspect he's new to Grand City. If he's been here long, he's been off everyone's radar."

"What sorta of game is 'e running out in the docks?"

"No idea," I said as Henry ashed his cigar. The smell quickly got old. It smelled washed, yet ill, like a nursing home, a scent not intended for those with long-term plans.

"So you 'ave no idea what sorta get up this, you said 'is name's Clay, did you?" Henry said as I took a double jump. "But you know you want to go after this bloke... Ooh, I see it now."

"This one is personal," I said as Henry made a double jump on me and was a move away from getting kinged.

"I'm willing to bet that's the reason you're walking funny, at least funnier than the last time I saw you."

"Something along those lines, Henry."

"There's no *something* about it. You want blood."

"I don't want blood. I have enough to suit me fine."

"No you don't. You forget that I've been around, maybe even longer than you 'ave. I've seen enough dogs in my day who've buried the reasoning part of their brain out behind the shed with the 'umans' tools. I can tell you've been doing some digging, 'aven't you? Oh yeah. And you got that gleam in yer eye that tells me you ain't gonna rest until you get yer revenge; and the revenge yer looking for won't be quieted by Clay being yanked away into the back of a truck. The revenge you want, the revenge you need, can only get done by getting yer 'ands dirty."

"You don't know a thing about me, Henry."

"Yer a dog, ain't ya? Then I know ya. Maybe you been around people so much that you think you be just like them? People can be wronged by someone or something and let it go. They can forget about it, but us, we dogs, no matter 'ow much time you spend with people, yer still a dog. They might be talking to ya and communicating with ya, but at the end of the day, yer still taking orders from them. King me."

"All I want is my fair shot."

"There ain't no such thing as a fair shot, Fritz. You should know that."

"What about checkers? I thought you were all about fair shots."

"That's why they call it a game. It's not real life. King me again. Told you a smoke would 'elp you with that thinking cap."

"Let me spill it out for you. Regardless of my intentions, I've seen dogs like Clay a million times before, and you have too. Grand City isn't big enough for two dogs to have an operation like what you have here and whatever and wherever you may have elsewhere. It may not be today or tomorrow, but you know that Clay is going to one day see you as hindrance. I'd take care of it now. That's one less problem you have looming down the line, so all I'm asking is that if you hear anything, feel free to pass it my way. If you don't mind."

"I 'ave to tell ya, Fritz. I didn't get to where I am today by 'elping out the coppers. But I guess since you say you ain't one anymore, then sure Fritz. If I 'ear anything, you'll be the first to know. Old times' sake."

"Thanks," I said, getting up to leave.

"Game's not over, mate. You can't leave."

"You're too good for me, Henry. Checkers isn't my game."

"Why didn't you say so? We could'a played anything. Name it. Take a seat, the night's young still. Have a drink with me. Come on, it's not like yer on the clock no more. What's yer game, Fritz?

"I don't play games, Henry. You should know that by now." I turned my back to Henry and walked out the same way I walked in.

"Like I said, Fritz, that face of yers is right close to that flame."

## CHAPTER NINETEEN – A LOT HAPPENS IN A MOMENT

Several hours had passed since last call at Henry's. The sun was hours away, and we still hadn't left South Side. The stench appeared gone. More likely, it simply permeated through us. We hunkered down in the corner of a nearby parking lot. Nipper fought to stay awake while laying on a flattened piece of cardboard. I sat alongside a dented, mid-sized sedan with a boot on the front driver's-side tire. Ernie was at the bottom of a nearby dumpster digging for scraps. I had no idea if anything was accomplished at Henry's. And what were Nipper and Ernie doing out here with me? Why did I drag them out here with me?

What had I hoped to learn that I didn't know already? Clay was at the docks while I sat next to a junk pile. Why didn't I just go to the docks and be done with it? I knew where to find him. I could've gotten the jump on him if I wanted to. Not that I would have done it that way. A fair fight was a fair fight even if my enemy didn't share that sentiment. There was no honor in sneaking up on Clay. Revenge only counted when it was done face to face. Anything less than that and Clay still won.

All my conversation with Henry told me was that I'm a lousy checkers player. Even if he knew something, there was no way he was going to tell me, so what was that all about?

It was nice to feel like a cop again, but I knew it wasn't real. I knew I was just getting a high, a quick fix. It wouldn't be a high if I didn't have a low to compare it to. That low is where I was when we left Henry's. I wasn't a pretend cop anymore. I was back to being just another dog sitting on his ass.

I picked up the scent of a cat who circled around us. He carried something warm and edible with him. I smelled a familiar cat panic from him, but it wasn't the hostile panic scent you usually got from cats. This guy was anxious. He eyeballed me, but he wasn't interested in attacking. He did not seem particularly frightened of me. That was curious. He was stupid if he wasn't.

He crept closer and slid between a few cars in a crisscrossing pattern. As he approached, he never broke his view even while batting his package in front of him. Nipper paid no attention, and Ernie was distracted, talking to himself in the dumpster. I kept my ears low, my eyes opened and empty to signal that I was no threat to you, buddy.

"You're fine," I said. "Feel free to scoot on by. Say hi if you want to because I'm not interested in sniffing beyond what I have already. Whatever you've brought with you, it's all yours. The last thing I care about is an alley cat."

"Huh?" Nipper said. The cat took his attention back and forth between me and Nipper. "Is everything okay with you?"

"Not talking to you, Nipper."

"You talking to me?" Ernie said.

"No."

"Okay. We're just in here getting some food. I'll be out in a few minutes."

*We're?* I thought.

"If you gotta get somewhere," I said to the cat, "don't let us get in your way. You won't get any trouble here."

"You sure?" the cat said as he poked his head out from under a VW Bug with a complete set of flat tires. I nodded back at him. I can't tell you what makes a cat good looking, but I can tell you what made one look like a train wreck. It was this feline: clipped ear, skinny arms, and a few patches of fur that must've been on vacation. He sprung out from under the car, stayed low to the ground, and swung clear of me to leap up onto the rear end of the car I was leaning against. I was not happy with this cat taking the high ground on me. "Sorry, I have to go inside."

He pushed his wad of what I had determined to be moldy string cheese into a hole in the car's roof and followed it down. I stood and looked in the rear window, and I dropped back down immediately. How I missed it, I don't know. There was another cat huddled up in the back seat, and she was about to give birth to a few kittens in there.

I slowly rose my head back up so I could see in. Her back was to me, but the other cat could see me if he'd wanted to. He was busy tucking a towel in around her. They had a box down on the floorboard on its side, torn open to look like a bed with another small towel and some newspapers lined across it. The mother took heavy breaths and uncomfortably moaned. I caught myself being as still as possible. I didn't want to breathe. She looked like she needed all the spare air that was available.

I saw the total look of helplessness on the guy's face. He wanted to help; he wanted to with every fiber of his being, but he couldn't, and he knew it. Made me think that the ordeal was tougher on him, which is a pretty ridiculous idea now that I say it. He could walk away if he wanted to. He could leap out of that backseat with a "sayonara." She was the one who was stuck.

Then his face contorted, and he looked uglier. She licked herself, and the first kitten was out. It was little more than a tiny blob of fur with its eyes closed and its arms and legs tucked in. She licked herself again, and he gently scooped up the kitten and placed it in the box, nudging it in the corner. It took its first quick little breaths. I felt like my presence surely violated a bond or something between these cats, but I couldn't take my eyes away.

A second kitten came out, this one with a flash of different stripes of fur across its face. The father, he had to be the father, gently placed it next to its sibling in the box. A third one followed, and the mother spent more time licking herself. This time the father didn't bring the kitten over to the box. Instead, with none of the care he gave the first two, he picked up the kitten and jumped out of the car, down just a few feet from where I was. He looked startled when he saw me. I just looked at him.

"What are you doing?" I said.

"This guy didn't make it," he said. "I'm sorry, please excuse me."

He set the limp kitten down behind the rear tire and went back inside the car. I examined the kitten. No signs of life; no movement, no breathing, nothing. Something about that image wasn't right. This was an impossible scene. If it was real and this little cat was born dead, then what was the point of any of this? Why this one? Who decided that it got no shot at living a life? I wasn't convinced. It made no sense for there to be a slippery lifeless body lying right in front of me, and I'm supposed to accept that there's nothing there and that nothing ever was there? I knew that it did not work that way. I nudged him and rubbed his head with the dry part of my nose.

"Come on," I whispered. I could feel him cooling off, so I exhaled warm air up and down his tiny body, trying to compete with the twilight morning cold. I blew on his head and face and nudged him harder. Then it coughed. It coughed again! Another, and then he gurgled for breath. His throat convulsed and tried to open. I rolled him over, but no luck. I took a deep breath, loosened and relaxed my jaw as much I could, and picked him up. I kept his face pointed down and shook him hard enough to dislodge the fluid. Who knew a few drops of phlegm could be so vicious? He was breathing and crying. He would be okay at least for that moment.

I felt the little guy relax as I sat him down away from the tire out in the open. He lay on his side while I watched him for a moment. A single moment in time and it was just me and this little fella. This cat who would probably grow up to be a real pain in the ass, or he might get lucky and find somewhere warm to live, but I didn't waste my moment thinking about that.

Did I save his life? Maybe. I gave him a hand when he needed it. That was my job. That was good enough. Hopefully, he doesn't remember those harsh few minutes that began his life. Fortunately, I won't forget them. He'll never know I existed. If I hadn't been procrastinating alongside some junk car in South Side, he'd have found his end underneath the broken rear axle of said junk car. How's that for not making any sense?

I looked back into the car. The two kittens nibbled on the string cheese, and mom tended to herself. I looked at the dad and gestured toward the hole in the roof. He looked confused, so I gestured again with my best *get your scrawny butt out here or otherwise I'm coming in and you don't want that* look.

"Umm, hi," he said as he jumped down and kept his distance.

"You forgot someone," I said.

"I told you, he didn't...Oh my!"

He grabbed the kitten with the tenderness he should've given him to begin with and brought him back inside. He placed him next to the mother, who started nursing it.

"Thank you," the father said, poking his head out of the hole in the car.

"Don't be so quick to give up on someone," I said.

"I'm sorry."

"I'm not the one you need to apologize to."

"Okay. Hey, ummm, you don't have to if you don't want to, but I feel like if you want to give him a name, you probably should have the first shot at it."

"I've never named anyone before," I said, looking inside at the two kittens huddled together on the newspaper, the comics section. "Ziggy. Call him Ziggy."

"Okay. Thanks again."

He disappeared, and I left them alone. For all I know, it'll turn out to be a fitting name. Maybe it won't. I went over and sat by Nipper.

"Something going on over there?" Nipper said, yawning.

"It's nothing," I said. "Hey Ernie, did you say 'we' a few minutes ago?"

"Yeah," Ernie said.

"What're you doing?" Nipper said.

"Getting food. While you two were napping, I was starving again. There's plenty of good grub in here. If you want some, you better get in here while the getting is good. Me and my new friend here have about eaten all the good stuff."

"Who are you in there with?" I said.

"Don't know his name. He's busy eating. Oh, I almost forgot, Knox and Gash told me about Clay."

"What?" I said. "They did? How do you forget something like that?"

"Yeah. I don't know. Seems like they knew him pretty good. No one else would talk about him, but Knox said he's always at the cat races and always bets big in the tenth and cleans up huge."

"That's it?" I said.

"Well, yeah. They wanted to know why I was asking so many questions when I just asked if they'd heard of him, so that was it. Those are dogs you don't push the issue with. I'm not stupid. Oh no–" Sirens suddenly engulfed us. Did they find us? How? Did someone from Henry's rat on us? Who would they have ratted to? I couldn't go back now. "How did you deal with the noise of that for so long? It hurts so bad it's making me angry."

"Don't move," I said. "Stop making noise."

A quartet of Grand City squad cars pulled up to an apartment complex near the lot. Footsteps pounded the pavement surrounding us. If they got closer, our cover wouldn't hold. And there was Nitro. He was let out of the second-to-last car. No sooner did his paws hit the concrete than he spun and saw me.

"What is it?" Nitro's partner said, releasing Nitro to investigate. Nitro ran over and stayed on the other side of a nearby minivan. He pretended to examine the car.

"Well, well, well," Nitro said. "You never know who you'll run into on the job. Don't worry, I won't bring the rest of the boys over here, but it does make me wonder what you're doing at this hour out in South Side?"

"Leave me alone, Nitro," I said. "You should probably be working."

"I *am* working. Unlike you."

"I'm not doing anything," I said. "Why don't you get back to the call?"

"Who's your friend?" Nitro said.

"We're working a case," Ernie said from inside the dumpster. "Tell them to shut that siren off. We get it, you're here."

"What? Who? You know what, Fritz, I don't even want to know what's going on with you."

"Good," I said.

"But humor me this," Nitro said, "what kind of case are you working on? Is someone stealing bones from the convalescent pound's holiday party fund?"

"There's that humor I've missed so much," I said.

"We're chasing criminals," Ernie said.

"If whoever you are in the trash wants to keep talking, you better show yourself."

"You know anything about that dog, Clay?" I said. "If you do, you could help me."

"Why would I want to do that?" Nitro said. "What? He's someone you want to bring in? You're a piece of work, you know that? You gotta let it go, Fritz. This isn't healthy, this obsession you have going on. At first, I thought it was part of the grieving process or whatever you want to call it, but you sound like one of those conspiracy nuts who say they only use one dog for the same character on a TV show. And you know as well as I do that any information on a pending case isn't just handed out to any Fido Q. Citizen. So, sorry, I can't help you." Nitro's partner yelled out at him and whistled. "Back to work. I'll be seeing you, and by that, I mean hopefully never again, you dig?"

"Yeah, I dig."

After a few minutes, the squad cars cleared the scene. Ernie got out of the dumpster and said bye to his dining companion. I felt comfortable sitting there in a parking lot in South Side. That's how I knew it was time to leave. The three of us wandered off into what was left of the night.

"I think it was possum actually," Ernie said. "It was dark, I couldn't tell. It stunk in there. Nice guy though."

As we walked, I imagined it was Scamper whom Ernie was talking to in that dumpster. I pictured his mangled teeth biting into some raw meat that would hopefully make him sick. I imagined the fear he would've felt when he realized that it was me just on the other side of that dumpster. Ernie wouldn't know what was going on, just another derelict mutt scrounging for food.

"You want us, eh? Well, we're not hard to find," I imagined Scamper said, once we were out of earshot. I heard him laugh like a buffoon. I fantasized that he'd run to the docks to find Clay lurking in the shadows.

"I saw them," I imagined he told Clay. "They were right there. He's coming for you, Clay. They were at Henry's looking for you. He's not scared of you."

As we continued out of South Side, I felt Clay's eyes watching me, hovering in the air above me without a body. I felt him stalking me, planning his attack, where he'd bite me, how he'd pin me down, whether it'd be quick or if he'd let it linger. That wasn't imaginary.

"So, now what?" Nipper said.

"You guys like to gamble?" I said.

## Chapter Twenty – The Tenth Race

I spent the third Friday of every month of my rookie year, except for the summer, at Chester A. Arthur High School. Officer Hart and I took part in the Junior Officers' Club from 12:00 until 14:00 hours. We took the kids out and made them run for a half hour and do an assortment of exercises. Officer Hart then answered questions and would cover basic law-enforcement techniques. Their favorite questions were how many times Officer Hart had to shoot somebody and how many times I got to bite people.

"He likes biting people, right? I mean, dogs like to bite living stuff, right?"

"What's it like to hit someone, like, with your nightstick? Are you afraid, like, you'll break your stick on someone's head?"

"Are you allowed to, like, run red lights and, like, not get in trouble? I'd totally do that!"

"How come they only let you have a moustache? I would think, like, a rad Fu Manchu or Lemmy chops would be scarier. Could you imagine if, like, a dude with, like, a full-on psycho mountain-man beard pulled you over? Dude, that would be so scary!"

"Have they ever thought about purposely giving the dogs rabies because, no, listen you idiots, think about it. What's crazier than a rabid dog? Plus, maybe, like, enough spreading of rabies would, like, create some zombie things. I don't know."

For the better part of the twentieth century, Grand City was among the elite of the state's many educational standouts. We boasted a high school graduation rate in the ninety-ninth percentile of the country. But then too many schools were built in areas that required too many good-paying jobs to live in. A few too many stock market crashes forced enough "daddy's bosses" to make difficult cuts, which forced many of Grand City's growing population to find refuge in neighboring cities. Suddenly, those good schools didn't have enough good kids to populate them. A couple years of this domino effect and they had to board up a school or two.

Chester A. Arthur was the first to get the wood-panel-on-the-windows-and-deadbolt treatment. It was a popular decision with the mutts of Grand City who always needed a large abandoned place within the city limits to throw their bones away at the cat races.

Fortunes were won and lost, mostly lost, by daily betting on the cats at Arthur High School. The three of us entered the school through a vent in the old music building. We passed by the trophy display case, which now charted the history of the cat races at Arthur High Racetrack. The first official race was held four years ago (though dogs have organized underground races across the city for decades) and was won by Minty Fresh, a three-year-old American shorthair.

At one time, Cat Racing was the largest sport in the canine world, having topped even ball-chasing and wrestling. Some races, such as the Annual Labor Day Stakes, drew thousands of dogs who'd escape for a day to toss their bones to Lady Luck at the track. Prior to going with Nipper and Ernie, my only time at the track was on a day off I had from work. I was able to sneak out to make it over to catch the inaugural Four Tails Cup to see what the big deal was. Maybe it was because I didn't bet, but I failed to comprehend how these hounds could get so riled up over something so trivial. Then again, I ran races where first prize determined who went to jail.

The trophy case was lined with photos of purebred cats with wreaths around their necks. There were clods of dirt from famous races and other various race-related trinkets scattered about. Ernie stopped to examine every item along the Cat Racing history timeline.

"Whoa, Nipper! Did you know that the record time for the mile has dropped more than twenty seconds over the past two years? Before that, it took twenty years for the record time to drop even four seconds. Man, these cats are getting faster and faster. You think you could beat them? I mean, I think I could. Oh man, check this out. The actual claw clipper used by Snarlgauge the night he won the Triple Claw." Nipper didn't stop to look. "Aw, come on, doesn't this stuff interest you? It's history."

"I don't know about that," Nipper said. "There's no way to prove that's the actual nail clip or that they didn't just get dirt from outside and say it was from the finish line of some race. You know, guys like your friends back at that club used to run this place. Probably still do."

"Well, I don't care what you guys think," Ernie said. "I think it's cool."

At the end of the music building there was a double doorway that took you outside to a patio area at the edge of the football stadium. From there, you went around the corner to the main ticket booth. There were a few dogs, all non-ticket holders, who hung around outside the entrance to the stadium, trying to hit dogs up for spare bones as they left the stadium. A collection of permanent down-on-your-luck types who'd just as soon rob you than see if they could talk you out of a few bones.

"How are we going to get in?" Nipper said. "None of us have any bones."

"I got this," Ernie said. "Watch and learn, old pal." He approached the ticket booth and stuck his nose under the glass, looking up at the ticket seller, an older mastiff, who stood up and stretched her back. "Long day? How are we doing so far?"

"How can I help you, sir?" she said.

"Oh, I don't need any help," Ernie said. "Just stopping by to see if we're on track to top last month's figures. Last month was a strong month for us. You look tired in there. You need a break?"

"No sir," she said, suddenly straightening up. "I'm sorry–"

"It's okay. Are you new here? I've never seen you before."

"I... Well, I've been here a few months now," she said. "I'm sorry. I don't think we—"

"I'm Ernie. Remember? We met three weeks ago. Normally, I run the museum up front. I'm a walking encyclopedia on the history of the races. I still remember when Fly Swatter made that epic comeback in the third all those years ago. What a race. Anyway, the boys upstairs liked me so much they've got me overseeing the ticket booth now, so I just wanted to stop by and check in. Crowd looks really good today."

"Oh, I think I remember now. Okay. Yeah. It's been a good day so far."

"Very good," Ernie said. "Keep up the good work. Who's your supervisor now? Is it still Elmore?"

"It's Maxy."

"That's right. Maxy. I'm gonna put in a good word to Maxy for you. See if maybe I can swing you a raise down here. I can tell you're working hard. Can I get you anything? You need water, some snacks, anything?"

"Wow," she said. "Thank you, Ernie. And no, I'm doing good in here."

"Don't mention it," Ernie said as he started to walk away but stopped and turned back to her. "Oh, hey, one last thing before I forget. I got a couple of boys here with me. They're from out of town and they're, ahem, *connected* with the fellas upstairs, if you know what I mean. How about we take care of their tickets for them, on the house, if you catch my drift? By the looks of it in there, we're having a good day in there, so don't worry, I'll smooth it out on our end with Maxy."

"Of course," she said. "How many do we need?"

"I think we can manage with three," Ernie said as she gave him the three passes. "I'll take care of the rest."

"How did you do that?" Nipper said, clearly impressed and a little spooked by how well Ernie, who rejoined us, pulled that off. "What if you get caught?"

"Getting caught? What are you talking about?" Ernie said, looking back and winking at her. "Obviously, I work here. Just ask her. Come on, let's go."

"I have to admit," I said as we gave our tickets to the attendant and were officially at the races. "That was good, Ernie. That was solid, professional undercover work."

"And here they come speeding around the third and final turn," the Public Address Announcer said through speakers with far too much squeak to them. "It looks like a swirling tornado of feline fury, folks, as they come down to the wire where it's King's Surprise out in front. Oh! Now it's Turnip's Treat ahead by a whisker. No, it's Catman making a late run, trying to pull everything he can out of his utility belt of tricks. It's a three-cat race as they approach the finish line. It looks like it's going to be a photo finish. Here they come. At the finish, it's... It's... It's... Hold on to your tickets folks... By Joe, it's Turnip's Treat by a whisker, followed by Catman and King's Surprise. Whew! What an exciting race, ladies and mutts. Win pays two-and-a-half to one, the trifecta pays thirty-two to one. The tenth race is up next in ten minutes. The ten in ten. Place your bets."

A typical losing dog's post-race reaction flowed in the following manner. They cried primal screams of dejection as the unthinkable happened yet again. The screams subsided and ended in an extended sigh, punctuated by a series of deep breaths and exhales as their head and shoulders dropped to the ground. But then, just as all hope was nearly lost for good, a renewed sense of determination fell before their eyes because there was still another race to be run. A chance to win it all back and then some with a bigger bet that would make up for the loss. All they needed was a moment of clarity to turn that daily race program to the right page and pick the cat destined to win the very next race. They slapped their paw on the winner's name and floated to the nearest pay window to lay a fresh bet. *Got 'um this time*, they thought.

"I love it!" Ernie said. "Can't you just feel the excitement? It just reaches in and grabs you as you watch those little cats run. You want to chase them, you want to bite 'em, but most of all, you want your cat to win. Then you just want to hug it. Where do you get all this emotion in one shot?"

"We're here to work," I said. "Keep your eyes open."

"How will we know when we see him?" Nipper said.

"Big, black, mean, ugly, and with a sidekick," I said. "You see that, you give me a holler."

"Hey partner," Ernie said to a Bassett hound with bloodshot eyes and his nose deep into a hooch-stained program, "who do you like in the tenth?"

"Oh, I don't know," he said. "I've been cold all day. I'm down three hundred and fifty bones. My wife is gonna kill me."

"I hate those days," Ernie said. "But hey, all you need is one winner, right?"

"That's what I keep telling myself."

"Hey, this Willow cat looks good," Ernie said to the hound. "Year-and-a-half tabby. Good odds and is on a streak. What do you think?"

"Looks okay. Besides, my name is Winston, and I share the first two letters of my name with this Willow, so yeah, it makes as much sense as any other bet I've made so far. Thanks, buddy."

"Ernie," Nipper said.

"What?" Ernie said. "Me and my buddy here are looking at the tenth. He needs an extra eye on the lineup. That's the race we're supposed to care about, right?" Nipper went over to the two of them and yanked Ernie by the collar away from Winston and the program. Ernie pulled back and showed his teeth for a split second and didn't retreat. "Back off, Nipper. I love you like a brother, but don't you ever put your teeth on me again. What's your problem?"

"I'm sorry," Nipper said. "I'm not comfortable here. I don't like this place and I don't like why we're here."

"Nipper," Ernie said. "Look around you. There's tons of dogs here. No one cares about us here because no one knows we're here except us, so relax."

"The sooner we get done," Nipper said, "the sooner we can go home is all I mean."

"I know," Ernie said. "That's why I was trying to have just a little bit of fun first. I'm not stupid. I know this is probably my last time ever coming here, so I'm not in a huge hurry to leave."

There was no sign of Clay by the betting windows. If what we were told was true and Clay only bet the tenth, then he must have already made his bet and was off watching the events unfold somewhere else.

"Guys," I said. "That's enough. Follow me. I want to see something."

The pre-staging area was thirty yards from the betting windows. All the cats were in individual pens and were in the open so that the gamblers could get a closer look at who was racing and what their demeanor was like a few minutes prior to race time. A particularly well-groomed collie was interviewing Willow, the front-runner in the tenth, from the first pen.

"Sadie-Jane here with KCFG news," she said into a microphone tucked neatly into her collar, "and I'm standing here with Willow, perhaps the biggest name in all of Cat Racing at the moment, a tabby who has rattled off seven straight wins and is everyone's favorite to take home the Triple Claw this year. Willow, what are your thoughts heading into this next race?"

"Complete and utter domination," Willow said, like it was a chore. "When I race, it's as if there are no other cats on the track. A lot of cats will hiss and raise their tails to try and intimidate me, but when you have the tools that I have, there's nothing they can do to take me off my game."

"Sounds like winning has given you an expanded ego. How do you keep up your training if you—"

"Let me stop you right there," Willow said. "Here's the thing. You say it's ego, but it's just confidence. I know I can run faster than any other cat they put up next to me in that starting gate."

"There's been a new, and some say unorthodox, cat who has created a reputation for himself at the track in recent weeks and has fared especially well in the tenth. Any thoughts on this Clay's Pigeon?"

Ernie nudged me. "Hey Fritz, you need to see this cat over here."

"Ernie, if you can't control yourself here," I said, "maybe you should wait outside."

"You need to back off, man," Ernie said. "Would you just listen and follow me. Nipper found something."

"There you have it," Sadie said in the background. "A confident and ready Willow eager to get her paws on the track once more regardless of her competition. This has been Sadie-Jane, live from the races."

Ernie led me down the row of racers who were all stretching and limbering up for the race. Nipper waited for us down the row; he stopped me a few feet away from the end cat, out of its eyesight.

"Take a peek," Nipper said. "Don't let him see you."

"Oh my," I said.

"Yeah," Nipper said, "if anyone knows a lousy costume, it's me."

The cat at the end was larger than the others and kept its face hidden under a book. Its ears were too long to begin with and were pinned up straight. I saw the zipper to its fully encompassing cat fur coat end below its chin.

"It's his sidekick," I said.

"Who? Clay's?" Nipper said. I nodded. "So that's how he wins. He cheats."

"We have to do something to stop him, don't we?" Ernie said.

I looked up to the clock above the pens; there were only a few minutes left until the start of the race. I had an idea. It made as much sense then as it does now. I gestured for Nipper and Ernie to come close.

"Nipper, you see that closet over there?" I said. "I want you and Ernie to get in there. You have two minutes to get Ernie looking like a cat. Whatever you can find, make it work."

"Umm, and then what?" Ernie said.

"Isn't it clear?" Nipper said, with a tinge of glee. "You're racing those cats over there."

"I can't do that," Ernie said.

"Relax," I said. "You're not racing to win. I just need you to stay close to Scamper. You can do that, can't you?"

"He's a Jack Russell, isn't he?" Ernie said. "They haven't made one of those yet I can't chase down."

"How is he getting into the race?" Nipper said.

"Leave that to me," I said. "You guys better hurry. Get going."

The two of them split toward the service closet. I went to sit behind a rusted rack of old race forms near the bathroom. Sadie-Jane was on the other side of the rack. She couldn't see me from her side.

"Excuse me," I said over her shoulder. I lowered down and deepened my voice to a whisper. "Don't look back at me. You've heard about all the performance enhancers that are being thrown around this track, haven't you?"

"No," she said. She started to turn around.

"I said don't move. I'm risking a lot to talk to you right now. I have it on good word that the cat in pen six is on a cycle of felineondrineoxide right now."

"Felineo...What?" Sadie said

"It's a super-powerful strain that's brand new and nearly untraceable. There's your scoop. Make haste." I turned the corner and vanished into the male restroom and took position. I watched from there as Sadie stormed over to pen six and tried to get everyone on the record. Of course the cat denied everything and called Sadie a liar and a hack journalist.

One thing to note about cats, they're as moody and emotional of a creature as any I've ever encountered. They'll hold a grudge for a lifetime. Once you get on their bad side, there's no going back. And poor Sadie, so blinded by the thrill of breaking a big story, well, the cat became so irate that he jumped the wall and went after her. It took a dozen track officials to pull the cat off and send the clawing offender back to the locker room. Don't worry about Sadie. They were only minor scratches.

"Did you see that?" a Dalmatian said on his way into the bathroom.

"You can never trust a cat, can you?" I said as I went out to the main stands where Nipper was already out waiting in the center of the third row.

"So?" I said. Nipper was perfectly and unnaturally still, like someone so clearly guilty.

"It's good," Nipper said, opening his mouth just enough to snap out the words as quickly as he could. "I can't help but think we just broke a lot of laws."

"You know why Cat Racing is so popular?" I said. "It's because while there are rules, the thing is, no one really cares too much about them. And pretty much, this whole thing is illegal. It's like the bone lenders. There's no one to regulate this stuff, so of all the supposed laws you're worried about? Basically, they don't exist. No rules and dogs? No one bats an eye at that."

"What if they find out what we did?"

"What if they do? What's the worst that could happen? You think we're the first people to exert some outside influence in a race where there's money to be made with the gamblers? Nipper, if there was a race today where someone wasn't trying something suspicious, well, that would be suspicious. And besides, it's been a long time since a dog was killed for fixing a race or two."

"Killed?"

"And besides all of that," I said, concluding, "take a look around here. You have a bunch of dopes with their noses buried in racing programs who are picking ripped tickets up off the ground looking for a dropped fortune. A bunch of malnourished jerks who only bark up until the moment they start coughing up years of tobacco and hooch. I mean, do you see anyone around here who looks like they'd be able to do anything even if they thought you cost them their last bone?"

Nipper looked around. The more he scanned the mutts walking around, the more I could see him begin to relax. And then he looked nonchalantly toward the top of the bleachers, the cheap seats. He froze.

"Yeah," he said. "That guy up there."

"What guy? Let me–" It was Clay. He sat alone in the last row at the very top of the stands like an eclipse. No one else was even close to his vicinity, and that's saying something because the top seats at the track are among the best if you want to actually watch the race instead of yelling at the cats, which Ernie says is nearly as fun as betting on them.

Say what you will about the decision-making skills of perennial gamblers, but even they knew to keep their distance from the big guy in the good seats. He hadn't seen us and looked as if he couldn't be bothered by the goings on of mere track hounds. His eyes were trained on the track. No program. No snacks. No hooch.

"Attention, patrons of Chester A. Arthur Cat Track, may I have your attention for an update regarding the tenth race?" the Public Address Announcer said, interrupting the goings on at the track with a screech in the speakers that made all of us wince, except Clay, whose face compressed into focus at the announcement. "We have just been informed of a last-minute scratch in the tenth race. It seems that Parrot's Foe has been indefinitely suspended by the Feline Racing Association for undisclosed actions unbecoming a racing professional. I have also just been informed that we will have a replacement in the race by the name of... Let's see here, uh, it uh looks like, oh, here it is. Replacing Parrot's Foe in the tenth race will be a newcomer to the track, a four-year-old male...*mutt?* Wait that must be a typo, so we'll just say he's a four-year-old, um, they probably meant to say Manx, likely feral, who goes by the handle...Saucy's Hero. Again, Parrot's Foe out and Saucy's Hero is in for the tenth race. Race starts in two minutes."

Clay relaxed his face and resumed his post atop the stands as he intensely watched the setting like a general on the battlefield.

"That's him," I said.

"I know," Nipper said. "Ernie's in the race. He's Saucy's Hero. I came up with that. He didn't like it, but we didn't have time to argue."

"No. That dog up there. The one you just saw. That's him. That's Clay."

"Why didn't you say he was part bulldozer?"

"Let's not get melodramatic," I said. "It's the angle we're at. You put anyone up there at the top and they'd look bigger."

A mastiff down on the inside of the track blew a trumpeter's call, and the cats made their way to the track. Willow was out front. She was followed by two other lean wirehairs, then Scamper, who lay low and ducked behind the others as much as possible. A couple more racers entered and then it was Ernie who brought up the caboose of this train. He was covered with dirty mop tops over his body and head. He walked slowly to keep them balanced. Broom thistles stuck into hastily chewed gum that was plastered onto either side of Ernie's face gave the illusion of cat whiskers. While the cat next to Scamper engaged in a last-minute stretch, Ernie took its place in the starting gate.

"Hey," the cat said. "You're in my spot."

"No," Ernie said. "I'm in *my* spot. You see how that works. There's one open at the end. Take that one."

"That's not how it works," the cat said as a track official blew his whistle and yelled at the cat to take his place in what would have been Ernie's outside gate.

"Go up there," I said to Nipper.

"By that thing?" Nipper said.

"If I go, and he sees me, our plan is up."

"What exactly is our plan again? I thought you wanted to get him. Well, there he is. Who cares about the other one racing? You can go arrest him now. Aren't you going to arrest him?"

"It's not that easy," I said.

"Hey Fritz, look, I'd be afraid of him too. I *am* afraid of that dog."

"Who says I'm afraid of him?" I said.

"You're not even looking at him," Nipper said. "I don't blame you."

"Go up there," I said. "He doesn't know you from anyone else here."

"Me? Can't you go undercover or something? Isn't that how the cops do it?"

"I go up there, and there will be a fight," I said. "I'll be at a disadvantage because he has the high ground. When that happens, and it will, because as you know, he and I have fought once already, so when that happens, can I count on you to jump in and to get my back at a split second's notice? Can I do that, Nipper? Can I count on you in that moment?"

"I don't know."

"Well, you can count on me. Trust me; he's not going to make a scene over someone he's never seen before. And no, I'm not afraid."

"Fine," Nipper said as he begrudgingly took baby steps up the bleachers toward Clay. I kept my back to them and watched Ernie while training my ears toward Nipper and Clay. All the cats were harnessed into the starting gate except one who was batting a mud ball around.

"You ever get nervous?" Ernie said to Scamper.

"Shut up," Scamper said. "I'm concentrating."

"It's my first race. Any tips for how to get started?"

"What did I just tell you? Oh my goodness, what kind of cat are you?"

"I don't know. A fast one?"

"You're the ugliest looking thing I've ever seen."

"Maybe you should find yourself a mirror, pal," Ernie said.

"Quiet down!" the Track Official said to both of them. The official made a final walk of the starting gate, having flung the mud-playing cat off into its gate with a crash.

Nipper stopped three rows short of Clay and sat less than five dog widths off to Clay's left. Much closer than I'd expected him to go.

"Hello," Nipper said, looking over his shoulder to Clay. "Who's your bones on?"

"Do I know you?" Clay said.

"Me? Who? No. And you? Let me think. Eh, I don't know. I would think I'd remember if I met someone, you know, as uh, you know, with your presence and the voice, that voice, still echoing in my ears... So, no, I don't think you know me. At least for sure I know for a fact that I do not know you, Mister... What's your name?"

The starting bell rang. The gates sprung open with a metallic snap. The cats hurdled out and chased the giant ball of stringy yarn on a long pole racing in front of them.

"And they're off," the Public Address Announcer said, barking through the speakers.

"Come on, Ern– I mean, Saucy's Hero," Nipper said, shouting. Some of his excitement was that it gave him a reason to turn away from Clay. Out of the gate, Ernie kept up with the pack. Willow pulled out to an early lead. Above me, Nipper held his ground. And there I was in between them doing absolutely nothing.

Nipper was right. I was a coward.

Within the span of a few minutes, I had talked two dogs into risking their health and their home to fight my battle. They even trusted me that I was still looking out for them. I turned over my shoulder and made eye contact with Nipper. He winked and nodded at me because he was holding up his end of the plan. His confidence rose as each moment ticked away and he wasn't getting mauled by a dog that I should've kept him as far away from as I could.

"As they begin the first turn, to no one's surprise, Willow has taken the early lead," the Public Address Announcer said, "while Clay's Pigeon and Saucy's Hero are threatening to break ahead of the pack of these wild racing cats."

"Wait for me," Ernie said, yelling ahead to Scamper.

"Doesn't work that way, stupid," Scamper said, firing back. Ernie pushed forward. His head was only inches behind Scamper's tail. As the first turn straightened out, Scamper flicked his leg out in an attempt to wing a cheap shot across Ernie's face.

"Do that again, and I'll take it home for dinner," Ernie said.

"You'll try," Scamper said.

"Heck of race so far, huh?" Nipper said as he tried to engage a non-responsive Clay. "I said it's a great race, isn't it?" *Stop it, Nipper.* "Who's your money on, pal? Me, I like that weird-looking one. Almost doesn't even look like a cat. That one right–" Clay's head pivoted on its axis like a heat-seeking cruise missile aimed squarely at Nipper. Nipper stopped cold. Clay's chest expanded out at least a full foot with an inhale of pure fury. "Like I was saying, good race. Never mind me. I'm going to stop talking. Probably forever actually."

"On the straightaway," the Public Address Announcer said, "it's Willow pulling away with only two cats still hoping to make a go at the champ."

"Hey Willow," Scamper said, neck and neck with Ernie, both of them only a foot away from a focused Willow. "If you know what's good for you, you'll start to slow down on the next turn."

"Not a chance, loser," Willow said, hissing back at them.

"You've got about a minute to change your mind, cat. And if you don't and you win this thing, you'll have a very angry Rottweiler waiting for you in the back when no one is around."

"So that's how you do it!" Ernie said.

"Do what?" Scamper said.

"Would you two shut up and lose with some dignity still intact?" Willow said, punctuating her missive with a kick of speed as they rounded the second turn.

"You'll regret this," Scamper said, pounding his paws into the dirt as he tried to keep up with the much faster Willow. Ernie stayed right there step for step with Scamper. A slight stumble caused Ernie's makeshift mop top on his head to shift off to the side. It blocked his sight and caused him to bump Scamper on the outside. "Watch it, jerk. Do it again and that Rottweiler will be waiting for you too."

"I got news for you," Ernie said. "We know all about you and that Rottweiler."

"What? Who are you? And what is wrong with your head?"

"On the final turn," the Public Address Announcer said, "it's Willow with a growing lead on the inside of the track. Clay's Pigeon and Saucy's Hero, the late-minute scratch, are behind Willow and ahead of the rest of the pack. There looks to be some roughhousing going on as the cats make the turn. Keep it clean out there, you stinking cats."

The crowd noise picked up as the cats approached the finish line. I focused my ears on Nipper, though I was positive his attempts at conversation were all but finished. *Come on, Fritz. Do something. Nipper's right. What are you waiting for? He's right there. He's distracted. You have one more charge in that body, don't you?*

But all I needed was for my leg to buckle as I hopped the bleachers. Then what? I get mauled, get tossed back into an ambulance, back to the hospital, back to the backyard at Officer Hart's house. Or worse.

The nubs and splinters from the bleachers stuck into my legs and tail. They pinched and stabbed me, like they were daring me to get up. *What do you got, cop?* You know this bench isn't comfortable. It's not designed to be. At least stand up and watch the race, the splinters teased, because you're the only one here who is still sitting down. You're afraid he's going to see you, is that it?

You held your own the first time you fought him. Or was that how you chose to remember it? It was the other one who bit you from behind. Who knows what would've happened if he hadn't done that, right? Oh, now wait a second my friend, why are you even asking that kind of question? A cop doesn't say "who knows?" He knows. A cop knows that he's taking the criminal down. There's none of this *maybe* stuff going on.

Maybe you'd forgotten how surprisingly strong he felt as he pushed you and pinned you on the asphalt. You didn't forget how tight his bite was and how you felt him trying to finish you with that bite. There was no playing, and there was no holding back. You knew in that moment that he was squeezing until your lights went out.

Do you remember not being able to get up when you wanted to? Do you remember that feeling of complete powerlessness for the first time in your life? How about the realization that another dog had absolute control over the rest of your life? Does knowing in your gut that you were seconds away from your final breath and that you had no choice in the matter haunt you? It's crippling isn't it?

But hey, you know all about crippling. There's no need to waste our time on that. You know crippled. You've known crippled since that night. You've acted like every step didn't hurt. Most of them don't, but that one, that one out of however many steps you take in a day, it could be the first one, the last, or somewhere in the middle. That one step is waiting to awaken; the one that reminded you that you're weak.

Every time you stepped and the pain didn't appear, there was no relief because you were still waiting for it. Waited on the pain. The pain that you knew was there. The pain that wouldn't go away. You wanted to scream at it and beg to know what it was waiting for and to just show up for good already. Then again, it wouldn't be pain if it wasn't torturing you. Worst of all, you knew damn well that if you tempted it enough times, it might've taken you up and showed up and stayed for good.

But then you figured that it might as well have hurt with every pace, every breath, and every moment because it was there with every thought anyway. Whether the pain terrorized your leg or not, it had the entirety of you in its clutches. And if you couldn't beat Clay when your body wasn't letting you down, what was going to happen when it was? You knew what would happen.

I remained seated and invisible. In a moment of total relief, I felt nothing.

Out on the track, Ernie was as alive as he'd ever been. He was running for his life out there under some misguided obligation to me, a dog he barely knew. Nipper was alive too. He was up there, in way over his head, but he was alive. He was excited. He was scared. His senses fired on all synapses. His heart pounded, and he was as ready as he could be, regardless of the outcome. To a blind eye, I was doing the exact same thing as Nipper was. We both sat on a bleacher and watched a cat race, but we might as well have been on opposite sides of the planet.

"Last warning, Willow," Scamper said, hollering out down on the track.

"Now's as good of a time as any," Ernie said, and with a whip of his neck, Ernie flung the mop top into Scamper's face. Scamper stumbled and nearly lost his footing. The mop head hung over his nose like a long mustache. "I've never liked bullies!"

"You're not a cat," Scamper said, ramming into Ernie as they came out of the final turn, biting at Ernie's face. "Let me see those whiskers."

"And here they come into the homestretch," the Public Address Announcer yelled. "Leading the way is Willow with Clay's Pigeon and Saucy's Hero engaged in a bitter war of attrition. From my vantage point, it looks like they're trying to bite at one another. Something looks wrong on Saucy's Hero, like part of his head is missing and is hanging off of the nose of Clay's Pigeon. This has to be one of the craziest races and finishes we've ever seen at the track. These two cats surely have some bad blood between the two of them. Look at them battle each other like a pair of gladiators. And you know what we dogs say about a good cat fight? If there's no winner left standing...We all win!"

The crowd roared as Ernie leaned down and got a glancing bite on Scamper's arm, tripping him up. As Scamper went down in the mud, he sunk his teeth into Ernie's tail and sent them both crashing into the guard railing. The dirt flew into the air around them like a tornado. By the time it became clear enough to make anything out, Ernie had Scamper mounted. As Ernie went in for the bite, he looked down the track at the approaching tsunami.

Ka-Boom!

"Oh my, there's a ten-cat pileup on the track. The rest of the pack just slammed into Pigeon and Hero. What a terrible sound. Listen to those cats screech and hiss. It's an explosion of fur, but look, there's Willow crossing the finish line, the only cat not caught up in the fray."

The pandemonium spread to the stands. Dogs howled and barked at the track as the officials and security guards restrained the patrons from charging over the fence onto the field. Dogs bit and pawed at anything they could – the bench, the fence, a random dog next to them. Clay stood and paced back and forth on the top of the bleachers, knowing that he was the target of this melee but not sure why or who was coming for him. The only thing he could pinpoint was the strange dog sitting too close to him.

"Who are you?" Clay demanded.

"I'm not a cop, that's for sure," Nipper said.

Then our eyes locked. Clay looked down on me while my back was to him, and I sheepishly peeked over my shoulder. I saw the contempt and pity he had for me.

"Well, well, well," he said, snickering at me. "Look who it is."

The cats on the track shook off the dirt and collectively got back to their feet. Scamper was gone, having taken the opportunity to vanish into the melee. Ernie's shoddy, makeshift costume was also a casualty of the crash. He went around in circles looking for Scamper, unaware that the cats had surrounded him.

"He's a dog!" one of them said. "Cheater!"

"He could've have gotten us killed."

"Wait a second," Ernie said as he realized he was outnumbered nine to one. "I was trying to help. The other dog was cheating. I'm one of the good guys. I was stopping him until you all crashed into us."

"There's no such thing as a good dog," one cat said.

"You didn't stop *him*," another cat said. "You stopped all of *us*."

They unsheathed their claws and pounced on Ernie. They swiped at any part of him they could, like a swarm of piranhas incited by a drop of blood.

"This must be your puppy," Clay said, referring to Nipper. Neither of us said anything back. "Awww, how cute, Fritz. You have a little lackey to do your dirty work. And let me guess, that dog out there on the track that has his paws full with those cats at the moment is yours too? Ooh, that one's gonna sting. They're really tearing him apart."

"Ernie!" Nipper said as he sprung to his feet and pushed his way through the rioting dogs to the fence, then jumping over it to help Ernie on the field.

"Fritz," Clay said, coming down the steps toward me at a deliberate pace, "I was looking forward to the day when I'd see you again, but now you just had to go and ruin it by being all pathetic and, dare I say, a sorry sack of what used to be a dog. Is this how you envisioned it playing out? Now see, I was hoping to finish what I started, but it looks like I don't have to.

Maybe I gave you too much credit. I could tell you were old, but I didn't think you were this old. By the looks of you, it'd be like mauling a mouse at this point. Where's the fun in that? See you around, Fritz."

Clay strutted right past me and waded into the riot. He disappeared into the chaos. The track officials used laser light pointers to distract the attacking cats and successfully wrangled them up into pens. They ignored Ernie and Nipper, who remained in the center of the track.

And I sat still on that rotten bench not doing a damn thing.

## Chapter Twenty-One – The Post Race Wrap Up

Within minutes, the races continued once more inside the stadium. As I walked out, the Public Address Announcer explained that there would be no refunds on the tenth race and that the results stood. Nipper and Ernie were forcibly escorted out of the stadium by a trio of Irish Setters, confirming for me a long standing rumor that it was indeed the Irish who pulled the strings behind the scenes at the cat races.

Their scratches and cuts weren't as bad as I thought they'd be. Beyond a long scratch on the top of Ernie's head, nothing else was visible on him. Nipper had a few marks along his sidewall, but they'd both be fine. Ernie looked exhausted.

"What was that line you said about having my back?" Nipper said. "Because all I saw was me going up to Clay and then when Ernie was in trouble and needed help... Hey Ernie, did you see Fritz out there trying to peel any cats off of you?"

"Nope," Ernie said. "Wait, you saw Clay? And you sent *Nipper* after him? That doesn't make any sense. No offense, Nipper."

"None taken, believe me," Nipper said.

"I was undercover," I said. "I thought I explained that already."

"You weren't undercover when Clay saw you," Nipper said.

"What happened?" Ernie said.

"Nothing," Nipper said.

"Aw, come on. Tell me."

"I did," Nipper said. "Nothing. Nothing happened. He didn't do a thing."

"That's not true," I said.

"Oh, it's not?" Nipper said. "Maybe you should explain what exactly it was you did because we both risked our necks out there and now while I did see you sitting on that bench, clutching it like a puppy who caught his first stick, and I know Ernie and me aren't big-time cops, but if there was something else you were doing there, please enlighten us."

"Was it your leg?" Ernie said.

"He was scared," Nipper said.

"You guys don't understand what I'm going through," I said.

"What you're going through?" Nipper said. "What *you're* going through? What about what we're going through? Ever since you've graced our lives with your presence, you know what we've gone through? Huh? We left our home because of you. We haven't had a real meal in days because of you. I made a spectacle of myself in front of everyone I know because of you. Scarlet thinks I'm a fool because of you. We've been chasing criminals and hanging out with lowlifes because of you. Ernie was forced into a cat race and then attacked, and you have me doing your dirty work, so no, I guess we don't know what you're going through."

"We were so close," Ernie said as he sat down and struggled to reach his wounds to lick them. "I had that little jerk right where I wanted him. Little weasel. Man, one more second. So, what's our next move? We got 'em on the run."

"There is no next time," Nipper said. "We're going home."

"He's right," I said. "You guys should go back home."

"But Fritz? Wait, Nipper. I know you're mad, I mean, look, I'm mad too, but it's not Fritz' fault—"

"Yes it is," Nipper said. "One hundred percent it is. You didn't see him up there. I'm not exaggerating when I said that he did nothing. He just sat there and threw us to the wolves."

"Go home," I said. "I'm sorry. Get yourself cleaned up."

"Aren't you coming with us?" Ernie said.

"I don't have a home," I said. "I don't deserve one."

"You got us," Ernie said.

"Nope," I said. "I don't have anybody."

"Then if that's how you feel," Ernie said. "Nipper, let's get out of here. Those setters said we had a few minutes to disappear or they'd make us disappear for good."

"Fine with me," Nipper said. "Let's go."

"You sure you don't want to go home?" Ernie said as I turned around and walked away. I didn't care where I went or where I ended up. I'd never left Grand City. Never in my life. I may have been on a call in a neighboring city or driven through one on a vehicle pursuit, but I'd gone to bed and woken up every day of my life in Grand City. Always in service for someone else.

I'd thought all along that I was Odysseus on my path back home. As the stadium, as well as Nipper and Ernie, fell into the abyss of my periphery, I acknowledged what I had always known. I assumed that all I had to do on this quest was to avoid humans, not get run over, catch Clay, and then it would be done. I'd go back to my home. It had to end that way. It just had to.

My home, and the only home I ever wanted to go back to, wasn't in Officer Hart's backyard. Up until that exact second before Clay looked down at me, I thought Grand City P.D. would take me back. They'd see the error of their ways and would welcome me back to my kennel. I would pick up right where I'd left off. Once they all saw how I'd brought down Clay, they'd know that they had acted in haste and that nothing was wrong with me and that I was better than ever; better than any other dog they had chomping at the bit in training. That was my home, and that's where I was going.

Then with no warning, and in the wag of a tail, my blinders were tossed aside, and I acknowledged what I'd known all along. They'd replaced me with a dog who was younger, faster, and a stronger version of me at my best. The same way I had done to Lincoln with no apologies a lifetime ago.

They didn't care about you, and they never did. No matter how well you did your job, and regardless of your record, all you ever were was a potential liability. You anxiously waited your turn until you became the weak link in the chain. Then they fixed the chain and threw away the old parts. The only thing you could do was prolong the inevitable because nobody came out unscathed. Everyone gets replaced and tossed away.

The moment they decided that your service was no longer up to par, you ceased to exist. You're no longer a living, breathing creature who feels joy and friendship and fear and anger, you're a service provider. That's what you were there for. To make someone else's job easier.

Let's say that it had played out at the track the way it should have. That I didn't procrastinate when I saw Scamper dressed like a fool in that pen. I should have never dragged Nipper and Ernie into it to begin with. I had already hedged my bets. I was just another gambler at the track.

If I'd done it the way I should have, I'd have hurdled that fence and tore the costume off Scamper. I'd have squeezed him up against the corner of his pen so hard that he could barely exhale. I'd have demanded right there for him to tell me where Clay was and that if he tried to stall I'd bite one of his nails off. *Answer me! Where is he?*

Fritz, I don't know what you–

Clay would announce that he was right behind me. I'd drop the quivering sack and go after Clay with no fancy talk. I'd take out his legs. I'd waste no time paying him back by closing my mouth on his knee. His bones would crumble in my mouth. As he yelped in agony, I'd pin his neck down with extreme prejudice.

I'd tear him open and show him to that reporter. I'd challenge her to use every adjective she had in her arsenal to describe it. The other dogs, who at first were excited for me to take Clay down, would tell me that enough was enough. I'd dare them to stop me, and I'd make them take pity on Clay. Take pity on what was left of him and then tell every dog they knew in Grand City to be afraid of me.

Would that make me a cop again? All that would prove was that I was just a dog. A cop wouldn't behave like that. No matter what course of action I took at the cat races, I was nothing.

I was not Odysseus. I was not on a quest. I wasn't going home. I was old. I was beaten down. I was tired. I was Argos. I waited for my master to come home. And then I was going to roll over and die.

I thought about Nipper and Ernie on their way back home as they reentered the maze of homes on that cool night. They were lucky. They had their little piece of land that was theirs, the back yard. Ernie took his time, using his scratches as an excuse, saying his legs were tired from the race. He was just in no hurry to get back. He suggested that they stop on the way to visit Scarlet and Saucy.

"Sure," Nipper said. "If you want to go say hi, let's go."

Ernie woke up Saucy by scratching the fence. She was excited to see him even if it was just through a broken piece of a wooden fence.

"Shouldn't you be on your big case?" Saucy said. "What are you even doing here?"

"I just wanted to come by and visit," Ernie said. "We haven't played together for a while."

"And whose fault is that?" Saucy said.

"You think it's mine?" Ernie says.

"Well, it's not mine."

"He needed our help."

"Where is he? Should I wake Scarlet?"

"He's not coming home," Ernie said.

"Is he—" she said, gasping.

"No. He's fine. Or so he says he is. There wasn't much else we could do, so we left. He didn't want to come. Whatever. You should have seen me though, Saucy. You would've loved it. Nipper made me look like a cat and then we snuck into the cat races and I was doing really good chasing after this dog who was a real jerk, but then it turned into a huge mess and the cats attacked me and the dogs in the stands went crazy and then Nipper had to come help me and then they threw us out of the track. And Nipper, he got right in the face of Clay, *the* Clay. Not even Fritz did that, but Nipper did. Oh, and I saw Knox and Gash too."

"I think you guys should leave," Saucy said.

"What? Why?"

"I don't want to hear about what a great time you've been having while I've been stuck here with the beauty queen."

"I thought you'd appreciate the story. I thought you'd be happy for me."

"See you later, Ernie," Saucy said. With no other stops to make, Nipper and Ernie walked in silence the rest of the way home until they got back to their street and Nipper stopped.

"Do you think I'm brave, Ernie?" Nipper said.

"I don't know what you mean."

"It's a yes-or-no question. Just be honest with me. I heard what you said to Saucy."

"Yeah, sure, Nipper."

"Really? You think I have guts?"

"Sure, Nipper. The way you jumped in there when those cats were clawing at me was pretty cool."

"But those were just cats. You don't think I'm a coward?"

"You went up and sat right next to Clay when Fritz wouldn't, that took some courage. Hey, it's not like you need to impress me or nothing. But to answer your question, no Nipper, I do not think that you are a coward."

"So much for one last adventure, huh? We'll have to do it again sometime, right?"

"We'll see," Ernie said. "I don't know."

"What's wrong?"

"Why was Saucy so mad at me? And why do I care so much?"

"I don't know, Ernie. I don't know. You're probably asking the wrong dog to give you any advice about that stuff. You think I could have been a cop?"

"I don't know, Nipper. Why does that matter?"

"Just wanted to ask." They continued and passed under a streetlight right out in front of the Hart house on the corner. A rattling came from behind them.

"What do you think, Clay?" Scamper said as Nipper and Ernie turned around and were inches away from an angry Clay and Scamper. "Could he have been a cop? I don't think they'd ever let a pathetic mutt like him wear a badge."

"Watch your mouth," Ernie said.

"Tough talk from such a little dog," Clay said.

"What do you two want?" Nipper said.

"Where's Fritz?" Clay said. Nipper looked to Ernie for what to say and do. "Let me rephrase the question. Where's that broken-down, hobbling ghost of a dog? Last thing I was going to do was tear his throat out with a hundred witnesses. But two witnesses? I can handle that."

"We don't know where he is," Nipper said, with too much gumption. Ernie closed his eyes and took a deep breath knowing what kind of mistake Nipper had just made. "In fact, we haven't seen him in hours since we left the track."

"That's too bad," Clay said.

"Yeah," Nipper said. "You'll have to keep looking somewhere else."

"That's not what we had in mind," Scamper said.

"I wasn't just looking for Fritz," Clay said. "The two of you cost me a lot of bones today."

"Maybe you shouldn't have been cheating," Nipper said. "Then we wouldn't have had to do anything. Besides, we don't have any bones between the two of us, so again, you'll just have to go somewhere else."

"That's what I was hoping you'd say," Clay said. "Because now I get to have a little bit of fun."

"Yeah, it's time for us to have a bit of fun," Scamper said, chiming in safely behind Clay.

"Just know that I can hurt you too," Ernie said, his voice trembling as he positioned himself in front of Nipper and faced Clay. "You can bet on that."

"No, you can't," Clay said, circling Nipper and Ernie as he closed what little distance was left between them with each turn. Ernie crouched down, ready to strike, while Clay strolled nonchalantly. He drew an invisible wall around Nipper and Ernie. In a moment of pure desperation or genius, Nipper barked non-stop as loud as he could.

"You trying to scare him?" Scamper said. "You must be the most inept mutt I've ever seen. Look at him. You're going to strain your itty-bitty little voice there. Why can't a dog just shut up and get mauled with honor? Why is that, I wonder?"

Nipper was in his own world. He barked with a passion he'd never felt before. Like he knew that suddenly there was a good chance he'd never see tomorrow unless he kept shouting with everything he had. The sheer volume began to unnerve Clay and made him stop his rounding. He lowered down to attack.

The light on the front porch of Officer Hart's house flipped on and sent a cloud of light behind Nipper and Ernie that flooded Clay. Officer Hart appeared in pajama pants. He took a few steps beyond the porch with his hand extended parallel to his brow like he was staring into the sun. He said "ow" as he stepped onto a particularly pointed piece of cracked driveway. Nipper slowed the pace of his manic barks and let out a final barrage in deliberate succession.

"Nipper?" Officer Hart said. "Is that you? Come here. Where's Fritz?"

Clay turned his locked jaw toward Officer Hart and approached.

"Leave him alone," Ernie said.

"If I were you," Scamper said, "I wouldn't look this gift horse in the mouth, and I'd take the chance to escape."

"Get out of here," Officer Hart said to Clay, who responded with a growl. Officer Hart swore to himself and reached down for the hose curled up in front of the house. He pointed it at Clay, put his thumb partially over the spout, and turned on the water full blast. Clay stopped at the end of the empty driveway just outside the range of the water. Officer Hart flipped his wrist up and sent a freezing waterfall onto Clay's head. While Clay shook the dripping water away from his eyes, Nipper took off and made it into the house. Ernie followed but stayed next to Officer Hart at the start of the driveway.

"Aww, sorry about your plans," Ernie said.

"This isn't over," Clay said as Officer Hart blasted him straight on in the chest. Clay backed off the sidewalk into the street.

"Get the other one too," Ernie barked to Officer Hart. "Get him too. Right in the face. Give him pneumonia."

"Okay," Officer Hart said as he gave Ernie the single best and most relaxing pair of behind-the-ear scratches he'd ever felt in his life. "Calm down, Ernie. They're going away. We got 'um. I'd hose the runt down, but he was smart enough to run away across the street. Come on, let's go back inside and get you guys some food."

As Ernie went inside, and while Officer Hart rolled the hose back up, the Intimidator pulled into the driveway. Mrs. Hart held her face in her hands for a long moment before shutting the engine off and getting out of the car. She took a few stumbled steps before she stopped in front of Officer Hart.

"Why is the driveway all wet?" Mrs. Hart said.

"Where were you?" Officer Hart said. "I was worried."

"I told you I was working."

"Do you think I'm stupid?"

"Are you going to explain to me what you're doing up this late? Don't you have to be at work in three hours?"

"Those aren't the clothes you went to work in."

"I brought a change for after the gym," Mrs. Hart said.

"You brought clothes for after the gym that are nicer than what you went to work in? Is that your story? Are you going to stick to that? I'm tired of this. The dogs are home. I think Fritz is out here too somewhere. I'm going to look for him."

Mrs. Hart walked past the two of them. She tried and failed to stand erect and walked like a zombie.

"That's a good boy," Mrs. Hart said to Ernie as she patted him too hard on the top of his head like a bongo player. "You're a good doggy, Ernie. You were always my favorite. I like you."

## CHAPTER TWENTY-TWO – LIFE IS A JUNG MAN'S GAME

Meanwhile, my wandering took me to the edge of town, beyond even the far side of the Trio-3 Screen Drive-In, to the North Grand City Industrial Train Depot where a dozen or so men tried to both work and stay awake. The ones who succeeded in their endeavor hadn't noticed the hobbling dog who passed through.

A loading area three train cars back from the end was void of any human activity. The ramp that led to the next-to-last car was still lowered down. I decided to open my eyes somewhere beyond Grand City for the first time in my life. No one saw me sneak onto the half-empty car. No one saw me find a spot to hide in between the crates, which were placed in the car with no apparent intent or design.

I found a spot in the corner and wanted to be asleep before the train awoke. I heard a shuffle and a thump like something else had jumped onto the train. I couldn't smell anything, but I felt a weight on me that told me I wasn't alone. Something followed me.

"Who's there?" I said, facing my shadow.

Just me.

"Who are you?" I said.

You know who I am, my shadow said.

"I'm getting real tired of playing these talking games that everyone else seems to enjoy. I ask a question, you answer. And you answer with a statement, not some other question asking me why I asked that or why I'd want an answer."

You're awfully testy.

"I've had a bad day."

No, you haven't.

"This has been the worst day of my life."

You learned something about yourself, right? How bad could it really have been then?

"There's no lesson in what I learned today."

I don't believe that for one second of one second.

"How can there be a second in a second?"

I don't know. You're giving yourself a headache here. Don't you have enough aches?

"You don't know anything about my aches."

I know that these aches of yours define every breathing moment of your life.

"Who asked you?" I said. I imagined what this shadow looked like – sagging face (especially below the jaw), bright spots of decay on the nose, fallen ears with a reaction time south of a molasses drip, faded fur sprinting from the nose to the eyes, broken teeth, a shrinking gum line, bony arms with nasty veins showing from paw to shoulder, hips with the stability of shattered glass, and a tail with all the efficiency of a frayed shoelace.

You asked me, my shadow said. I don't want to bother you, so if you want me to shut up all you have to do is just turn back around and do your best to pretend that I'm not here. In the meantime, I'll stick around and just get bigger. Should you ever want someone to talk to, I'll be here. Great plan you have going on, by the way.

"I don't have any plan," I said. "That's why I'm here."

Make no mistake, Fritz, not having a plan is no different than executing the most detailed course of action. Not having a plan *is* your plan. You may not know where you're running to, but as long as you run from something, that's good enough for you, am I right?

"Who says I'm running from anything?" I said.

I do. I knew that the moment I saw you. That's why I've been following you. If you're running toward something, there better be something you're running from. The farther and faster you run, the bigger I get.

"I've never seen you before."

But you know I've been there. You've just been too afraid to turn and face me.

"You're crazy."

Says the dog talking to a shadow. Whatever you say, pal.

"You have a better idea?"

It's not my place to have a better idea. You get on a train to ride the rails and find somewhere new, and I just happened to be in the same car as you.

"You wouldn't understand. I used to be something."

We all used to be something. So what? Some of us were cops. Some were firedogs. What's your point? You used to be a puppy. You used to be this. You used to be that. What are you now? That's the only thing you should be worrying about. So, what is it? What are you right now?

"I'm nothing. I'm an ex-cop with nothing else to live for. Everything I've been was ripped away from me, and there's nothing, not a thing, that I can ever do about that."

Is that it?

"I'm a broken and crippled dog with nothing left to offer anyone, not even myself."

And?

"You know if that ramp wasn't there, I wouldn't have been able to get into this car."

But here you are. Now what?

"There's only one thing left for me to be that I haven't been yet. The sooner that comes, the better."

What are you waiting for?

"Pardon me."

Get it over with. If there's only one thing left to do, do it. If you're nothing, it should be easy.

"You don't scare me."

I'm not trying to scare you. All I wanted was for you to realize that I'm here. If you want me to go, all you had to do is look at me. Since you've done that, I suppose it's time for me to get off this train. What do you think?

The car jerked, and I sprung back to my feet. It crawled along the tracks as the engine sputtered to life. I didn't want to sit down anymore. I walked over to the side of the car and looked out. Grand City slept in the distance. I had to be there when she woke up. I had to.

I backed myself against the cold railing on the opposite side of the car. My chest rippled with anxiety. The final train whistle blew, and the engine rumbled through the floor into my feet. The rumbling shook me loose. My legs pushed away from the rail and off I ran toward that opening in the train car. The light reflected into the car as we passed a blank screen at the drive-in. My shadow was gone. I sprinted toward the moonlight that beamed through the door. I jumped.

Everything was beautiful. I looked down and saw myself glide above the ground as the moon's spotlight blurred everything around me. There was nothing except me. I was in the air and was something greater than a dog who jumped from a moving train. I couldn't feel anything on my body. Not the air on my hanging tongue. Not my ears pressed down along my head. Not my tail perfectly aligned with my spine. Not my outstretched arms reaching for everything. And certainly not my wonderfully damaged leg.

I took a breath through my nose, and it was the greatest air ever inhaled. It was air created for only me, as if it knew to be there and to wait for me until I needed it more than anything else in the world. It washed my lungs and inflated my body as the train ricocheted behind me, stabbing through the still night.

I landed hard on the ground into a patch of grass and soft dirt. I exhaled every bit of that magical breath. The flashing light from the last train car turned off toward the mountains. A slight breeze caressed my extended ears. Air reentered my nose like data entry, and everything shifted back into crystal focus. I felt my body again. My face was warm and healthy. My arms, embedded into the ground, pulled themselves free. My chest and ribs expanded with plain old air like they always had. My tail hovered above the ground, ready to guide me back to life. My leg waited for me to buckle under the pain. It hurt. I won't pretend it didn't, but I stood there in the darkness, and I was going to keep it that way. I'd be damned if the pain didn't respect me. If it was a fight that the pain wanted, I would be thrilled to oblige.

If you listen to enough advice, you'll inevitably hear that you have to live like it's your last day. I'm telling you right now, that is the single biggest line of nonsense ever uttered. Living everyday like it's your last is how you wind up on a train headed to nowhere.

I shook my leg out to let it know that I knew it was still there but that I had other things to concern myself with. I had no idea where I would end up at the end of this, but when I finally rested, it was going to be at home.

# Chapter Twenty-Three – The Lady in the Back Yard

The sun was up by the time I returned to Officer Hart's house. I took cover behind the boat in their neighbor's driveway. Mrs. Hart flung the front door to the house open with a swollen duffle bag in each hand. She tossed both bags in the back of the Intimidator and slammed the trunk closed with the fury of a game show contestant spinning the big wheel. She adjusted her sleek dark dress and pushed her hair down. She grabbed a cigarette from her purse that hung high off her shoulder. She lit the thing and took an obnoxiously long drag off the stick, savoring as she held her breath. Mrs. Hart exhaled and wiped the smoke away from her face.

Simon came out of the house and looked the best I'd ever seen him. His shirt was clean and tucked in.

"I told you to leave the game in the house," Mrs. Hart said as she snuck another quick, concealed puff.

"But it's just for the car ride," Simon said. "I won't bring it inside. I promise."

"I told you no," she said, with an exhale that she wanted to enjoy more than she did. "We're only going to be in the car for fifteen minutes."

"*Fifteen?* That's forever. Please, Mom. That's like half of a whole cartoon. Come on." She ignored him and dropped the partially finished cigarette under the front tire. She drove the point of her heel through the lit end like a corkscrew and took out two pieces of gum from her purse. "Can I have a piece of–"

"No. Not in the car."

"Come on–"

"I'm tired of cleaning your gum off the seats. This car is worth a lot of money, and every time you do that, it ruins the value."

"Okay, Mom. Sorry."

She revved the engine and honked the horn, which startled a sulking Simon. After a second series of honks, Officer Hart came out of the house looking great from the neck down in a light suit. From the neck up, he was a wreck.

He held Missy in an oblong crate in his left hand. His right hand pleaded with Mrs. Hart to calm down while he locked the front door. Missy spun inside the crate and forced Officer Hart to carry it with both hands as he placed her in the back seat next to Simon. A crate within a crate.

They drove away southbound from the house. As they curved out of sight I walked over to the fence to the back yard. I looked in through a break in the fence posts. Nipper and Ernie sat and ate at their bowls.

"Was it just me," Ernie said, "or do they seem particularly more mad at us than usual?"

"It's not just you," Nipper said.

"How long you think it'll last?"

"Hard to say. We've never done anything this bad, she said. Which, come to think of it, what did we do that was so awful anyway? Okay, sure, we shouldn't have escaped, but we came home."

"We didn't all come home," Ernie said.

"And whose fault was that?" Nipper said.

"Maybe they're mad because Fritz didn't come home? She didn't seem to care, but he didn't sleep last night. He was up watching the TV and just pacing across the house. He was even punching the air a few times, and then it looked like he was crying. He's probably worried about Fritz."

"He'll get over it," Nipper said. "You heard the kid. He was hoping we'd not come back so he could get a rhino in the yard."

"Nipper, you smell something?" Ernie said.

"Just a fresh meal. I know we weren't gone long, but man, you miss the simple things."

"No, not the food. Hey, where do you think Fritz went? You think he's gonna get that dog?"

"He had his chance, Ernie. Remember? As in yesterday? No, I don't think so, and no, I don't have the faintest clue as to where he's headed or where he went. Sorry."

"I don't get why you don't like him so much."

"You're right. I didn't like him when he first got here. This is our home, and he just shows up and expected us to welcome him because he's some cop. But then I trusted him and went along with his ridiculous plan because I could see how important it was to him, and you liked him, and I didn't want to lose you as my friend, so I played along with his scheme. Then what happened? He left us high and dry, Ernie. Strung us up and threw us to the wolves. And you know what, yeah, I did start to like him, but he went his way, and we went ours. There's nothing we can do about that now."

"Hey," I mumbled through the fence.

"It's weird, though," Ernie said. "It's like I can still feel him. Like he's here."

"Ernie," I said.

"Like I can hear him. I can still hear his voice, calling out to me."

"You're crazy," Nipper said. "Wait a second, I heard him too. Ernie, I think your strangeness is finally rubbing off on me. Or maybe we're just famished and hallucinating."

"Hey!" I said.

"Fritz?" Ernie said as he stepped toward the fence.

"It's me," I said.

"I knew that was your scent," Ernie said. "What're you doing here? You come back home?"

"Not yet. We still have a case to put on these dogs, and I can't do it without you guys."

"No dice," Nipper said. "I'm done playing your games."

"You better watch out," Ernie said as he pushed his face right up to the fence to sniff my nose, then he tilted his head sideways and put his eye and all its darting lines across it up to the fence. "They're going to see you standing out there."

"They just left," I said. "This is our chance to get out of here."

"Did you ever think that maybe we don't want to leave this time?" Nipper said.

"I want to go," Ernie said.

"That's because you always want to go," Nipper said. "Nothing's ever good enough for you, Ernie. We've got it all here. Food, water, when it rains we can go inside, they pamper us with toys and treats, and on their holidays we get the leftovers."

"And it's boring!" Ernie said, with more passion and fury than I'd ever heard from him. "It's the same thing around here every day. You get up, you walk around, you take a nap, you eat the same food from the same bowl, the exact same little dry chunks of food, you can't get a good run here, you get to *play* with the little spazz from inside, which to him playing means hitting you and throwing robot parts at you and then him wondering why you don't feel like chasing them. If you do anything fun like dig or bark or try to climb the wall, you get yelled at, so sorry if that sounds like the good life to you, Nipper, but to me it sounds like a life spent wasted. I agree, we're safe here, but it's way more fun out there."

"I didn't know you feel that way," Nipper said.

"I do, and I can't help it," Ernie said.

"So, what are you going to do about it?" I said.

"I'm out of here," Ernie said as he flickered between the fence posts and went to the front corner of the fence that separated Officer Hart's yard from the neighbor's. The fence gently wiggled in front of me. Ernie cursed and barked and kicked the fence.

"He fixed it?" Ernie said. "That plank has been broken ever since I've been here, and he picks *now* to fix it? Did you know about this, Nipper?"

"I didn't even know the fence was broke to begin with," Nipper said.

"How do you think I'd get out to visit Saucy all those times when you were sleeping?"

"Ummm, because I was sleeping."

"Nipper, we have to go with Fritz. Whether you want to or not. They came here looking for us. They're gonna come back."

"Who came here?" I said.

"Your friend and his racing dog," Nipper said. "They were waiting for us, or they followed us, or I don't know, but they showed up out of nowhere last night and he came out from inside and hosed them off and they disappeared."

"Is this for real with you now, Fritz?" Ernie said.

"It is," I said. "It's my fault that the two of you were in danger. And I'm going to fix that. I've never been in the habit of putting my friends in harm's way. I'm not starting now. We're ending this."

"Stand back," Ernie said as his voice echoed back to the other end of the yard. I moved to the side and lost peripheral vision on Ernie through the breaks in the fence posts. After a couple of deep breaths, Ernie's paws slammed into the ground as he hurled himself toward the fence. Nipper shouted as the impact of Ernie crashing into the fence split the air. Shards of wood blasted into the front yard while Ernie pulled the rest of his body through the hole made by his shoulder and skull. As Ernie climbed through the hole, he pushed out the rest of the broken fencing.

"Whew," Ernie said as he shook himself off. "My head's spinning a little bit."

Nipper stood at the opening in the fence and looked at us on the other side of the smashed fence. He knew Ernie just gave him no choice.

"You coming?" I said. "Ernie did the hard work. It's plenty large enough for you to walk through. It's up to you, Nipper."

I expected another righteously indignant speech from Nipper. I expected more coaxing from Ernie. But there was none of that. No hyper-dramatic moment of *should I or shouldn't I*, no trepidation in his face, and no inner monologue as far as I could see.

"Let's go," Nipper said. He walked through the hole Ernie made in the fence, even breaking off a piece of fencing that wasn't necessarily in his way. "It is more fun out here."

"Wait a second," I said as we escaped out of the maze of homes. "You had a way of out there the whole time I was here?"

"Yeah," Ernie said.

"Why didn't you tell me?" I said. "It would've been a lot easier than escaping from the park."

"Yeah. It would have, Ernie," Nipper said. "Would have been a lot easier. On all of us."

"But how much fun would that have been?" Ernie said. "I thought your plan sounded cool. Besides, I didn't think I'd ever have gotten Nipper to just sneak out through the fence."

"You're probably right about that," Nipper said.

We navigated our way out of the neighborhood at a brisk pace, not quite an all-out run, but we weren't dragging our cans either.

"So where were you?" Ernie said.

"It doesn't matter," I said.

"Come on," Ernie said.

"I was on a train talking to my shadow. I finally faced it, and it went away. Then the train started to move, so I went to one end of the car, and I jumped off when the train was going. I flew through the air and walked all night back here."

"Okay," Ernie said. "I get it. Yeah, and I was driving a car too. A real nice one. Power steering with the top down and music blasting. You're right. I guess it doesn't matter."

We were a block away from the main street out of the neighborhood when Ernie abruptly turned right and sprinted toward a nondescript single-story residence on the corner.

"One condition for all of this," Ernie said as he stopped behind the house. "Saucy comes with us. And don't even think about giving me the 'It's too dangerous' speech or a 'we don't have time for this.' If I'm going to risk the worst trouble I can think of back home by wrecking their fence, and you know what I'm talking about, I'm making sure she comes with me."

Nipper and I stayed on the sidewalk and watched Ernie try to jump up onto the wall to get her attention. We tried not to listen while he pleaded with her and explained how he ran headfirst through the fence to get here. Ernie didn't bust through that fence just to escape the humdrum life of the backyard. He didn't do it to go on some quest with me. He was going make sure that there was never anything that would keep him away from being able to see Saucy whenever he felt like it.

We watched his head fall between his arms while he was up on his hind legs against the wall. He looked like he would push that wall over if he could. We tried not to stare while the kick in his step vanished like a gust of wind stealing a napkin from a picnic table.

"She's not coming," he said as he returned to us. "She has to go with Scarlet to the dog show today. She always gets in these lousy moods whenever they all go to those stupid things. Scarlet this and Scarlet that. Scarlet is supposed to be so pretty, and no offense to you dogs, but I just don't see it. I can see where others might think she's pretty, but she doesn't do it for me. I try to tell Saucy that, but she never listens to me. So, now great, I break down the fence, they'll probably *fix* me when we get home. I've heard horror stories of dogs getting fixed for far less. And for what? Saucy can't come with us, and then she says that even if she could get away, she doesn't know if she'd want to in the first place."

"I'm sorry," Nipper said.

Scarlet was led out of the house on a sparkling leash by a lopsided buoy of a human female in an ill-fitting dress. She continued to brush Scarlet on their way to a tiny car that didn't look much bigger than one of Simon's toys. She let Scarlet in the front seat of the car and buckled her in.

"Saucy!" the buoy hollered back toward the house. "Let's go. We can't be late for your sister's coronation. Isn't that right my Scarlet-sparlett-barlett-darlett-garlett? She is the most precious little doggie there ever was, isn't she, Scarlet-pooh-pooh-pooh-pooh? Saw-see!!!"

Saucy appeared and got into the car from the driver's side and lay down in the back seat. No seat belt or sing-song for her. The car turned on with barely a sound, and they pulled away.

"So?" Nipper said.

"Whatever," Ernie said. "Now what?"

"There's only one thing we can do that makes any sense," I said. "We're going to that dog show, Ernie."

# CHAPTER TWENTY-FOUR – THE 34TH ANNUAL GRAND CITY DOG SHOW

The Grand City Knights were the lousiest team to ever play pro basketball. That didn't stop the city council from passing City Amendment CFDR 234.5a, a local tax increase that paid for the construction of the Grand City Sports Arena, a decision that cost every councilman their job over the course of the following two election cycles. As one of the first expansion teams in the early days of professional basketball, Grand City assumed the position of league punching bag. It was a role we didn't relinquish until the team moved five states east, where they found a new town, a new name, and a new mascot. The team remained terrible and still is now, but at least they're someone else's problem.

The arena, however, remained an eyesore and a problem for Grand City. A night working an event at the arena meant a night of sniffing burnouts who stunk like rotten foliage from cheap drugs at some concert for a second-rate band who hadn't recorded a hit in decades and were too old to play anywhere better. Or so said the officers I worked with.

It was either that or tamer affairs such as the Grand City Dog Show. A place for the high-society types to use us as a proxy to show off how posh they were for a panel of human judges. For years, I was forced to make appearances at this side show and to take walks around the indoor carpeted track between show rounds when people went to the bathroom and got nachos. It amazed me how many people showed up every year to watch this thing, to watch some moron like a papillon win *Best in Show.* Some prize. These people wouldn't know a real dog from a comic book character.

The parking lot was packed by the time we made it to the arena. We needed to hurry to be able to sneak in unnoticed. Ernie was nearly plowed over by a speeding sedan as it claimed one of the few remaining parking spots. Ernie barked obscenities, and the driver barked back at him. Three aisles over, Officer Hart held Simon's hand as they walked toward the arena. Mrs. Hart and Missy were nowhere to be seen. Simon looked back over his shoulder, and we made eye contact. Shoot.

Simon's face lit up, and he pulled away from Officer Hart.

"I said I would buy you ice cream once we sat down," Officer Hart said, "so stop fussing, Simon. Or maybe you don't want ice cream?"

"Dad, I–"

"We have to hurry," Officer Hart said. "If your mom looks up and doesn't see us, I'm never going to hear the end of it."

"Fritz," Simon said. "It's Fritz!"

I dove behind a car and crashed into Nipper and Ernie as I knocked them out of sight.

"Again?" Ernie said. "Do eyes just stop working at this place? I'm trying to walk."

I poked out just far enough from behind the car to watch Officer Hart turn back toward the arena as he dragged Simon away. I reemerged from the car and stared at that little cretin who kept trying to turn his head back. When our eyes met once more, I rearranged my face into the most frightening concoction I could. I showed him every tooth I had and puffed out my fur as far I could. He didn't look back again. That felt good.

The three of us were then free to make our way to the service entrance. Inside, all the show dogs and their human partners prepared themselves to get ready for the big event.

We walked by the staging area where all the sporting breeds were stationed and waited on their introductions to proceed down to the floor area. The humans were trying to sneak in last-minute brushes and wipe downs. One man in an ill-fitting suit with pants just a smidgen too high over a pair of not quite running, but not quite dress, shoes, used a toothpick on his cocker spaniel. The dog looked to be enjoying the tooth picking more than he should have because that is the sole jurisdiction of one's own tongue.

"Get out of the way," a thin man with plastic-looking hair said as he shoved Ernie out of the way so he could lead a golden retriever in severe need of a haircut out into the arena.

"That's it," Ernie said, then stopped and addressed the rest of the dogs waiting in line. "I've already had enough of this place. You know, you types have never impressed me, trying to play dress up with the humans and those stupid leashes up under your chin that you know aren't comfortable. You all make me sick, you know that? Were you ever real dogs, or have you always been some human's toy, huh? Not me. I'm a real dog. I bite things. I bark. I mark on whatever I want, whenever I want to. I'll do it right now if I want. No one's claimed that table. I'll do it, and no one will stop me. Look at you, a bunch of sheep from where I'm at, right Nipper? Tell 'um. Baaa-aaa-aaah. Baaa-aaa-aaa-aaah. What are you gonna do about it? Nothing. You gonna shut me up? Nope, and I'll tell you why. You don't want to lose your spot in line to try and win the approval of strangers. Worse than that, you wouldn't want to disobey your masters, would you?"

"Whose dog is this that won't shut up?" a square-shaped lady said as she led a Labrador by. "He's really starting to upset my dog. Someone needs to get him on a leash."

"Whew," Ernie said as I pulled him away from the crowd of people, a crowd that, while self-absorbed in their worlds, took notice of the portly mutt with the broken teeth who lectured them. "I needed that. I just let them have it, you know? I don't even know where that came from. It just erupted from me like I couldn't control myself."

"I'm glad you had that therapeutic moment," I said, "but we came here to get Saucy, and that's not going to happen if we get tossed out."

"I never thought you were the smartest dog in the world, Ernie," a voice said from behind us. Saucy found us. Ernie's posture immediately slumped. "But I didn't think you were this stupid. I figured *you* would know better, Fritz. What are you three doing here?"

"I came to get you," Ernie said.

"I thought I made myself clear," Saucy said. "You guys should go off on whatever quest you're on now."

"We're back on the same quest," Ernie said. "I'm not going without you. I already told them either you come with me or I don't go, and I can't really go back home right now because they're going to be mad at me because I, kind of, pretty much, ran through their fence."

"You really ran *through* the fence?" Saucy said. "I thought you were exaggerating."

"I really did," Ernie said. "I have the hallucinations to prove it."

"Just to come get me?" Saucy said.

"Pretty much."

"Ernie, I can't disappear right now. I came here with Scarlet. Eventually they're going to realize that I'm not around. I'm supposed to be scouting the competition for her. If I'm not back pretty soon, she's going to throw a fit, so I don't know what to tell you."

"I guess we're staying here then," Ernie said. "Don't worry, we'll play it cool. I won't make a scene. No one will know we're here."

We stayed a few yards behind Saucy as we blended back into the crowd of dogs, show officials, arena staff, and other frantic humans. The echo of all the footsteps in clunky shoes slapping the linoleum gave me a headache. We rounded a corner, and I picked up a familiar scent. Within moments, I'd placed it. The Perp from that night in the alley.

I salivated as my jaw crept open. I knew that he was nearby. It had to be him. I was certain, even in the sea of hair and fur products, colognes, and perfumes. And if The Perp was there, I had a decent suspicion of who else was not far behind. I didn't say anything to Nipper or Ernie, and I pulled several steps away from them to the outside of the crowd to scan for anything suspicious. Saucy told Nipper and Ernie to stay away while she went back to report to Scarlet.

There The Perp was. He stood between Scarlet and was talking to Saucy and Scarlet's human. A leash dangled off his wrist and led directly around the neck of Scamper, primped, proper, and with a phony smile plastered on his face.

"Who's that with Scarlet?" Ernie said as I got as close as I could to The Perp without Scamper noticing me. I kept my tail to the wall to prevent a sneak attack.

"You have a lovely dog there," The Perp said. "I'm sorry, I didn't get your name, Missus?"

"It's Sheena," she said. "And it's Miss."

"I didn't want to be forward," The Perp said as he set Scamper down on the ground. "And this is Scamper. It's his first time competing, so I'm just hoping he doesn't make a fool out of me. I think I'm more nervous than he is."

"He looks frisky," Sheena said.

Saucy nudged Scarlet, who tried to shake off the touch.

"Well?" Scarlet said. "Is there anyone here for me to be concerned with?"

"Who's this?" Saucy said, referring to Scamper.

"I don't know," Scarlet said. "Looks like an amateur entry."

"Excuse me?" Scamper said as The Perp grabbed a crate from a nearby table and stepped closer to Sheena and Scarlet. "I can guarantee you'll eat those words before this day is over. And she calls me an amateur...Lady, if you only knew what was going on right now, right in front of your pretty little face."

"Just be glad we're not in the same category," Scarlet said. "I've made a career of making pups like you look foolish on the big stage."

"I swear I hate every single dog at these things," Saucy said.

"Look at you, Miss Always-the-Bridesmaid," Scamper said. "With looks like yours, I'd work on that personality if I were you."

I crept closer. Saucy had provided me with an excellent cover. I scanned the floor again, and there was no Clay in the immediate area. For all I knew, he was watching me in plain sight. If he was, would he have let me get within striking range of The Perp and Scamper? He wouldn't.

"Come to think of it," Scamper said, "we could definitely use a dog like you too. I bet you think you're a lot tougher than you really are. In fact, I think it's safe to say you're a triple threat. No looks, that's without question, no personality, that's apparent, and I'd be willing to wager that the brain in that wooden skull of yours has the street value of a sack of wet cement."

"That's enough!" Ernie said as he came out of hiding and towered over Scamper. "Sorry, Saucy, I know you said to lay low, but I've never been good at sitting around watching my friends get treated like that. Especially by a scumbag like this dog."

"Look who it is," Scamper said. "Where's your goofball buddy?"

"I'm right here," Nipper said as he appeared next to Ernie.

"Well, what do you know?" Scamper said. "Sometimes, fate has a funny way of working in your favor."

"For no personality," Saucy said, "I sure have a lot of friends."

"It looks like you have a whopping two friends, so my assessment of your personality stands. Two more that we could use as live meat."

"Make it three," I said, growling. Scamper turned to me. We had him surrounded. "Lay down, and keep your mouth shut." Scamper slowly nodded and nervously lay down. None of us moved. Sheena looked down and noted how well behaved Scamper was.

"Cllllllaaaaaaaaaaaaaaaaaaayyyyyyyyyyyyyy!!!!!!" Scamper said, suddenly barking with every breath in his lungs, ending the sweet moment of his silence. The Perp shoved Sheena with both hands while holding the crate. She tumbled over some chairs and landed with a flop. The Perp wrapped his arms around Scarlet and forced her into the crate. Scarlet tried to fight it, but The Perp violently shoved her in head first. Too many people swarmed to the scene to take pictures and videos with their phones for me to attack The Perp. I couldn't jump in, jaws wide open, into a human salad.

Scamper bit Ernie in the face. A stream of blood fell from Ernie's eye. The Perp ran toward the nearest exit. He carried Scarlet in the crate and barreled through anyone who stood in his path. Scamper escaped through the crowd. He darted between anyone's legs he could trip up. Nipper, Ernie, and Saucy took off after him. I went to cut off The Perp at the exit. Nobody tried to help apprehend The Perp, even as Sheena screamed that he had her baby. They shielded their prized dogs and got out of his way.

Then Clay found me. He cut me off out of nowhere.

"Look who decided to show up again," Clay said as he took a seat in front of me.

"Where's he taking her?" I said.

"Ah, now that is the question," Clay said, "is it not, Fritz? Quite the quandary this poses to you, doesn't it? Do you do the right thing and try to save her? I say *try* because there's no way I let that happen. Or do you let her go and instead try, and fail one more time, to get that revenge on me? While you decide that, he'll get away with her, and the scene around us will calm down, and the area will be quickly surrounded by your former employers, which then provides us with a less than ideal combat setting. So, if you're going to attack me, get it over with while no one is paying any attention to us."

He sat there with a grin on his face and wagged his stump of a tail. It was the first time I got a good look at his face in the light. I saw the spots in the fur by his nose and at the corner of his eyes. His eyes weren't cold and empty of feeling. They were old like mine. Their life of intimidation took a toll on them, and they just wanted to blink. Clay sat slightly off to one side, and his head hunched forward. The skin on his chest was loose, and his jowls hung low and were bloated. His arms and legs were still bigger than mine, but I could tell they weren't as big as they once were. His whiskers weren't steel rods that shined in the moonlight; they were no different than my aging set.

Clay wasn't a monster. He was once a puppy who fought with the other pups to nurse from mommy. He was once an anonymous member of a litter who stumbled over feet too big for his little body. There was a time when his fur was soft, too short, and puffed out over thin bones instead of laying flat on well-maintained muscles. I saw that dog plain as day, and it allowed me to see exactly who Clay was – another dog, just like me. I smiled at Clay, and he didn't know what to say. If I had to, I could kill him.

"Clay!" The Perp said, over the swarm of people, as he neared the service entrance with Nipper, Ernie, and Saucy in tow. "Come!"

"Sorry, Fritz," Clay said. "A good soldier follows his orders, but please feel free to try to catch us. In fact, I'd love it if you did. It'd be my pleasure for you to see what he does with that beauty queen. If we're lucky, we'll get to do it to you and your little cadets there too."

He sprung to his paws and rumbled his way through the people who were all too quick to get out of the way of a barking Rottweiler. Instead of heading toward The Perp, Clay raced toward the arena floor. I hoped Clay didn't think that I wouldn't chase him through an ongoing dog show. He turned left and went through the tunnel and into the middle of the show. He knocked over a cotton-candy vendor who was taking a break. I vaulted the vendor and gained ground on Clay while running on the artificial turf.

"I got to be honest with you," a voice from the other side of the turf said, "we've never had a K-9 officer quite like Nitro. He's smart, he's very fast and obedient, and was the top dog in his class. We're pleased as punch to have him on the force. He's the best dog I've ever had the pleasure of working with."

Nitro turned away from the camera as Clay sprinted by them toward the other exit off the floor. Nitro's partner kept talking to the camera. I couldn't help myself.

"How's it going, Nitro?" I said as I stopped and stood next to him.

"Tell me this isn't happening," Nitro said.

"Sorry," I said. "It is."

"I am on camera right now at this moment."

"Technically," I said. "*We're* on camera at this moment."

"What are you doing here?" Nitro said.

"Remember that night in the alley with The Perp and the Rottweiler and the night you took credit for my scent? That night? That dog that just ran through the show here? That's him. And, oh yeah, The Perp from that night, yeah, he's here too. While you're busy doing your whole press thing here, I'm gonna go get them both. Just thought you'd like to know that. See ya around." Clay disappeared off the floor, but I knew where he was headed. "Nitro, one last thing and then I'll leave you alone. They like it when you bark at the end of the interview. Just once, though. It makes them think that you're talking to them and that you really like them. Gotta run."

And I did. I lost sight of Clay, but his scent was still in the air. I slowed down and followed it out of the sports arena. I circled the perimeter and caught up with Nipper and Ernie at the north side of the arena as they chased a fading trail of burnt rubber toward the exit.

"Wait," I said.

"We're losing 'em, Fritz," Nipper said.

"They took Scarlet," Saucy said.

"I know," I said. "I know. Just hold on. We're not going to chase down a car, so everyone just catch their breath and calm down."

"Clay got in the car too," Ernie said, panting. "They threw Scarlet in the trunk."

"We have to go rescue Scarlet," Saucy said. "We're not going to do it standing here. You let them get away."

"No he didn't," Ernie said. "How many times have you ever outrun a car, Saucy?"

"Never," Saucy said. "But if there was going to be a first time, that was it, and he tells us to stop? No wonder you guys can't stand him."

Concerned humans and arena security guards came out of the arena with serious looks on their faces that poorly complemented a complete and total lack of any idea of what they were supposed to be doing or looking for. The fattest one of the bunch ordered the others to look for a guy carrying a dog.

"At a dog show?" a less fat one said. "That could be anyone."

"Everyone just take a deep breath," I said as I closed my eyes and drew in a deep inhale like I was trying to sandblast my lungs. The others didn't follow my lead. Ernie was nervous because Saucy was anxious. Nipper looked around and expected us to get caught at any moment. "Trust me. Do it. What do you smell? You smell that, don't you, Saucy? That musky stench of dead fish and salt. Come on, how about you, Ernie? You smelling that?"

"I smell pigeons," Ernie said, after a quick sniff. "Filthy scavengers. They always get the good stuff from the dumpsters."

"I smell gasoline," Nipper said. "And rust."

"This is what is putting you in such a good mood?" Saucy said.

"Sure does," I said. "Because you know what that all smells like, don't you?"

"The docks!" Ernie said. "That's where they're going with Scarlet."

"We can see them from here," Nipper said.

"So, what are we waiting for?" Saucy said.

"My thoughts exactly, young lady," I said.

We followed the scent, but we didn't need to. The cranes and cargo holds from the Grand City Docks could be seen poking out over the Grand City Arena. From afar, it looked like the arena was a massive baby spider, with the circular dome in the center and the tentacles of the docks sticking out of the top.

I know what you're saying right about now. "Look, Fritz, you expect us to believe that you three went to the dog show and that Clay, Scamper, *and* The Perp from the beginning of the story were all there? Not only that, Nitro managed to make an appearance? Come on, how gullible do you think we are?

And then, to make matters worse, the docks were only a quick jog away?"

I'm telling you, they were there, and I dare you to procure a copy of any Grand City map you can find; the evidence will be right there in front of you. Go ahead and accuse me of stretching things to make it all fit together, but the truth is the truth, as much as we all wish it wasn't sometimes.

# Chapter Twenty-Five – The Docks

Parking lot 3f at the dockyard was nearly empty. The security booth was locked and unmanned. The guard arm was up in the *come on through, we're not charging for parking today* position. A few tow trucks hugged the fence. A couple of dented limos with "For Rent" decals and several coats of dirt stretched out sporadically. The only car I was interested in was the fifteen-year-old sports car closest to the pier entrance. The one that smelled of burnt gas and had a fresh pair of skid marks coming from the rear tires.

"I have Scarlet's scent," Saucy said as we stood next to the vehicle. "They can't be far from here."

She was right. I picked up Clay's scent along with The Perp's. I looked down the dock and couldn't see anything besides makeshift offices and stacks of cargo crates large enough to hold a dozen Intimidators.

"Disgusting," Nipper said as he looked down at the caked pigeon droppings that stained the cement.

"We should split up," I said.

"I thought that wasn't a good idea," Nipper said, very quickly.

"They could be anywhere around here," Ernie said.

"We'll cover more ground if we go in teams of two," I said. "Nipper, you and I will start that way toward the pier. Ernie and Saucy, why don't you two take a look around the warehouses. See if you can get inside and look around."

"Easy," Ernie said. "There's not a door made that me and Saucy can't find a way around."

"I can go with them," Nipper said with a jitter in his voice.

"Why?" Saucy said. "The teams aren't fair with a girl on one side?"

"This isn't a game," I said. "The dogs and person we're after are serious. They're not playing around. If they've taken Scarlet for the reason I think they have, none of them will think twice about permanently stopping another dog who gets in their way. Those are the stakes, so if anyone here wants to go back, this is your chance. No one, especially not me, is going to think anything different of you. Ernie?"

"I'm in, Fritz," Ernie said.

"Saucy?" I said. She looked like my speech ruffled her. That's what I wanted. They needed to know what they were about to get themselves into.

"I got your back," Ernie said as he brushed up against her. "I would never let anyone, person or dog, hurt you."

"Okay," Saucy said, "Me too. I'm in."

"Nipper?" I said.

"You want me to go with you, Fritz?"

"That's my plan."

"I'm ready," Nipper said.

"All right then," I said, feeling more like a coach than a cop. "I want you two to lay low, stay hidden, quiet, and keep your ears and noses open. If you see Clay or The Perp, don't engage them. If you find them, double back to get me and Nipper."

"What if we find Scamper?" Ernie said.

"If he's by himself?" I said. "Then do what you have to do. Come on, it's getting dark."

"I'll see you soon, Ernie," Nipper said. "Good luck."

Nipper and I went toward the piers and Ernie and Saucy vanished into a sea of cargo holds. I kept a few paces ahead of Nipper.

"You want to know what my first memory of anything is?" Nipper said, not giving me a chance to answer. "I remember living somewhere that was hot and dry all day, and it stayed hot late into the evening. They kept a whole bunch of us in the kitchen, fenced in with each other. I don't remember how many of us there were, but enough to feel cramped and enough to where the only place for me to sleep was under the lip that came out from the cabinet in the corner next to the little dark thing they stick onto the floor to trap the baby roaches. At first, I was there with my two brothers and three sisters. I woke up one morning and my sisters were gone. A day later, a brother was gone. Pretty soon, I was the only one left from my family.

"And it's not that they were just disappearing or something. Sure, that's what I thought the first day when I woke up and the place was empty except for the food bowl and the flies trying to pick at your ears. Then a new batch of fresh German shepherds, who could barely open their eyes yet, was dropped off. Every day, people were there standing on the other side of that thin wooden gate. They looked very serious and pointed at us. The new ones would all run to the gate and jump up, pushing each other and biting at each others' tails. Someone would point at one of us, the people would shake hands, disappear, and a few minutes later the pointed-at puppy was scooped up, placed in a crate, and never heard from again.

"After a few times of this, I stopped going up to the gate when some random human showed up. That's when I'd go eat; when no one was watching me. You learn not to talk to anyone and to not waste time making friends because there's a better than average chance that before your next meal that friend, your new acquaintance, was getting scooped up.

"Eventually, I was the biggest one left. Not that I was big or anything, but you get what I'm saying. I thought that'd give me an advantage and that it was finally my time to get called up to the big leagues. I was getting tired of living on a kitchen floor. I got to be able to understand them better when the men would discuss and analyze us, and there it was, blurted out of thin air like the flush of a toilet.

"'What's with the big one?' a prospective buyer said.

"'He's not a pure breed,' the puppy purveyor said.

"'Good luck with him. No wonder no one's taken him.'

"I don't remember how much longer after that, but one day I look up and a lady who smelled nice was reaching over the top of the gate to scratch my ears. I knew she wasn't going to pick me, so I bit her. She thought it was funny and scratched my face, so I bit her again. She still thought it was funny and kept scratching, so I licked where I'd bitten her. She said she wanted to call me Nipper and put her fingers near my mouth so I could bite them again while she laughed at me.

"'I want the big one,' Mrs. Hart said. 'The big one is my favorite.'

"At last, Fritz, I was the best. It was my turn. I was floating as they opened the gate for me. They opened it for me; first time that had ever happened. The others all got picked up, but I was walking out on my own paws. I went with them as Officer Hart signed the papers.

"'Glad to see him go,' the man said. 'I was afraid I was going to have to give him away for free pretty soon.'

"Officer Hart joked about coming back in a week for a cheaper price on me. I think that if Mrs. Hart hadn't smacked him in the back that he may have considered it. Officer Hart said that he knew he was getting a good deal, the police discount. And that's my first memory, realizing that I'm everyone's last pick. Even then, I was a joke. My name is one big joke. Every time I hear it, that's what I think."

"I didn't have a choice either," I said as the film from the restless ocean mist slapped into the pier. The residue splashed up on my paws and made my claws itch. "I wasn't picked out of your kitchen, but from the moment I was born this has been all I've ever known. This is it. Right now. Tracking down people who don't deserve their freedom anymore. I chase, and I hunt, and no one gets away. All I know is that right now, Nipper, you and me, we're alive, and we're hunting. We're alive right now in this moment, and that's what I'm hanging on to."

"You could have taken Ernie instead of me. I understand. I would have taken Ernie if I was you. We're gonna find him. We're going to face Clay, aren't we?"

"Yes we are, Nipper. This is going to end today. It'll be okay. Trust me. I want to explain something to you. There's a reason why you don't cross paths with retired police dogs. Once that job's gone, that's it. There are no golden years. There is no sunset to walk into. No time to relax. It ends. I don't know why, but I know that everything goes black and one day you don't wake up. It was happening to me. You want to know why I didn't do anything at the track when I had the chance? Because I didn't want it to be over. I was afraid that when we were done that, sure, you and Ernie would go back to the backyard and have a great life, but for me, that would have been the end. That's what happens to police dogs. We are the job, and when that job is gone so are we."

"Then what are we doing here?" Nipper said. "Let's go home. It doesn't have to end."

"I can't. This is who I am. I'm going to be alive for as long as I can. This is the only way I know how to. And when this is over and we get them and we get Scarlet back, I don't know what'll happen, but I'm not afraid anymore. I'll worry about the future some other time."

"I'm sorry, Fritz. I would've made a lousy cop."

"Nipper, this isn't a training exercise in the backyard. We're playing for keeps. I wouldn't have brought you with me if I didn't think you had the bankroll to play the game."

"Aw, I love me a mixed metaphor," a voice I knew to be Clay's said as it clung to the shadows. "How touching. How sweet. The only way to show affection is to mask it with some human talk. Me, I don't mix my messages. I'm about to bury a few dogs at sea."

"Where are you?" I said.

"I'm here," Clay said as his voice bounced off the cargo trailers, skimmed off the water, and hung in the air over us like puffs of smoke. "I'm there. I'm everywhere, Fritz. Wherever there's a dog begging to be mauled, I'll be there too."

"Show yourself," I said.

"I don't know, Fritz. Looks like you have me outnumbered. Maybe I'll just keep you distracted while my accomplice gets away with your little girlfriend."

"Scarlet!" Nipper said. "Where is she?"

"Don't worry about where she is," Clay said. "It's where she's going that's the real treat. I wouldn't know from personal experience, but I have it on good word that fighting dogs love it when they get to practice on a pretty little thing like her. Relax, hero. Sometimes the practice dogs make it through a training session alive. The only problem is that you're not going to recognize her after the fact, unless earless, tailless, missing a paw or two, and plenty of facial scars is your thing. Eyes are probably going to be gone too, but hey, whatever floats your boat, I say."

Suddenly, The Perp emerged from the shadows, still holding Scarlet in a crate. He swung her like a purse and took off through the maze of cargo containers. We ignored Clay's voice and went to pursue The Perp. Clay stepped out from behind a crate and blocked our path. The Perp whisked himself away behind a stack of containers, six-high.

"Attack!" The Perp said as the echo of his footsteps grew larger.

"You heard the man," Clay said, standing perfectly still. "I feel bad for you, getting caught up with Fritz. It's a shame because you really have no business in this world of real dogs. You'd have been better off in that yard of yours, but unfortunately you got dragged into this by Fritz, and now you're going to pay the same price."

"What do I do, Fritz?" Nipper said. "He's getting away with her. They're going to kill her."

"Then you better go get him," I said.

"That's your plan?" Clay said. "Send the reject after the guy you couldn't get? You know what, I want to see how this plays out. Be my guest. Go ahead. I won't stop you. Try to catch him."

Nipper turned to me. I don't know what he wanted me from me. Permission? Last-minute advice? Me to say no? A better idea? Maybe none. Maybe all of that. Or something else. So, I nodded.

"Run," I said.

"What about you?" Nipper said.

"We've got some unfinished business here to attend to," I said. "Just me and Clay."

Nipper stayed well clear of Clay as he sprinted past and barked his way in the same direction of The Perp.

"That was touching," Clay said.

"No more running away."

"Not planning to, Fritz."

"This won't be like last time."

"Wasn't planning on that either."

"I'm not letting you walk away."

"Fritz, without the burden of the badge, I wouldn't respect you if you did. Not that I respect you to begin with."

"No backup this time," I said. "Just you and me. Let's do this if we're going to do it."

"I think your biggest problem," Clay said as he sat down like he didn't have a care in the world, "is that you've spent too much of your life around humans. Only humans care about things like being fair and one-on-one and rules and you can't do this or that, but you got to remember that dogs ain't like that. I don't know what you thought you were going to find here, but there's just one rule I adhere to. I go home and you don't. You're up, boys."

Their scent told me that I was in trouble. As the gravity of the situation pressed down on me, Knox and Gash walked out on either side of Clay, sights and jaws aimed at me.

"Meet our two newest recruits," Clay said. "A couple of blue chippers ready to make their name in the dog-fighting world. Just imagine when word spreads that they took out a police dog. Consider it a good thing, Fritz, that we won't say anything about you being old, retired, basically crippled, and not putting up much of a fight. It's better for the marketing."

While I drew a blank as to what to do against three monsters, Ernie and Saucy had covered a fair amount of ground to no avail until they passed a warehouse with some lights on and an opened side door. As they tiptoed through the door, they heard a chorus of muffled whimpers that were unmistakably canine.

"I think we found something," Ernie said.

"You think?" Saucy said.

"You think it might be haunted?"

"Are you being serious right now? I genuinely can't tell."

"Depends on if you think this place is haunted. The sounds? Could be ghosts, right? I don't know. Look at this place; it looks like a place that would be haunted. There's an echo, it's dark, there's no one around here, and it smells like hundreds of wet dogs. Granted those *could* be actual wet dogs. I don't know what I'm thinking. I just don't want you to be scared."

"I'm not," Saucy said, stopping. "Wait a second, what's that?"

"What's what?"

"That thing. You hear that, Ernie?"

"No. What is it?"

"Come here," Saucy said as she crept close to Ernie. She put her ear up in the air and kept it by Ernie's head like she was directing him where to listen.

"I don't hear anything," Ernie said.

"Shhh. It's right...THERE!" Saucy barked into Ernie's ear and sent him flying back in terror. He crashed into a file cabinet. The sounds of the collision clanged all the way down the warehouse.

"Very funny, Saucy," Ernie said.

"You practically begged me too."

"'Ey, you 'ear somt'um?" a voice clearly born east of Grand City said. Ernie gestured toward a staircase that led to a second-story catwalk. "'Oooo's down there? I coulda swore I 'eard some dogs."

"That can't be him," Ernie said as Henry's voice seemed to follow them up the stairs. They watched Henry lumber toward where the two of them had stood moments ago. The obtusely elongated shadow of Henry's flat face poked through below as Ernie and Saucy looked over the edge of the catwalk.

"We're surrounded by dogs that won't shut up," a voice said, one that Ernie had no trouble linking to Scamper. The end of Henry's shadow stood still for a moment, and then it returned with a mumbled curse back to where it came from. "Get back over here so we can get these shipments loaded."

"I don't believe it," Ernie said. "What's Henry doing with him?"

"Should we go get Fritz?" Saucy said.

"Not yet."

"He said just to see who was here. Let's go get him."

"We will. I just need to know what's going on. Keep quiet, and we can follow them from up here. They're not expecting us. We'll be safe up here."

Saucy sighed and followed Ernie as they hugged the edge of the catwalk and kept a healthy distance behind Henry as he went back toward Scamper.

"Oh my god," Saucy whispered. She pointed down the walkway, and they both saw where the cries were coming from. Crates upon crates upon crates, stacked on top of one another, some packed with as many as three little dogs. Most of the dogs were sedated or drunk and were barely older than puppies. The crates stunk so bad they made the pet stores in the mall smell like roses. "Ernie, look. What are they doing?"

"I don't know. Stay here."

"Ernie, don't."

"I said stay here," Ernie said, with a finality that startled Saucy. She took cover on the catwalk while Ernie walked into the open. He found another staircase that descended across the other side of the warehouse.

"Henry?" Ernie said as he got closer than Saucy would've liked.

"Mr. Tubbs?" Henry said. "What brings you about these parts? You shouldn't be 'ere."

"What are you doing with him, Henry?" Ernie said.

"Just doin' some business. Why don't you just turn right around and disappear? Pretend you ain't seen a thing 'round 'ere. Sound good?"

"He's not leaving," Scamper said. "He's going in one of the crates too. He's seen too much. Plus, he owes us for lost earnings."

"Henry, these guys are criminals," Ernie said.

"So'm I, Ern."

"But they're actual ones, Henry. You just run a club."

"Sorry, bloke. That bobby came poking 'round me place asking too many questions, so I 'ad to reach out to get me some protection. Turns out, we 'ave a partnership worked out that's mutually beneficial to all involved. They look out for me place. I 'and 'em over the mutts who won't pay the tab. Mutual, y'know."

"You have Knox and Gash," Ernie said. "What other protection do you need? Where are they anyway? I should talk to them."

"I sold off Knox and Gash to these blokes to be big dog fighters. Me new partner 'ere promises myself a percentage of their fightin' purses. In return, I 'elp round up scabs and strays for training, and no one bats an eye at me club anymore. Win, win."

"Fritz wasn't coming after your club. He didn't care about your operation."

"Once a cop, always a cop, I say. They always find a way to care. Either today or tomorrow, 'e'd be back for me."

"I'd feel much more comfortable," Scamper said, "if the two of you would play catch up with him inside a crate."

"Not a chance, pal," Ernie said.

"Sorry, Ernie," Henry said. "A deal's a deal. If 'e won't let you go, there's nothing I can do. Nothing personal, bloke. I always liked ya. Always paid the tab."

"And to answer your other question," Scamper said, "Knox and Gash should be taking care of your buddy out there as we speak."

"Nipper?"

Speaking of Nipper, he was gaining on The Perp as they raced down the pier. He picked up the scent quickly and was in foot pursuit. The Perp was headed toward a security office at the end of the pier.

"Hurry!" Scarlet screamed. Nipper excused the shrillness in her voice. He understood, he told himself.

We'll get back to him soon enough.

Clay kept a few feet behind Knox and Gash as they slithered toward me, ready to attack. They had me backed up to the edge of the dock, a step away from falling into the ocean.

"Nowhere to go, Fritz," Clay said.

"Think he'll jump?" Gash said.

"I hope not," Knox said.

"Don't worry," Clay said. "He's got too much pride to go down without a fight. He's probably still trying to figure out how to make this fair."

"I'm going to take one of you with me," I said, stalling. "Of course, the three of you can do whatever you want to me, but I'm gonna make sure that only two of you will be able to celebrate. Whoever wants to be the one who misses the party can come first."

Knox and Gash stopped and looked at each other. The ocean water splashed against the back of my legs.

"I don't want to go first," Knox said.

"You don't have to," Clay said. "What are you waiting for?"

"We gotta decide who's going to attack first," Gash said. "We gotta figure out who's got the best chance against him."

"Take your time," I said. "Don't make any hasty decisions."

"You can both attack him at once, you idiots!" Clay said. An explosion of knowledge spewed across Knox and Gash's faces. They took matching deep breaths and turned to me in sync.

"Nice try, cop," Knox said.

"Your tricks won't work on us," Gash said as they approached and took position on either side of me.

I think this is good time to explain something. Sometimes in life things just happen. Whether you're looking for them to happen or not. A day is nothing more than a series of random happenings. Some of them are good, some aren't, and most don't make any difference at all, just another blink of the eye that doesn't obstruct your view or a sniff that doesn't pick up a scent.

Things happen that make you think you have an invisible friend looking out for you, while some lead you to believe that you've been cursed and are paying a penance for a crime you didn't commit. It's like the waves at the beach; they're going to run through you no matter how much you try to control them, stop them, or try to get out of their way. That's what random things in life are like. It's life. It's a wave.

In my case, at that moment with no outs, and with the fuse lit toward my final breath, my wave was a German shepherd who I despised up until that moment. But when I saw Nitro speeding toward us faster than I could ever run in my prime, there was no one else I wanted there. Gash didn't see it coming. None of them did. The absolute crash of bones into bones was startling. Nitro didn't slow up as he plowed into Gash's side and inserted his jaws into Gash's shoulder. They violently slammed into Knox, and the three of them tumbled off the pier into the ocean. Nitro only let go of Gash moments before he splashed into the cold water.

"I'm okay!" Nitro said. "Did you see that? I totally took out two at one time."

"That just happened," I said as I stepped away from the pier and growled at Clay, who grunted a sort of half-hearted acknowledgment. "Now where were we?"

I leapt in and attacked Clay.

"Nothing personal, Tubbs," Henry said as Scamper dragged an open crate to where they were.

"I thought we were friends, Henry," Ernie said.

"We still are, Ernst. Me club comes first. Everyone knows that."

"Put him in," Scamper said. "We don't have time to waste with this street fleabag."

"You want to send your friend away somewhere where I'll be fed to a fighting dog?" Ernie said as he walked into the crate and sat down. "Is that what you want? Fine. You do that. You do that to your friend. Let's see how you live with that. Just remember, I always pay my tab."

"Apologies, mate," Henry said as he slammed the door in Ernie's face.

"That didn't go as planned," Ernie said, his voice trembling. "Ummm, aren't you going to see the error of your ways? I just sacrificed myself to point out your mistake."

"No mistakes here, dummy," Scamper said. "Lock him up."

Scamper's order was never obeyed. Ernie has a forty-pound mutt who took a flying leap off a second-story catwalk to thank for that. Saucy glided through the air and landed flush on Henry's spine, knocking the wind out of him.

"Get out of there," Saucy said in a primal scream to Ernie, who awoke from whatever altruistic trance had overcome him. Ernie head-butted the crate door open, pounced on Scamper, and pinned him to the ground.

"I've been waiting to do this," Ernie said.

"Please don't hurt me," Scamper said.

"I thought I was some street fleabag."

"I was wrong about that."

"No you weren't. I hate baths."

Ernie snagged Scamper by his collar, nearly snapping it off. He yanked Scamper off the ground and dragged him in front of the open crate. Ernie spun around and mule-kicked Scamper in the mouth, sending him and a few errant teeth into the crate. Saucy locked Scamper in. The other dogs surrounding them in the crates erupted in cheers, yells, hollers, and howls at this unforeseen change in events.

"We have to free them," Saucy said.

"How?" Ernie said. "They're locked in... Wait a second. This has worked for me in the past. Sheesh, I promised myself I'd never do this again."

Ernie trotted several yards away and lined himself up with the wall of crates. He howled liked a banshee and ran toward the wall of crated dogs. Ernie tucked his shoulder, pushed hard off his legs, and flung his body, skull-first, with reckless abandon, into the center of the stacked crates. For a brief moment after impact it looked like a cartoon where gravity was slow on the pickup. The crates hovered in the air momentarily while the dogs inside went from instant elation to an immediate fear for their safety. The rational laws of the universe returned, and the crates fell hard to the floor, their flimsy metal doors breaking off in the process. Any doors that didn't break open on impact were pulled open by Saucy or by another freed dog. They were banged up, a tad woozy, but the misfit dogs were okay.

"That was pretty cool, Ernie," Saucy said.

"Remind me to never do that again," Ernie said. "Seriously, that was the last time."

"I can't breathe," Henry said, not having regained his breath from Saucy's landing. He coughed and convulsed uncontrollably as he rolled away from the others.

"What about him?" Saucy said.

"What *about* him?" Ernie said as the freed dogs surrounded Henry and weren't concerned about making sure he was okay. "Just another rat from the gutter as far as I'm concerned. Fritz was right. This time it was for real. And it looks like there's no one here to save you."

"No 'ard feelings, whadda ya all say, right? Tell you what, 'ow 'bout you all get a lifetime free tab at The Dogcatcher's Net, on the 'ouse. A one-time-only-like special."

There were no takers among the two dozen dogs who stuck around to *tend* to Henry.

"Should we do something?" Saucy said to Ernie.

"What can we do?" Ernie said. "They're free dogs. They can do whatever they want to him. We didn't see anything."

"You can't just leave," Scamper said, with a mouth that was now short a few teeth. "You can't just leave me like this."

"You're right," Ernie said as he spotted a pull-down power switch off in the corner, one that looked like the kind they use to flip the switch on the electric chair. "We can't just leave you like *that*. Let's see what this does."

Ernie jumped up, grabbed the handle in his mouth, and pulled that lever down. A machine connected to the handle whirred to life with a high-pitched fervor. A giant crane swooped down from the ceiling and squeezed its grip around Scamper's crate. Scamper was lifted with ease, and the crane followed a track along the ceiling and stopped over an open cargo container marked with strange lettering ("looked like a bunch of scribbles," Ernie said later). The jaws opened, and the crate fell into the container with an echoing metallic thud that rang their ears.

"Did you know that was going to happen?" Saucy said.

"Nope. But sometimes, like Fritz says, you just have to go for it."

Look, I don't believe that either, but this was the story as relayed to me straight from Ernie himself. Who am I to question him on his story? It was his moment of glory and he earned it. If he says he shipped Scamper to China, then as you're reading this, Scamper is being chased through the streets of Beijing by a chef with a meat cleaver. We should be so lucky.

For the record, Saucy didn't correct the story when I asked her about it. And no, Ernie wasn't around when I asked her, so who knows?

Nipper caught up with The Perp at the end of the pier.

"Would you hurry up, please darling?" Scarlet said.

"I'm trying my best here," Nipper said. "I almost got him."

"Wait, is that you, Nipper? I was hoping that was Fritz coming for me."

"You got me," Nipper said as he smelled the same fear coming off The Perp that I did that night in the alley. It's repulsive and insulting, and there's something in it that makes you want to eat it. Nipper wondered if he was really there to save Scarlet, was he there to catch The Perp, or was he chasing him for a whole other reason that might not be so black and white? Nipper was a few feet from The Perp, seconds away from catching him, and then what? He'd never bitten a human hard before. He'd play-wrestled with Officer Hart but barely put any pressure on a bite. Could he bite with vicious intent on a human if he had to? What would it taste like? Would there be blood? There'd better be if he was going to bite hard enough to stop him. There was only one way to know. "And I got this, Scarlet."

The Perp threw Scarlet's crate to the ground.

"Scarlet!" Nipper barked as he watched it roll over and over several times before skidding to a halt. The Perp flung open his jacket, reached inside, and pointed a shiny gun right at Nipper's charging, wipe-open mouth. The gun went off. It exploded next to Nipper's ear. The immediate heat from the barrel singed the fur on Nipper's neck. Shreds of fur along his tail were sliced off as the bullet whizzed by.

Nipper had an instinct that any dog, police or otherwise, could be proud of. He sunk in the bite of his life around The Perp's forearm and tackled him hard to the ground. He wasn't thinking about Scarlet or if she was okay. The bones in The Perp's forearm bent in Nipper's mouth. The crack and the release of their natural tension vibrated through his teeth. The Perp cried out in agony and tried to reach for the gun that fell from his hand when his head bounced off the concrete. Nipper straddled his prey and tore at the limp arm in his mouth. He was no longer the dog he'd been before. He tasted blood. The adrenaline turned Nipper into a wolf. Scarlet, dazed but otherwise no worse for wear, loved what she saw.

The Perp stopped squirming and was still crying, but Nipper held on to that bite as long as he needed to. Not even the oncoming sirens stopped him.

Clay got the first bite on me. I expected both of us would go for an immediate throat bite. Clay, instead, went low, shooting under me and grabbing hold of my good leg. My body came down on top of Clay. I spun my leg out of danger before he could tear at it. I went for his leg, right above the knee, but he too spun to safety.

"Little slow?" Clay said. We both aimed high for the second go around. The air screamed out of our lungs as our bodies crashed into each other. His arms squeezed my ribs while our skulls bashed into the sides of one another. Clay pushed me into a block wall. I lost my balance as my one leg couldn't hold both of us up. Clay got to his feet faster and went for my neck. I tucked my head in just enough time for Clay to only rip a hole in my cheek. I was on my side, and he was above me. I landed my first real bite on his front arm, holding on to it for a few seconds, long enough to tear off a patch of fur and skin and pull him off balance to the ground. We both got to our feet and clashed again. I got his ear and tried to tear it off.

Clay wrapped his arms around my torso again and flung me to the ground. I crashed on my bad leg, and it popped out of socket once more. *Oh no, no, no, no, no, no,* I thought. Not now. Clay stepped back and shook off his arm that I'd gotten a hold of. I gingerly got back to my feet but couldn't put any pressure on my leg. I couldn't charge him again. Clay knew I was done. He knew I couldn't attack him with one leg. I could still defend, but when you're fighting not to lose, even if you're successful, you still don't win. And in this fight, there was only going to be a winner.

"Wanna trade?" Clay said as we stopped, inches apart. Our eyes connected, every sense heightened. We were one dog in that moment. We shared the same emotions, the same fury, the same pain, and the same fear. We both fought the urge to walk away, but I wasn't going to let him, and I wasn't going anywhere. "My arm, your leg? What do you say?"

I'd never been in a fight like this, ever. Clay was a mess; he was covered in holes along his arms, legs, and face that all spilled blood with every heartbeat. I imagined I looked the same way. Probably worse. There was a gust of wind, and the salt from the ocean stung as it danced across bite marks that I didn't know I had. The warm blood trickled down my face. I couldn't close my jaw all the way, but I could still bite.

I was next to the wall and braced myself against it to hold me up.

"Time to finish this," Clay said.

"Take your best shot," I said as a last-minute idea showed itself in my mind.

"Looks like we know who the stronger dog is after all, don't we, cop?"

Clay shot in at me with everything he had. He catapulted himself off the ground and aimed right at my throat. I took a breath and smiled. I put every ounce of my weight onto my bad leg.

My leg crumbled and I fell to the cold ground as Clay sailed over me. He implanted his nose, face, and cranium into the cement wall behind me with a dull thud. His dead weight landed on me, and I felt his wilted body spasm in shock. I pushed him off me with my leg. Sure, the dog in me wanted to finish him. It would've been easy to take that one last bite, but Clay said it himself. He was right about one thing. I was a cop. The cop in me knew that wasn't the right way to handle it. It was over. I won.

"Yeah, but we know who's smarter," I said. Like Nipper, I too heard the sirens approach.

Grand City PD was on the scene in minutes. An anonymous citizen reported the gunshot, and they were chasing after Nitro, who, it turns out, had escaped from his partner at the dog show. That won't look good in the final report. Nitro managed to swim toward a breakwater and got himself stuck out there.

I took cover around a corner as animal control treated Clay. They scooped him up and took him away. The Grand City guys stood around and tried to figure out how to get to Nitro without getting wet. They decided on calling in the harbor watch, who were only twelve minutes out.

"Suspect down," a voice piped up over the officers' radios. "He's in custody at the end of the pier. Request backup. Looks like he was taken down by a German shepherd. Uh, definitely not one of ours."

*Good dog, Nipper.*

I was done taking cover. A sunset had formed in the direction back toward Grand City proper. I had another hour or so of good light left in the day. I figured that was as good of a direction as any to limp toward. I'd see Nipper and Ernie back at home.

"Hey wait," Nitro said, barking to me. "Come on, Fritz. Help me get out of here! I'm freezing."

"Sorry," I said, knowing he'd be dry and safe in a few minutes. "No can do, pal. I'm going home. Besides, I'm retired. By the way, I appreciate the assist out there. Thanks, Nitro."

## Epilogue – One More Place Left to Mark

"Ten?" the beagle said to a trotting, plump Pekinese as they picked up the pace to keep up with the rest of the pack. "Are you sure? I heard it was more like a gang of fifteen."

"It wouldn't surprise me either way," the plump Pekinese said.

The two fell back into the group of dogs that followed Nipper around the dog park but remained at a respectable distance from Nipper and Scarlet. She clung to Nipper's side and took every chance she could to nuzzle into his neck while they walked. Some of the dogs simply said hi to him. Some welcomed him back. A few apologized to him. One even said he secretly liked Nipper's song. Some had questions about what kind of gun it was and if Nipper saw any pound time. Others still asked if there was anything they could do for him. Scarlet stopped and addressed them all.

"Look fellas," she said as the reigning queen of the park who'd finally found her king. "All you need to know is that this dog standing here next to me is a hero. He was brave and strong and quick and ruthless, and he alone saved me from certain doom. If you've heard a rumor about what happened, let me tell you, I promise that it doesn't do justice to what Nipper did. Now why don't everyone here leave us alone and think about what you might have done if you were in a similar situation? And then you think about what Nipper here did for me."

I saw Nipper smirk to himself. Sure, he happened to save her in the process, but she'd never know that Nipper had to save himself first. Scarlet planted a nice long kiss on Nipper for everyone to see and gawk at. The dogs soon scattered and resumed their miscellaneous dog park activities while Scarlet led Nipper to one of those quieter parts of the dog park.

Ernie and Saucy had found a corner of the park back around by the trees where they roughhoused together. Ernie let her win, and suddenly, with him lying on his side, he stopped flailing his arms like an eager puppy and looked at her. She too stopped and sat down next to him, genuinely wondering if something was wrong.

"You're not a street fleabag," Saucy said.

"I know," Ernie said as he rolled over and looked as sophisticated of a dog as he was ever going to be. He placed his paw on top of hers and just kept it there. "It just sounded cool at the time."

I'm positive that the same thought passed through all three of our heads. It's about damn time, Ernest Tubbs.

There was one dog oblivious to any of the drama and intrigue at the dog park that day. Missy was allowed in for her first official visit within the hallowed outer fence. She had a stick, some dirt, a grass stain across her back, and plenty of room to run. I've never seen a dog so happy just being a dog. I'm not saying I got emotional watching it, but then again, maybe I did.

She was under the watching and moderately concerned eyes of Officer and Mrs. Hart, who stood together along the outer fence. Simon played a video game in the Intimidator. They didn't give us any grief about escaping. The fence was repaired, Ernie's hole was covered again, but it was okay. They were more concerned with getting me fixed up... and not in the way that Ernie was afraid of (which also did not happen). My wounds looked worse than they were. I healed up nice and good. I've had worse.

They weren't talking, but Officer and Mrs. Hart stood next to each other at the fence. He put his arm around her, and she leaned into him. I don't know any better about the human way of doing things, but that seemed good enough for now.

As for me...

The outline of the moon shined down on me through the clouds, but there was no time to ponder its meaning. I was back in pursuit. Flat terrain, grass. A piece of cake. My target would be in my grasp in another step or two. All I needed to do was jump. I've been here before.

I suppose Grand City wasn't as bad off as I'd thought. So what if there's nowhere new for me to mark? What that really means is that this city was mine. I've claimed every inch for my own. I could go anywhere and know who's who and what's what without thinking twice. Some of the streets and buildings weren't what they once were, but who was? And who'd want to be?

It wasn't that Grand City stopped growing; it was me who stopped looking for something new. I was afraid of running out of wisdom. That's one thing you learn when you think you've said everything you have to say – it's time to go out and find a new story and some new wisdom. So, on second thought, I think there are still a few places left in Grand City where I haven't left my mark yet. I suppose I should start looking.

Before I could do any of that, it was time to take this guy down. He didn't need to help me by hanging his arm out in my direction, but I'll take it. Down you go, good sir. I'll never get used to the taste of metal, cotton, and dried leather, but that's what Grand City made their protective training suits out of, same as when I was a pup. For all I know, I bit into this same arm piece years ago when I was the trainee.

Officer Hart blew his whistle. I let go and sat down next to him as we faced a fresh line of K-9 recruits and their prospective partners. For my effort, Officer Hart fed me a few treats from the bag around his waist. The officer in the training suit got up and said he was fine. Of course he was. I took it easy on him.

"Good boy, Fritz," Officer Hart said. The prospective officers lightly applauded me while the line of new K-9s stood still at attention. I nodded to them.

"That's how you do it," Officer Hart said. "Just like Fritz there. Clean, quick, and effective. I'm biased, but he's the best dog to come through this academy, and there's no one better to learn from. That's it for today. Class dismissed."

Officer Hart rubbed my ears while the prospective officers continued to practice basic commands with what daylight was left. I looked forward to showing them the obstacle course in the morning.

Grand City isn't going anywhere. And neither am I.

THE END

## Author's Note

For those interested in such trivia, Nipper, Ernie, and Missy were my family's dogs when I was growing up. Nipper was some sort of German shepherd mix, and Ernie was.... Ernie. He was billed as a golden retriever, but he was orange, and that was the extent of any resemblance. He was a tough little guy who was furiously loyal to his family. Nipper could be a grump when he wanted to, but I've never seen a dog so happy to see you every morning. The two of them spent their entire lives, nearly fifteen years each, together as best buddies.

Missy came later into the fold, and, as such, she stayed inside the house while Nipper and Ernie had our backyard for their home. Their paths only crossed when Missy would bark at Nipper and Ernie through the window while the two of them couldn't be bothered by her. Only after Nipper had passed away and when Ernie was much older (and far tamer), did Ernie and Missy strike up a friendship of sorts. Or at least they would nap and eat spaghetti together.

In a bit of a creative role-reversal, it was Nipper who would escape from the backyard any chance he could, even as an old dog who could barely walk at the age of fifteen. If the gate was open, he was going to make a run for it. Ernie had no interest in an escape. His backyard was his backyard, and he liked it that way.

Full disclosure, my father was a police officer (and an emphatic NO to the question if the rocky marriage between Officer and Mrs. Hart was a reflection of our home life), and briefly considered becoming a K-9 handler. One of the reasons he passed was because we weren't sure how Nipper and Ernie would react to having a new "friend" at home. As an adult many years later, I thought what if? This book is the answer to that question.

I suspect this isn't the last we've heard from Fritz. During my "research" phase on this novel, I kept hearing stories and rumors about bodies turning up at the cat races. Maybe Fritz will investigate one of those down the line. We'll see...

## ABOUT THE AUTHOR

Bobby D. Lux has a Master of Professional Writing degree from USC. His fiction, non-fiction, and poetry have appeared here and there online and in print. He co-wrote the screenplay for "Up the Valley and Beyond," which played at the Cannes Film Festival in 2012.

You can visit him online at www.bobbydlux.com.

Facebook.com/DogDutyNovel
Twitter.com/BobbyDLux

#DogDutyNovel

28287448R00144

Made in the USA
San Bernardino, CA
06 March 2019